*HER REBEL HEART*
Published by JAMIE FARRELL
Copyright © 2017 by Jamie Farrell
ISBN: 978-1-940517-19-3

Printed in the USA.

Cover Design and Interior Format
© KILLION

THE OFFICERS'
*Ex-Wives*
CLUB

# *Her*
# REBEL
# *Heart*

# JAMIE
# FARRELL

*To Buttercup - may you one day reach the stars.*

# Glossary of Military Terms

Because Lance is a military pilot and Kaci is a former military wife, there are several military acronyms used in Her Rebel Heart. Here's a quick cheat sheet.

BCG – Birth Control Glasses, aka military issue prescription glasses
LT – lieutenant, the lowest rank a commissioned military officer in the Air Force can have. (Enlisted Air Force ranks go from basic airman to chief master sergeant.)
C-130 – cargo airplane
Herc – short for "Hercules." The C-130 Lance flies is formally known as the C-130 Hercules.
MREs – Meals Ready to Eat, aka military field rations
IP – Instructor Pilot,
Capt – short for Captain
USAF – United States Air Force
STEM – Science, Technology, Engineering, and Math. (Fun fact – this one isn't a military term! It's an acronym in Kaci's academic world.)
LEOs – Law Enforcement Officers, aka the local cops
ROTC – Reserve Officers' Training Corps, a training program to prepare officers to be commissioned into the military upon college graduation.

## Chapter 1

L ANCE WHEELER SHOULD'VE BEEN AT his wedding.
He had the rings. The church. The tux. The reception hall,
the caterers, and the flowers and cake and photographer. He had
next week off for his honeymoon.

But as of five days ago, he no longer had a fiancée.

As of an hour ago, he'd ditched his friends and their efforts to
cheer him up.

Somewhere between the time he'd met Allison and this past
Monday, when she'd decided her life was *going in a different direction*, he'd lost his taste for the party scene.

Would've rather been up at thirty thousand feet, just him and
his bird dancing between the earth and the sky. Flirting with the
heavens while he worked out this weird mix of pain, loneliness,
and a surprising tremor of relief. Unfortunately, his commander
had grounded him while he got his head back on straight.

So here he was, on a hard wooden stool on a lonely Saturday
night, a full beer taunting him on the bar.

This was what he was supposed to do. Get drunk. Find a chick.
Screw around.

Embrace bachelorhood.

Problem was, he couldn't remember how.

Someone shuffled to the bar beside him. "Gimme a tequila,
sugar. And if you got a chaser that'll make my ex disappear, I'll
take that too."

Lance twisted his neck to investigate and almost fell off his stool.

She couldn't have stood taller than five-four and had the right amount of curve on every inch of her petite body. The breasts under her pink T-shirt, the hips in her tight jeans, even her slender arms and neck had graceful arcs to them. Her blond hair fell in waves about her smooth, round cheeks, and her eyes were sparks of blue mischief even while her pink lips were drawn into a fierce line.

Her hands trembled. She fisted them and pressed them into the bar.

A fighter.

His groin stirred. So did his pride. Some guilt, too.

She flicked a glance in his direction.

He should've gone back to minding his own business.

But when she did a double take, her eyes widening and her lips parting, all of his blood converged south.

"Evening," he said.

Her knuckles were white, but she was smooth, coordinated grace when she nodded to his beer. "You fixin' to drink that? Because if not, I'd be happy to toss it on back."

An honest smile tugged his lips. *That* hadn't happened in six days. "All yours so long as I get to watch."

"It have anyone's name on it already?"

It did, but she wasn't there.

And the *she* in question didn't drink beer. Or do shots. Or say *fixin' to.* "Nope."

The blonde flicked a look over her shoulder. Her left cheek twitched. She slid onto the stool beside him, twisted so her knees touched his thigh, and pulled his beer to her spot. "Too kind of you."

"Anything to help a lady in distress."

Guilt stabbed him in the chest again, but he shook it off.

He wasn't married. He wasn't engaged. He wasn't dating anyone.

He was absolutely, one hundred percent single. He was free to flirt with a sexy blonde.

Even if being a bachelor was still a foreign sensation.

Was Allison out drinking tonight? Was she with someone?

And would it honestly bother him if she were? Why should he want a woman who didn't want him?

"You from round here?" the blonde asked.

"Today." Not much longer if he had his choice. "You?"

She chuckled. "Sure, sugar. I'm from round here today too." She angled closer to him, those perfect breasts mere inches from his arm.

He might've been out of the dating scene for the last three years, but he recognized a woman on a mission to make another man jealous.

And he didn't mind a damn bit.

Would've been doing the same if *his* ex were sitting in the bar, watching him.

The bartender delivered her tequila. She licked the salt off the rim with a dart of her quick pink tongue, tossed the glass back, and then expertly sucked the lime.

"You from round here just today?" he asked.

She winked as she finished the lime. "I'm from round the corner most every day."

He slid a glance around the bar. Two guys were playing pool. Couples and groups occupied nearly every other table. A few people looked their way, but Lance couldn't immediately pick out a jealous ex-boyfriend staring him down.

Just an older dude watching them.

Couldn't blame the guy.

The blonde reached up and plucked at his short hair. He'd even gotten his wedding haircut before Allison dumped him.

"Got a little piece of something up there," she said, but her eyes said this was all a game.

"You really want to make him jealous, don't you?" he murmured.

"If it was legal, I'd strap the man to a rocket and send him back where he came from. But since it's not, I'll settle for demonstrating for him that I'm moving on. That okay with you?"

"Sure, seeing as I'm here today."

"Awful darn nice of you." She crossed her legs and put a hand on his knee. "I'll owe you one. But I'm off men right now. Just so you know."

"Even just for…today?" The words slipped out before he realized he'd even thought them, but he didn't want to take them back.

Because her eyes locked on his, shimmering and intrigued, while her hand tightened on his knee. "What kind of girl do you take me for?"

"The kind who didn't just get up and walk away."

His heart knocked at his breastbone. His fingers shook. There was every possibility she would throw his beer back in his face.

Probably needed it. Would be a good wake-up call.

"You military?" she said.

"Yes, ma'am."

"Don't you *ma'am* me. What do you think I am, old enough to be your momma?"

"Old enough to be the sexy schoolgirl around the corner." He didn't even know her name, but flirting with this woman was making him feel more normal, less off-kilter and more focused than he'd been all week.

She'd probably shoot him down, but what the hell did he have left to lose?

"Just today, hmm?" She slowly licked her lips.

The sight of her tongue sent his remaining blood straight to his dick. "Today's all we ever have," he said.

Her other hand came to rest on his thigh, and she leaned all the way in to him. "So you know," she whispered, her breath hot on his ear, her spicy-sweet scent tickling his nose, "I'm not usually this kind of girl."

She leaned closer, those pink lips parting, her lashes fluttering down to touch her cheeks, and his brain short-circuited.

This sexy, outspoken woman wanted him.

*This could be a setup*, a hazy part of his brain whispered.

*She could be batshit crazy*, another part suggested.

But she was warm. She'd made him smile. And she'd also made him harder than he could ever remember being.

Because she was new.

Fresh.

The complete opposite of the wife he'd almost had.

Exactly what he needed tonight.

His body was on fire. She was gorgeous. A firecracker. And unlike a certain other woman no longer in his life, she *wanted* him.

He was a master of control on the flight deck of his C-130 Hercules, but his hands shook when he splayed his fingers over her back.

Her lips touched his, and instinct took over.

He angled his mouth against hers and tasted her lips. Her hands slid up his shoulders, up his neck, around into his hair, and her mouth parted for him. He plunged his tongue in, tasting salt and lime and sweet, hot heaven.

Allison's problem hadn't been Lance. He wasn't broken. She hadn't dumped him because there was something wrong with *him*.

There was nothing wrong with him.

He was strong. He was attractive. He was hot and hard and throbbing. He could have any woman on the planet, and the proof was right here.

With this sexy blonde practically climbing into his lap, her tongue in his mouth, her hands tearing at his shirt.

Allison's life was *going in a different direction*?

Fuck her.

Lance's life was going in a different direction too.

His life was headed in the direction of getting laid.

Tonight.

*Now*, right here, in some bar, with—

"Who are you?" he gasped.

He didn't know her. Her name. Her history. Why she needed to make out with strangers in a bar.

"You go on and call me anything you want." She hooked her hand behind his neck again, her touch hot and confident and sexy as hell, but also—

Wrong.

*Fuck.*

He didn't know her name.

He was kissing a woman, thinking about stripping her down and feasting on her most intimate parts, and he didn't even know her name.

On the night he should've been getting married.

To a woman whom, just a week ago, he'd sworn he would love forever.

"Don't stop now," she whispered.

Pled, really. As though she wanted to disappear into the oblivion of him as much as he wanted to disappear into the oblivion of her.

To not be whoever she was anymore.

To live a different life through him.

He jerked back. "Sorry," he muttered.

He couldn't look at her. He ran a hand over his stiff hair and fumbled off the stool.

He could still taste her on his lips, still feel the brand of her touch on his skin, still hear the rush of his pulse banging in his head as his life came back into focus.

The gut-wrenching, heart-bending, bleak reality of who he'd almost become.

"Sorry," he said again.

And before she could say another word in that sassy voice of hers, he charged out of the bar.

## Chapter 2

*Four weeks later...*

KACI BOUDREAUX MIGHT'VE BEEN BORN with the face of a Southern belle and the brain of a quantum physicist, but she had the heart of a redneck. And today, for the first time in too long, that heart was in hog heaven.

Twenty feet down the way, the macho team from Gellings Air Force Base pulled the lever to release their catapult.

A satisfying *thwack* of wood and springs bounced through the air, followed by the even more satisfying *crunch* of a pumpkin exploding upon takeoff. Orange innards soared a measly twenty feet beneath the crisp October sky and rained down on the dry grass.

She whooped—a good ol' rebel yell—and high-fived Zada Koury, her team's student captain. "We got this, ladies!"

The Gellings team had one more pumpkin left to chuck in the fall festival today, but their catapult had too much torque, and the gourds didn't have the surface tension necessary to withstand the force of the air pressure that came with the launch velocity. There wasn't a pumpkin in the world with skin thick enough to survive being launched off that thing. Kaci would've loved to see it loaded down with a watermelon, or maybe a cannonball—*man*, that thing would probably give a boulder wings—but she was more excited about pending victory.

Her students, all ladies from the Physics Club at James Robert College, were about to be the first all-female team in the history of the Gellings Fall Fest to take home first place in pump-kin-chucking. And for tossing a gourd over a third of a mile at that.

If there was one thing Kaci Boudreaux knew, it was how to design a catapult. She'd nearly gotten herself a juvie record with that knowledge. But Ichabod, the catapult her team had entered, had been completely designed and built by the students.

"This means no homework for a month, right, Dr. Boudreaux?" Jess Peterson, a freshman who'd jumped right into the Physics Club with both feet at the start of the semester, flashed an impish grin.

"Why would I deprive anyone of the fun of physics home-work? I'm fixin' to treat all y'all to some ice cream though."

The military boys were loading up their last shot. One of them snickered. Another shoved a third. Three more huddled over their pumpkin, rubbing it and whispering.

The judge said something to them, and all eight or nine backed up. Two of them wiped their hands on their pants.

"This is it," Zada whispered.

Kaci's team crowded together.

"Think it'll break again, Dr. Boudreaux?" Jess said.

"Darn near certainty." Kaci pointed to the catapult. "See how tight they've got it wound down?" She geeked out, rattling phys-ics principles and design theories until she realized she'd lost them, then fell silent and waited for that beautiful sound of wood cracking and pumpkin crunching into pie in the sky.

One of the guys pulled the release, and the catapult sprang straight with that perfect, reverberating *ka-THUD!*

But there was no accompanying squish.

No pumpkin guts.

Just a beautiful orange gourd slicing through the blue sky, a per-fect arc, perfect height, perfect angle, perfect speed.

"Nuh-uh," Kaci whispered.

"Wow," one of the girls murmured.

"That can't beat us, can it?" Zada said.

The black-shirted boys were all hollering, arms up, fists pumping, chest-bumping each other like Neanderthals.

Their pumpkin started its descent to the ground, a pinprick in the distance, too far away for the satisfying crunch of smashing pumpkin on impact.

And the boys were still hollering.

"That thing went a mile!"

"Did it land on the road?"

"If it did, that road's sprouting pumpkins next spring."

Zada angled closer to Kaci, her brown eyes thick with worry. "That went at least as far as ours, didn't it?"

It didn't make sense.

That pumpkin should've been guts on the ground before it ever took flight.

"Y'all did great," Kaci said to the team. "I am so proud of every single one of you."

"Great *magic formula*, Thumper," one of the guys crowed.

Several others hushed him.

The judge, a pretty lady in her mid-forties, winked at him.

The head judge's voice came over the loudspeaker. "Two thousand eighty-six feet," he announced.

The black-shirted bandits all erupted in deafening shouts.

The best Ichabod had done for Kaci's girls was a penny past two thousand.

Those boys had just beaten her girls by eighty feet.

"But—but..." Jess mumbled.

Given the materials, height, and leverage mechanism those danged military guys had used to construct their pumpkin chucker, not to mention the launch velocity and the way they'd cranked the arm down even lower for the last shot, it should've been physically impossible.

It *was* physically impossible.

Unless—

The rubbing.

They'd put something on the pumpkin to keep it from exploding on takeoff.

They'd lubricated it to reinforce the skin.

And the judge had seen them do it.

She'd *winked* at them.

Kaci's blood vaporized and her temper spiked madder than a wet bumblebee.

She didn't mind losing. But she minded losing to cheaters, especially when her students were being robbed of a prize they'd not only earned but needed. She had a hair up her butt to show those cheaters just how redneck she could be.

If Kaci had learned anything from her mother, Miss Mississippi and second runner-up in the Miss USA pageant, it was the power and advantage of chin up, shoulders back, and belle them to death first.

Then they'd never see the redneck coming.

"Y'all stay here and get Ichabod hitched up to the Jeep," she said.

She wanted to charge headfirst like a bull over the trampled fairground grass to show those macho, cheating dingbats how *this* lady handled problems. Instead she put a sway in her stride and a smile on her lips while she approached the other team.

The team's shirts all bore the logo for the Wild Hogs, Gellings Air Force Base's 946th Airlift Squadron. Military men in general made her twitch—especially lately—but flyers were enough to induce a seizure.

"Excuse me, gentlemen." She stopped at the edge of their group and ran her finger down the closest one's arm.

Eight close-cropped heads swiveled in her direction, and all their backslapping and pompous self-congratulations over their victory trickled to a stop.

She curved her lips into a coy smile. "I just wanted to say that y'all did a *spectacular* job today. I have never seen a pumpkin sprout wings like that." She batted her lashes. Lull them into safety, then get them to admit they cheated so they'd be disqualified. "Y'all must be *so* strong. And smart. Me and my impressionable young friends would *love* some pointers on how we could get our poor little thingie over there to work half as good as yours."

The one with the aviator sunglasses flashed a wolfish grin.

"Well, miss, it's all in getting the right torque."

"And a really good pumpkin," the fresh-faced one added with a snicker.

She treated him to a smile and a subtle tug on her pink V-neck, exposing the barest hint of cleavage. Four of the men went slack-jawed. Three more angled closer to her.

The young pups were so easy. They had a few years on her girls—couldn't be pilots without a good bit of schooling—but she doubted any one of them was pushing thirty.

"Y'all got a magic pumpkin?" she whispered.

"Close—" The fresh-faced one's voice came out on a prepu-bescent squeak. He cleared his throat and covered with a wink. "Close enough, miss."

"No magic pumpkin," Aviator Sunglasses said. "We've got something better."

No *magic pumpkin,* her ass. And she'd bet anything his *something better* was Vaseline or beer rubbed all over its skin. She fluttered her lashes while glancing at the pop cans, rags, and tools scattered about the ground. Had they used Coke?

"We're just a poor group of college kids doing our best on a small budget and limited brains," she lied. "We'd love to hear more about your methods."

Such an easy half lie to tell. And for a good cause.

Her girls were mostly second- and third-year students who had been busting their tails designing and building Ichabod since they'd all come out to the fall festival and observed the competi-tion last year. They'd lost sleep, boyfriends, and weekends for this. Every last one of them was on a scholarship or financial aid of some kind, and half of them worked part-time jobs to keep their heads above water.

And these men had cheated their way to the top and robbed Kaci's girls of splitting prize money that would've gone a long way toward next semester's books for each of them.

Not to mention the publicity of having an all-girls team win. Too few women believed they were smart enough to go into science and technology careers.

She tugged her shirt a millimeter lower. "We'd be *most* grateful if y'all would be willing to share a few pointers with little ol' us."

The flyers all shared a glance.

A guilty glance, in her opinion.

"Sorry, miss, but it's proprietary," the fresh-faced one said.

She fluttered a hand to her chest. "Oh, *that* kind of proprietary?" she whispered.

"What kind of proprietary?" a new voice said.

She turned. A tall, lanky, dark-eyed man with barely-within-regs jet-black hair had his legs spread and his arms crossed while he stared her down. He was in the same black T-shirt as the rest of the crew but, unlike his buddies, he had his dark gaze trained on her eyes with an authority and a confidence that seemed to be daring her to look away.

Her stomach dropped.

Bad enough they'd taken her girls' trophy.

But *he* was on their team? Mr. Kiss-and-Run? Mr. *In-Town-To-day-Only*? Mr. Left-her-with-his-tab?

This was *so* not her day.

She subtly shifted her posture to make her breasts stand perkier and waved a hand at the fresh-faced guy. Hell if she'd let *this* fly-boy see her sweat. "I was just asking your boss here if you strong, capable men might be able to help my little ol' group make our pumpkin thrower thingie better."

His lips twitched. Barely a fraction of an inch up, but it was enough to make her ovaries sit up and notice. Something hot pulsed between her thighs, and her brain train stuttered to an emergency stop.

Traitorous body.

"Aren't you with the Jim Bob team?" His accent was subtle— Southern in a Momma's-in-the-Junior-League way, rather than thick country hold-my-beer-and-watch-this—and his eyes had game. Take-no-prisoners, accept-no-bullshit, jump-right-in-and-play-along game.

Just as they had the night she'd first met him. The *only* night she'd thought she'd ever see him.

"Second place by a landslide?" he prompted.

The man needed to quit talking before her feminine parts over-ruled her brain.

He'd been a *damn* fine kisser. Until he ran away. Which was probably best for both of them, but she'd had a bad day. *She should've been the one leaving him.* "Oh, sugar, a man like you surely understands there's no glory in second place."

"Sure isn't. But you get a monstrosity like yours to fling a gourd that far, don't think you need any help from us."

"My momma always taught me it was proper to be sociable with your competitors."

His gaze dropped to her chest. And he didn't have to say a thing, but she heard the message anyway. *Your momma teach you to always use your boobs to get your way?*

It wasn't often that Kaci blushed—at least, unintentionally—but *this* man calling her out on using her feminine wiles spiked the temperature in her face.

As if he were innocent in the wiles department. "I'm doing my darnedest to deal with all y'all politely, but there ain't no way in hell that last pumpkin was normal."

"Because we busted the first two?"

"Because that eyesore of a catapult isn't physically capable of *not* busting a pumpkin on takeoff unless that pumpkin was juiced."

His lips finally spread into a full smile, but it wasn't a nice smile. "It's not an eyesore. It's mine. And it's physically capable of any-thing in the right conditions."

"Aha! You admit you greased your gourd."

He took one large step toward her, let his hands drop to his sides, spread his shoulders wide, and aimed a don't-insult-my-pumpkin-chuckin' warning glare at her. "I admit I made a better pumpkin chucker than you did, and that's it."

"By cheating." She clenched her thighs together and told her-self the excitement building in her chest was from the thrill of a challenge. Not from an irrational, sexually-charged memory about what those large, long-fingered hands had felt like on her body, or how his smoldering brown eyes had looked in the dim bar.

She should've known he was a flyer. Wild, unpredictable, and dangerous to that little organ pumping erratically in her chest.

His gaze stayed steady on her. If he recognized her, he was doing a dang good job of hiding it. "Only thing we rubbed on our pumpkin was luck. What are you? Senior in college? Grad student?"

Not anytime in the past decade. "Didn't your momma teach you it's not polite to ask a lady's age?"

"Word of advice, Pixie-lou. You want to build a machine like this, gotta get out of your momma's house and live a little outside the books."

*Pixie-lou?* The man was asking to have a firecracker aimed up his nether regions. "You have no idea—"

"*I* have no idea, but it's okay for you to come over here, flash your boobs at my friends, and accuse us of cheating?"

She refused to flush again. He'd liked her boobs just fine a few weeks ago.

Until he up and left in the middle of kissing her like she was his oxygen.

Lordy, she was about to have a hot flash. She gritted her teeth. "The laws of physics don't lie, and the laws of physics say it's impossible for you to stay within the rules of this contest and still launch an intact pumpkin that far. Your takeoff speed was too high for the surface tension of a normal pumpkin."

"Or maybe it was just right. We didn't grease our gourd. And even if we had, it's still within the rules."

She sucked in a breath.

*Was* it within the rules?

"Can't help that you didn't win," the fresh-faced one said, "but I'd be happy to comfort you tonight."

*Oooh*, these flyers were *so* stinking arrogant.

Her dark-haired, sinful-eyed nemesis smirked at her. "We're gonna go get our prize. Load her up, boys. Time to celebrate."

An irrational disappointment flooded her chest. "You're robbing eight hardworking ladies of a prize they deserve."

"Happy to introduce you to someone who can teach y'all how to be gracious losers. Good life skill."

Several of the men snickered while they broke away from her and headed toward the makeshift stage.

Her daddy never would've acted like that. And she was horrified that she'd actually considered taking that man home.

Thank *goodness* he'd up and left her panting at the bar.

"Hope that trophy keeps you warm at night," she muttered. "Because there's not a woman in town who'll take the job."

Except the judge, apparently. And half the women out here today.

And Kaci herself.

Lordy. She had issues.

The fresh-faced kid slapped the pompous, dark-haired loser-proclaimer on the back. "Thumper here ain't ever had a problem with that, miss. None of us do. But we appreciate your concern all the same."

The lot of them laughed at that.

*Thumper* didn't spare her another glance.

"They really built that themselves, Dr. Boudreaux?" Zada said when she returned to their group.

"So they say," Kaci said.

"And their pumpkin wasn't rigged?"

"Seems not. I'm still super proud of all y'all," Kaci replied. Were they right? *Was* it within the rules to pad the pumpkins? She hadn't looked—she'd simply assumed they used the standard Punkin Chunkin rules, even if this wasn't an official national contest.

But if they *were* right, then the only one acting like an ass out here today was her.

Her cheeks flamed up again. "We'll get 'em next year. Ice cream on me once we've got Ichabod put away."

"Rather have a beer," Jess muttered.

"And I'd rather not hear about it until you're twenty-one," Kaci chirped. "C'mon, y'all. Time for the awards. Let's get up there and smile like we mean it."

What else could they do?

But later...later, she would fix this. Somehow, she'd make it right for her girls.

⟨₂⟩

L ANCE SHOULD HAVE BEEN FURIOUS. Or at least irri-
tated.

He'd almost made himself forget the blonde from the bar, but there she was, stomping back to her team.

"Chick's batshit crazy, but *damn*," Juice Box said. The kid, real name Devon Grant, was fresh out of training and equal parts annoying and helpful. He was lanky and his light hair made him seem younger than he actually was. "I'd hit that."

Lance's hand curled into a fist. "Shut up and get to work."

Juicy slapped him on the back. "I'll give you first dibs, man. Telling you, get laid, you'll feel better." He sauntered off to help pack up the catapult.

The kid was so much like himself four years ago, it hurt.

Worst part, though, was knowing that he was reverting to who he'd been when he was fresh out of pilot training too.

Wanting to kick his own ass for tucking tail and running away from a willing woman. Wondering if he could get her name from the pumpkin-chucking organizers.

If she still needed to make her ex jealous.

Getting mildly and inexplicably ragey at the idea that he'd missed his chance.

Because if the woman had done anything else—besides accuse him of cheating—she'd reinforced his opinion of her from the night they met.

She was the utter, complete opposite of Allison.

And that was the one thing he hadn't found anywhere else in the past month.

Pony, the dark-haired, pirate-ish senior pilot in the squadron, shoved a tarp at him. The guy had a swagger that he'd earned and he didn't mince his words. "Chick's got balls."

"You sleep with the judge last night?"

"Nah." Pony flashed his signature crooked grin. "That was six months ago."

"We *didn't* cheat, did we?"

"Fuck no. Random pumpkin draw, same as everyone else. She was complimenting our wood."

Pony kept everyone honest and in line in the squadron, so Lance didn't have any reason to doubt him. Though rather new to Gellings himself, he got the impression Pony was as honorable in his personal life.

"Glad your modifications worked so well," Pony added. "Would've hated to lose to a bunch of girls."

Lance's shoulders bunched. "Say that in front of my sister, and she'll fly her fighter up your ass."

Pony laughed and went back to loading up the catapult.

Lance stole another glance at the blonde and her crew.

The night they'd met, he would've pegged her for being just out of college, maybe a couple years older. Wrapped up in the drama of having an ex-boyfriend, or maybe in pretending she had one so she could use a jealous ex as an excuse to make out with strangers in bars. But she was definitely older than the rest of her team. The diverse group of girls all had one thing in common—they seemed to be looking to the blonde for guidance and reassurance.

She'd pat one on the back. Get nods from two others. Make half of them laugh. All in the span of four heartbeats.

Her group kept their distance during the awards.

Probably best.

He didn't take well to being called a cheater.

An hour later, he was home. The place still smelled like sawdust and fresh concrete. The weekend his wedding hadn't happened, his mom and sister had quietly taken care of the boxes of wedding presents piled in the guest bedroom. They'd plastered the living room walls with photos of planes, some with Lance in them, some those inspirational crap posters. Cheri, his twin, had brought in University of Alabama throw pillows, fleece blankets, and bobbleheads to cover up the bare spots where Allison's knickknacks and her grandmother's crocheted afghans had been.

But within three days, he had known it wouldn't be enough. He needed to get the hell out of Gellings, out of Georgia, out of the South. He'd only asked to come here because he'd known Allison wanted to be close to home. Left to his own devices, he'd have gone anywhere west of the Mississippi. Overseas. New England, even.

Would've been nice if Allison could've decided she was done with him six months earlier. Out-of-cycle orders were hard to come by. Deployments aside, he was stuck here for at least two years.

So he'd made the worst-best decision of his life.

"Pony's pulling the old man card," Juice Box announced when Lance walked into the kitchen. Where Allison would've been waiting with fresh cookies on the counter and a chicken in the oven, Juicy was digging through the liquor cabinet over the fridge. "Says we're doing a bonfire at his place instead of hitting the bars tonight."

Lance tossed his keys on the granite countertop separating the kitchen from the living room. "Good. Had enough of women for one day."

"We'll find you one who doesn't talk," Juicy said.

Lance grunted.

"Not like that blonde. Holy *shit*, she was a hot mess. You think she gives good head?"

"Shut up, Juicy."

"You got marshmallows?"

The things he had to teach this kid. "You take marshmallows to a bonfire with the squadron, they'll change your call sign from Juice Box to Breast Milk."

"Can't say *breast* in a call sign. New Air Force, dude."

Taking a roommate had seemed like a good idea at the time. Lance didn't want to come home to an empty house while he waited for his deployment rotation to come up, and Juice Box had been living in an apartment with a leaky roof, questionable plumbing, and two hundred more a month in rent than Lance charged.

Having Juice Box here was like having a horny puppy that talked. He left shit everywhere, loved chasing sticks, had the attention span of a gnat, and tried to hump anything with legs and a pulse.

"Running low on beer again," Juicy said. "Hey, can we bring dates to the squadron picnic next weekend? Got a buddy whose sister goes to school over at the college here, and he asked if I'd watch out for her."

Lance's sister had never had any issues taking care of herself, but that didn't mean his big-brother instincts didn't spike when Juicy was talking about *anybody's* sister. "On behalf of your buddy, if you touch her, kiss her, say anything suggestive, or so much as imagine her naked, I will personally twist you into a human pretzel, light your hair on fire, and kick you off the ramp of my Herc without a parachute next time I'm in the air. Got it?"

Juicy grinned. "Lightning doesn't let you threaten her boy-friends, does she? Hey, when's she coming back to town?"

Four months.

Lance deployed in four months. He could tolerate this for four more months.

God only knew what Juice Box would do in the house while he was gone, but on some level, he knew having the kid here was better than living with a wife who didn't want him.

Plus, if the deployment went well and he played his cards right, he'd have networked his way into a by-name request from another squadron, and he'd be putting the house up for sale and getting out to see the world.

But in the meantime, Juicy was a good distraction.

Not as good a distraction as the blonde would've been, but life was never perfect.

## Chapter 3

JUST AFTER DUSK, KACI SAT at the edge of the fairgrounds with Tara Shivers, her roommate and sometimes partner in crime. Tara was an adorable brunette. She'd been a friend of a friend looking for a new apartment at the same time Kaci had moved here just under a year and a half ago. They'd both been newly divorced from military men, adjusting to a new town, and eager to get on with their lives.

Like too many military wives and ex-wives, Tara was overqualified for jobs that required little to no experience, but underexperienced for jobs that required her educational qualifications. So she was taking classes toward an accounting degree at James Robert while working nights and weekends at Jimmy Beans, the coffee shop just off base. She was moderately more levelheaded than Kaci, which had made her the perfect choice as an assistant to keep Kaci from going too redneck and getting herself arrested tonight.

"Are you sure this is legal?" Tara said from her perch in the back of Kaci's Jeep.

"Nothing illegal about improving a catapult." Kaci flung her knife into the dry earth. She pried off the pumpkin's top and shoved one of her ex-husband's old medals inside. "I'm so done with military men. They've died on me, divorced me, and now they've taken my girls' trophy. If I could put the whole lot of them in this pumpkin and launch them instead, I would."

Especially the one who'd given her the hottest kiss of her life and then run away. She'd shove him in that pumpkin first.

Pompous bastard.

"Can mine go in too?" Tara's flashlight bobbed in the night.

"Absolutely." Kaci patched the pumpkin back up, then loaded it into a slightly modified Ichabod.

Her girls were winning this contest next year, dang it. No more arrogant, dark-haired, hypnotizing-eyed flyboys would beat her team.

He'd been right.

Even if his squadron had juiced their pumpkin, it wasn't against the rules.

Not in this contest.

Which meant her girls simply had to have a better catapult. And she probably owed him and his team an apology.

*Without* kissing.

Sweet baby José, that had been the worst way *ever* to work off steam after a day of bad news. What she got for running out of tequila at home.

"So, ah," Tara said, "usually wouldn't you like to see where you're aiming something like that? It's kinda dark outside."

"Miles and miles of cornfield, Miss Goody Two-Shoes. Hush on up and help, or get out of my way."

Tara's laugh interrupted a hooting owl. "Miss Goody Two-Shoes? Have we met?"

"Stand back. I'm letting her rip."

Tara scooted farther back. "Should've brought night-vision goggles."

"You got a pair?"

"It's the one thing of Brandon's I didn't burn."

"Lordy goodness, girl. Why didn't you say so?"

"I didn't know exactly what you were up to."

"Huh." Kaci set the catapult, then stepped back and tugged Ichabod's release mechanism.

The sound of rattling wood as the pumpkin took flight eased the ache in her chest and the irritation in her belly and brain.

Tara was right. She should've brought night-vision goggles so she could see if her tweaks to Ichabod were helping or hurting.

A soft *thud* echoed in the darkness.

"Aaahh," she sighed.

Nothing like destruction and exploding pumpkins to lift a woman's burdens.

"I thought you already did this after your divorce," Tara said while Kaci grabbed another pumpkin and started cutting the top off. "Didn't you say something about a blowtorch? Or was that in one of my books?"

"This ain't about him. It's about military men in general."

"It's a conundrum. They're so hot in books, but such jerks in real life."

"Amen, sister." Kaci actually loved military men—for the most part, they were honorable and strong and handsome, just like her daddy had been. But there was so much about them she just couldn't swallow anymore.

"You gonna tell me what happened today, or should I guess? No, wait. Can I guess? Please?"

She fought against a smile and lost. In addition to being an underemployed former military wife, Tara wrote romance novels in her spare time. "Go on," Kaci said. "I could use a good laugh."

"The pumpkin-chucking contest was actually a recruiting event for a black-ops mission requiring a team of redneck engineers, and they didn't pick you?"

"Hush your mouth. You know I would've been first on that list."

Tara laughed. "There were vampires?"

"You can do better than that, sugar."

"Werewolves?"

"Getting closer."

"Ol' Grandpappy showed up with your secret love child."

When Tara had discovered Kaci's ex was thirteen years her senior, she'd given him the nickname. For that alone, Kaci would claim her for life. "Nope."

"Oooh, wait. Did Mr. Kiss-and-Run show up?"

Her shoulders hitched. She forced herself to snort in what she hoped was disbelief while she stuffed her pumpkin with an old pair of uniform socks she'd found in a box of notes from her grad student days.

"He *did*! Kaci! You need to spill. Right this instant."

Kaci plopped the pumpkin into Ichabod, checked the catapult's settings, then gestured for Tara to stay clear. "Firing."

She pulled the release mechanism, and Ichabod tossed that pumpkin like yesterday's gravy.

Watching that gourd fly off and disappear into the night sent a thrill through her veins almost as heady as if she'd been riding a rocket herself, though infinitely less terrifying.

Which was exactly what had sent her to that bar a month ago, looking for a distraction for her life.

What should've been the highlight of her career so far—being asked to headline a conference on efficient combustion at one of the largest physics symposiums in the world—had her shaking in terror.

Because going to the symposium in Germany meant she had to fly.

"Is he a werewolf?" Tara said. "Is that why he had to run away? Because he was about to shift into wolf form? No, wait. He has to take a wife so he can inherit his family business, so he's engaged, but he doesn't actually love her. Or—*oh*. Oh, no. He's dying, and only a kiss from his true love will save him, so he goes bar-hopping every night to try to find her, but his time's running out, and—"

"His team beat my girls," she said.

Tara flashed her light in Kaci's eyes. "Seriously? It was the guy from the bar?"

Kaci ducked out of the light. She grabbed another pumpkin and went to work hacking a hole around the stem.

"I heard a team from the base won," Tara said.

Kaci nodded.

"He's military? Stationed here?"

"Looks like."

"Oh, Kaci, this isn't good."

"It's just fine. He's gonna stay on his side of the base, and I'm gonna stay far, far outside of it. It was one night. And I know better than to get involved with another military man. Besides, he was a horrible kisser."

"You know what's crazy?" Tara said. "I know I was a bad military wife, but every time I see a man in uniform, I still kinda want to jump him."

"Girl, you got issues." As if she could talk.

"I'm not the one shoving BCGs in a pumpkin. *Crap.* Birth control glasses. *Dang it.* Military-issue prescription glasses. There. That's not too military, is it? I'm trying to quit speaking military. Did Ol' Grandpappy really wear those?"

"Yep. And you do me a favor and give me ten minutes' warning if you're fixin' to call him that to his face. I wanna be there."

"Won't happen. He doesn't come to Jimmy Beans anymore."

"Wish he'd do my office the same honor," she muttered. She could do with seeing her ex less.

"Rumor is he wants you back."

"He had a fling with his secretary after I left and realized how good he had it with me."

Kaci was also nearly certain he'd issued his ultimatum—drop everything and have kids now, or they were over—without actually intending to follow through on it. But even though her parents' marriage had been cut short when she was still in grade school, she had known without a doubt that husbands and wives shouldn't have to threaten divorce to get their way.

Also, Ron had been right when he dumped her.

She'd never loved him the way a wife should. "I ever tell you about the time he made a pass at my momma?"

"Omigod, *no!*"

"Said he thought she was my sister." Kaci loaded the pumpkin into the launcher. "That man just wants what he can't have. Just like they all do."

She double-checked Ichabod, then gave him an extra crank to see how much torque the catapult could take. "Fly good, magic pumpkin," she said.

She stepped back. "Ready?" she said to Tara.

"Oh, yeah."

"Great." She tugged the release mechanism.

"No, wait, *wait!*"

The pumpkin whizzed into the darkness and the catapult bounced, its weight thudding on the ground. "What? *What?*"

"Fire!" Tara pointed in the direction the pumpkin had just sailed.

An orange glow flickered on the horizon. Small, contained like a campfire, but still a fire.

Directly in Ichabod's firing path.

"Oh, *shit,*" Kaci whispered.

She didn't hear the pumpkin thud to the ground.

But she heard something else.

Voices.

Loud, surprised voices.

"What do we do?" Tara shrieked.

*Run.*

She wanted to run.

But her daddy would've skinned her hide six ways to Sunday if she didn't own up to her own messes.

"Get on up in the Jeep. I'm gonna go make sure nobody's hurt. And don't touch my pumpkins."

Kaci might have been thirty-four years old, and her daddy might've been gone too many years already, but that didn't mean she wasn't still scared to death of her momma. So she set across the field, praying everything was fine.

❧

L ANCE COULDN'T GET THE BLONDE off his brain. The whiskey he'd been nursing helped marginally. So did shooting the shit with his buddies about today's pumpkin-chucking contest. As did patting Gertrude, a stuffed wild boar they kept in the unofficial squadron bar.

Pony lived on the outskirts of town next to the fairgrounds. He had converted his backyard shop to a man cave and then opened it up for all of them to use. The building had water and electricity, and they all pitched in to keep it stocked with chips and liquor.

And the wooden bar tucked along the back wall kept taking Lance back to the night that he should've gotten married. To the sassy, intriguing blonde who'd been frank about wanting to use him to make her ex jealous.

To that moment he'd given in to weakness and thought he could be the kind of guy who made out with a woman without knowing her name.

She was more than a nameless woman, he'd discovered today.

In full daylight, she'd been undeniably gorgeous. Those blue eyes sparking, those pink lips pouty, and she'd known *all* the right ways to show off her assets.

She'd also been batshit crazy.

He shook his head and blinked at the flame glowing in the darkness. Pony touched it to the crumpled newspaper beneath the logs in the fire pit, and an old, familiar crackle joined the song of the night insects. A few of the guys had brought out one of Pony's homebrew kegs, and most of them were kicked back around the circle, taking in the stars overhead.

Allison hadn't *hated* camping, but she'd always preferred doing it from the comfort of a hotel room. Nothing stopping Lance from sleeping under the stars tonight if he wanted to.

He didn't regret that they hadn't gotten married.

He regretted that they hadn't parted ways sooner.

An odd *thump* sounded somewhere in the darkness.

"That you, Thumper?" Pony said.

Juice Box snickered and thumped his leg like that danged cartoon rabbit. "Feel better if you get some, old man. Already told you I'll let you have that blonde from today, but if you don't want her…"

"Life lesson number seventeen," Lance said to Juice Box. "Don't go for chicks who call you cheaters."

Which was advice he needed to take for himself.

The fire was growing, flames licking at the wood, popping and fizzing. Pony lifted his glass. "How 'bout that trophy?"

They all lifted their own cups and agreed their catapult had been a thing of beauty.

Damn good to be number one.

At something, anyway.

The bonfire was picking up steam, crackling and glowing merrily in the moonlight.

He inhaled a deep lungful of night air and campfire smoke. Would be a beautiful night to fly. Get up there in the sky with the stars, forget about life and love and women for a while.

Juice Box straightened beside him. "Whoa, did you see—"

Another *thump* landed, along with a *tink* just beyond the fire. The reverberations shook the air, and they dove for cover.

Lance went on full alert, peering into the darkness. Rain misted down around them, stars still sparkling in the clear sky.

"What the hell?" Juice Box shrieked.

*Fuck.*

Not rain.

Beer.

Lance shot to his feet, Pony at his heels, darting for the keg, watching for more incoming—incoming *what?*

Beer spewed out the broken connector on top of the keg, the whole thing coated in stringy orange gunk.

Pumpkin guts.

"That's my keg," Pony yelped. "That's my *homebrew.*"

"How do we stop it?" Lance said.

Beer coated his shirt and stuck to his hair and misted through the air. Someone popped up with a flashlight. Pony grabbed the pumpkin-slimed connector on the hose and yanked.

It didn't budge.

"That's fucking disgusting." He grunted and yanked again, and the connector popped off.

A spray of beer shot straight in the air, then bubbled down to a slow runoff and stopped.

"Are we under attack?" Juice Box said.

"Where'd it come from?" Lance said. "Juicy! What did you see? Where did it come from?"

"Ah, that way." He pointed west. "I think."

Lance took off at a jog, senses alert for pumpkins or other flying objects. He could make out a glow in the distance—a flashlight? Car lights?—but in the dark, he couldn't judge how far off it was. Yelling might make them stop.

Or it might tell the enemy where he was.

Probably stupid rednecks out joy-flinging. "Hey!" he yelled. "Who's there?"

Pumpkins didn't just fall from the sky.

Well, they could. But usually it would've been his crew dropping them off the ramp of his C-130, and much as the guys would've loved that, they still only dropped cargo, official or unofficial, when approved by the proper figures, and only under controlled circumstances.

There weren't any missions flying on base tonight. Aero Club wasn't running either. And they weren't under any of the normal patterns for the closest local airport.

"Put the pumpkins down," Lance called into the darkness while he continued to jog toward the dim light. "There are kids back here."

"Oh, *no*. Y'all got kids over there? They're not hurt, are they? We didn't mean to hurt 'em. I just got really bad aim, and I swear I thought I was facing the other direction, and—"

His heart slammed to a stop and his groin twitched. "Are you fucking kidding me?"

He knew that voice.

Those sassy tones had been haunting him for hours.

"Oh, no," she said again.

For the second time in less than twelve hours, Lance assumed battle stance while he stared down at the pint-sized blonde and her fantastic tits, ignoring the tingling in his chest and the hum of adrenaline spicing his blood.

"*Oh, no*, you got caught?" he suggested.

In a wink, she put the sass back in sassy. "Hush your tongue. Does your momma know you talk like that?"

Any other place, any other time, with any other woman, he

might've offered an *I'm sorry*. For running away that night. For kissing her in the first place.

But this woman?

This woman made him crazy. He'd talked to her for a grand total of ten minutes in his entire life, but it was enough to make his skin twitch and his muscles clench.

And to think he'd considered apologizing when he'd first recognized her this afternoon. "Does your momma know you're operating a pumpkin chucker without a license? In the dark? And aiming at a fucking *fire*?"

"Lordy goodness, you're fixin' to get your tongue washed down with a bar of Ivory, aren't you? And there's no such thing as a pumpkin-chucker license. Though if there were, I'd get one long before you and your ragamuffin crew."

Her eyes were large and dark tonight, and her chest rose and fell rapidly. Because she was afraid she'd gotten caught? Because she was afraid someone was hurt? Because she'd been running?

This woman running—dear God. His groin tightened.

That'd be a sight.

"Of the two of us," Lance said, "I'm not the one with a second-place trophy. Nor am I the one flinging pumpkins in the dark."

He couldn't be sure, but it almost looked like she was blushing.

"Well, so long as no one was hurt—"

"Someone got hurt."

That blush he'd thought he saw receded until her skin glowed paler than the moonlight. "S-someone's hurt?"

"Mildred." Lance couldn't help himself. Baiting her was too much fun. "She's dead."

"I killed someone's grandmother?" She punctuated her sentence with a squeak, and she swayed on her feet. "Have you tried CPR? Called 911? Are the cops on their way? The fire trucks? An ambulance? What are we doing just standing here? My momma was right. I should've given this all up after the pig incident, but I—why are you smiling?"

Was he smiling?

Well, damn.

He was.

He switched it to a scowl. "I'm gonna need to hear more about this pig incident."

"Who's Mildred?"

"Criminals first."

"Excuse you, Lieutenant Bossypants, I am *not* a criminal. Who in the Sam Hill is Mildred?"

"Captain," Lance said.

"Mildred is a captain?"

"No, *I'm* a captain. Captain Wheeler. And you are?"

"I'm standing here having some light dawn on me, that's who I am. Mildred ain't anybody's granny. She's probably your damn mascot, isn't she?"

"No, that's Gertrude. Mildred's on private property, though. And you blew her to bits. Pony's about to have a cow."

She thrust her fingers through her hair and turned in a slow circle, muttering something to herself about arrogant flyers and military clubs.

"Hope you've got an after-school job to pay for the damage," he added.

He was certain she wasn't a college kid, but if she wanted to call him an LT and suggest Juice Box was the boss, he'd happily question her maturity too.

Huh. Maybe meeting her wasn't about getting laid and getting over Allison. Maybe it was about finding some fun in life again.

"What is that god-awful smell?" She paused and stepped closer to him, sniffing. "It's *you*. You're drunk as a skunk. Raise my hand to sweet baby Jesus, if you're this obnoxious drunk, I'm glad I never got to know you sober."

"You killed a keg, a *good* keg, with good beer in it, and you think I'm the one not worth knowing tonight?"

"Mildred is a *keg*? Who names a keg? No, wait. Never mind. Suppose every man wants his girlfriend to have a name."

"Want 'em to be sane too. You must be lonely."

"You keep talking, I'm gonna start thinking you must be lookin' to have a pumpkin aimed up somewhere the sun don't shine."

Had Allison ever been this hot over anything? He couldn't remember. But he knew one thing—he was having a damn hard time stifling a grin. "Lady, you've got problems."

"Sure do. And most of 'em are penis-carrying members of the military. Tell you what, *Captain* Wheeler, you go on and send me a bill for that keg of beer. *Dr.* Kaci Boudreaux, James Robert College, Physics Department. And leave the pumpkin-chucking to us professionals."

She was a piece of work. A pompous, overeducated piece of work with the ripest breasts and the hottest mouth this side of the Mason-Dixon Line. "Where I come from, the rednecks are more qualified to chuck pumpkins than the professors."

"Ah. You must be from Alabama."

"If by *from Alabama*, you mean where smart, sane people come from, then yes, I'm from Alabama. Proudly."

"Nothing sane about rednecks, but I got both redneck, smart, *and* sane covered, sugar. If no *human beings* were injured, then excuse me. My apologies to your sweet *Mildred*. And have no fear—I'm picking a different cornfield next time."

She turned and swung those sweet hips, marching away in her shitkickers, and he had a crazy urge to follow her and kiss the priss right out of her.

But unlike her, he still had his sanity, so he turned his back on her and jogged back to the guys.

The keg had stopped bubbling over. His friends were squatting around the pumpkin slop.

But instead of mourning, they looked downright intrigued.

"That's the weirdest shit I've ever seen," one of the guys said.

"Not the weirdest, but up there," Pony agreed.

"What?" Lance asked.

They all burst out laughing.

Juice Box pointed to the slimy mess and shone a flashlight into the middle of it.

A cracked and bent pair of BCGs were nestled in the center.

Lance glanced back toward where *Dr.* Kaci Boudreaux had

marched off.

That girl truly did have issues.

And he had a masochistic desire to dig into them.

That blonde was a bad idea.

But he'd spent most of his life chasing good ideas. Maybe a bad idea was exactly what he needed.

⁂

KACI PUSHED INTO HER APARTMENT with Tara at close to midnight. She had an emotional hangover battling with a raging case of hormones.

That man needed a warning label.

He was so—so—

Sinfully delicious.

*Ugh.*

Irritating. He was irritating and pompous and a fricking *flyer*.

And surprisingly intellectually stimulating.

Probably because it had been too long since she'd had a good argument with anyone other than herself.

And she'd not only failed to apologize for calling him a cheater, she owed him an apology for killing his keg with a pumpkin.

She could've seriously hurt him or one of his friends too. And that, more than anything, had her heart in her throat still.

Tara paused outside her room. "It'll be okay, Kaci. Don't let him get to you. He's just a man."

Just a man.

Just a man with a voice she could still feel in her bones and a way of looking at her as though he could show her how to get to the moon.

Tara disappeared into her bedroom and shut the door with a click.

"Mmmrrraaaa?" Miss Higgs said. Kaci's ancient white Persian cat blended in with the chenille lap blanket tossed all cockamamie over the couch.

She dumped her bag, then plopped down and gingerly pulled

the elderly cat onto her lap. "Miss Higgs, I had a man try to convince me I killed his grandmomma tonight. And then he had the nerve to laugh at me. And he probably wouldn't even believe me if I *did* tell him I was sorry."

The cat lolled her head back and peered up through milky blue eyes as though she knew the real issue was that the man was sexier than basic physics principles, and he probably wouldn't be interested in kissing her again.

Which she shouldn't have been interested in either, but her basic biological instincts were obviously working double time to betray her tonight.

"Don't you give me that look," she said to the cat. "He didn't even have the decency to appreciate how far Ichabod must've flung that last pumpkin tonight. And I swear I was another mile down the road when we pulled over with that catapult."

Miss Higgs flicked her tail, which at her age meant the tip moved a centimeter.

Probably the cat was right. Kaci had a horrible sense of direction. She shouldn't be left unsupervised.

Or perhaps she needed to get back to concentrating on what was truly important—her job, her girls, and the conference in Germany.

She shivered. "I screw up everything I touch, Miss Higgs."

Apparently her story was boring, because the cat struggled to her feet and gave her the pitiful look of *please don't make me jump.* Kaci gingerly set her on the tan-and-white Pottery Barn rug Momma had sent. Miss Higgs paused on the rug before continuing her stiff-gaited walk to the bedroom.

She'd been a prissy, nose-in-the-air doubting Thomasina for nearly eighteen years, but she'd been there. Through high school and college, grad school, marriage, divorce. Across the country and back. Every night, she curled up next to Kaci's head and purred herself to sleep, though Kaci had to lift her onto the bed these days, and she kept a towel on the pillow to compensate for Miss Higgs's increasingly frequent accidents.

One day soon, probably too soon, she would miss that cat.

Miss Higgs flicked a look back at her, as if to say *you coming?*

"Go on, you pretty little hairball." She stood and shooed the cat toward the bedroom. "I'm coming."

She probably wouldn't sleep—not when she couldn't shake the sound of a certain captain's voice out of her head—but she'd try.

## Chapter 4

WHEN LANCE WALKED INTO THE squadron meeting Monday morning, he was greeted by a sideways glance from his commander. Lieutenant Colonel Santiago was a bull of a guy with thick muscles and thinning hair, relaxed until he had to be otherwise, and he'd kept a sharp eye on Lance since the wedding hadn't happened.

"Morning, sir. Happy to be here today." It was the same thing he had said every morning since he'd shown up for work when he should've been on his honeymoon. But since he'd never had much urge to visit Scotland for any reason other than it being Allison's dream vacation choice, missing the trip itself hadn't been a burden. If anything, he felt guilty at the sense of relief that had overtaken the pain at the loss of his fiancée. Now, though the commander had put him back on flying duty, it was habit to tell the older man that he was fine. "You hear we took home the pumpkin-chucking trophy this weekend?"

"Heard you beat a bunch of girls."

His cheek twitched. He would've liked to shove the phrase *a bunch of girls* inside a pumpkin and chuck it over a cornfield like *Dr.* Kaci Boudreaux had done to those BCGs.

For Cheri's sake, he told himself. His sister put up with more shit for being a female fighter pilot than he would ever understand. "Just barely, sir. Got lucky, honestly. They had a hell of a catapult."

"Hell of a leader too," Pony said.

Several of the guys snickered. And the murmurs of "crazy as

fuck" and "hotter than hell" made his cheek twitch harder.

He ignored the banter and settled into one of the last open stiff plastic chairs facing the projector. The rest of the room was lined with photos of C-130s signed by crews on various deployments since the squadron had been stood up.

Beside him, Pony was flipping through his phone. The colonel stood and cleared his throat, and the guys quieted and focused their attention up front.

A slide flickered to life on the screen. Lance's heart thunked down to his boots.

"Think you all heard," Colonel Santiago said, "but in case you didn't, our regular rotation has been delayed a month."

"What the *fuck*?" Lance muttered to Pony. Nearly six months until he could get out of here? *Dammit.*

Pony grunted. He was supposed to leave in two weeks. Six weeks now, by the sounds of it.

"Shove it," Flincher said on his other side while other groans and mutters went through the room. Flincher was a ruddy guy with Irish roots who'd buy you a beer so he could show you pictures of his little girl, and he was right behind Pony in seniority in the squadron. He fiddled with his platinum wedding band. "My wife's due when we were supposed to get back."

One of the hazards of military life.

Allison hadn't filled in any more details on why she'd wanted out, but Lance was certain his uncertain lifestyle had been one of her issues. When push came to shove, she hadn't been willing to get on the roller coaster.

The colonel cleared his throat again. "We're switching up our normal missions this week to compensate for the change in schedule. Make sure you check the board to see when you're flying."

The colonel's weekly briefing went like clockwork after that. The usual messages from base leadership, a safety briefing about keeping your head out of your ass, quarterly award nomination packages were due soon, don't push it on bottle-to-throttle time or crew rest. "One last thing," the colonel said. "Heard from the training squadron. They're expecting a shortage of applicants for instructor pilot slots in the next two years. Don't want to lose any of you here, but I want smart pilots in my birds. You think you'd be a good IP, come talk to me."

Figured.

Only job that could get him moved early, and it would take him half a mile down the road instead of across the country.

Be good for a guy like Flincher though. Keep him home with his family for a few years.

The colonel dismissed them. Everyone stood and stretched, moving about the room, but Lance nudged Flincher. "Want to switch?"

Flincher looked him up and down. "Switch?"

"Rotations. You're delayed. I want to get the hell out of here. Can't solve you leaving a newborn, but I can help you be here when the kid's born."

Flincher's bushy red brows bunched. "You serious?"

"Be doing me a favor, man." Get out of here in six weeks instead of six months? *Hell* yeah. "Might talk to Juice Box too. He's on the third rotation. Could get you a few more months."

"I'm due for orders by then."

Twenty minutes later, the colonel had approved the idea, and the paperwork was in motion. When Lance settled down to his computer in the line of cubicles in the squadron room, he was actually whistling to himself.

He was flying this week, and he'd be getting the hell out of dodge in six weeks. "Weather good?" he asked Pony while he logged on to his email.

"Not raining beer," Pony replied with a grunt. He was flipping through a webpage with kegs on it.

Lance's fingers curled around his mouse.

His brain was heading back into not-smart territory.

*Dr.* Kaci Boudreaux had *distraction* written on every inch of every one of her curves and lingering in every undertone of that sassy voice. And it looked like he suddenly only had six weeks to kill before he was out of here.

Six weeks could be a long time.

Or six weeks could be interesting.

"How much are they?" he asked Pony with a nod to the screen.

"At least a hundred."

A hundred bucks.

Huh.

He logged in, glanced at the weather, and then opened a blank document.

He wasn't flying until this afternoon.

Which meant this morning, he could have some fun.

K ACI WAS WADING THROUGH A stack of research papers Thursday afternoon when there was an authoritative knock at her office door. "Come on in," she called.

She looked up, expecting to see one of her Physics Club students or one of her grad students or maybe a freshman with a question about today's lecture on centrifugal force.

Instead, Ron Kelly stood framed in the doorway. "Got a minute?"

For the man who told her that if she didn't have his babies, he'd divorce her, then followed her across the country to invade her new life? Nope. "Office hours for students are Monday, Wednesday, and Friday from nine to eleven, and otherwise by appointment. Office hours for ex-husbands are never." She flicked a finger at the hallway. "Shut the door on your way out, sugar."

He shut the door.

But he stayed inside the room.

Usually the eight-by-eight, white-walled space was big enough, especially with the window letting in natural light.

With Ron standing before her oak door with his legs wide, hands tucked behind his back in parade rest position, the whole stinking physics building wouldn't have been large enough to put enough distance between them. "It's been over two years, Kace. Can I please have ten minutes of your time?"

He was handsome in a distinguished way—dark hair threaded

with the right amount of gray and subtle wrinkles that could've been mistaken for laugh lines about his blue eyes—but he'd put on a few pounds since his retirement and his suit coat didn't fit just right.

"Don't know that we've got ten minutes' worth of talking in us," Kaci said. "I can give you three, and that's only on account of my momma raising me to have manners."

"Being here the last few months has made me realize life's been boring without you," he said.

"Sorry to hear that. Don't you have a lecture soon?"

"May I?" He gestured to the utilitarian blue plastic chair she kept in her office for students, then lowered himself into it without waiting for a response. "I didn't mean to hurt you."

She assumed he probably hadn't. Even her injured pride couldn't work up the argument that Ron had ever been mean-spirited. Not to her, anyway. "But you still meant everything you said about me not being a good wife."

"I didn't say—"

"It's neither here nor there, because I'm not your wife anymore."

"I've been in counseling."

Her chin slipped down. The Ronald Kelly she knew didn't need counseling, and even if he had, he wouldn't have admitted it.

"I blamed you for all of our problems, but I never took responsibility for my own shortcomings. It would mean a great deal to me if you would come to one of my sessions with me."

The world had gone and turned itself inside out, and it was making Kaci's stomach do the same. "I'm taking a break from men right now."

"All I'm asking for is an hour." He spread his hands, a plea the Ron Kelly she knew never would've made. But she couldn't tell if the hard set to his lips was a determination to put in what it took to get her back, or an order that she do what the great Colonel Kelly dictated. "It would be good for both of us."

"Time's up. Lovely to see you, Dr. Kelly. Don't let that door hit you on the tuckus on your way out."

"Kaci—"

"And don't go pulling those prick stunts you did at the Academy with pop quizzes for material you haven't covered. Kids are here to learn, not have heart attacks."

"The real world doesn't hand out lollipops for second best and weak efforts."

Dear sweet Jehoshaphat, she'd married that. "Y'all have a good day. I got work to do."

His jaw clamped shut, and he stood and reached for the door. "Think about it, Kaci."

She'd think about it.

She'd think about it as long as it took her to think the word *no*.

She hadn't been unhappy in her marriage, but she'd been no more or less unhappy since her divorce. To her way of thinking, that said something about their relationship.

And she didn't entirely trust that his motives were purely personal.

He'd gotten his own bit of attention for a paper he'd written in corollary to the paper she'd written that had gotten her invited to Stuttgart, and she didn't much like the idea of him riding her coattails on his way to getting tenure first because he was a man and she was a woman.

In this day and age, gender shouldn't matter, but in academia, especially scientific academia, Kaci's male counterparts still refused to consider that women could be just as brilliant as men prided themselves on being. One of her fellow physics professors had suggested to the dean that he go to Germany in her place to present her research. Because the conference was too close to the holidays and *everyone knows women are busy then.*

The patriarchal baloney was one of the biggest reasons no one could ever know she was terrified to fly.

She had to find a way to get on that airplane without hyperventilating.

Somehow.

Someway.

She'd do it, dang it. She had to.

The door slammed shut behind Ron. A moment later, a tentative knock sounded, and the mail delivery girl peeked in. "You got mail, Dr. Boudreaux." She held three envelopes out in her chunky fingers, her sweet smile and bright eyes chasing away all the bad juju Ron had left in the office.

"Thank you, sugar." Kaci slipped the girl a fun-size Milky Way, then closed her office door and settled back at her desk to inspect her mail.

One envelope from *The Atom Report*, another from the University of Stuttgart, and one from…

Oh, lordy.

One from the 946th Airlift Squadron on Gellings Air Force Base.

At the thought of Captain Irritating, her belly did another flip.

One thing Ron had going for him—he was safe. He had his moments of being a pompous ass, but he'd never made her nerves twist and swirl like a tornado in her chest.

She grabbed her phone and hit Tara's number.

"Franco or Blake?"

She blinked at the phone. "Pardon?"

"I'm naming a new hero. Do you like Franco or Blake better?"

"I like any of 'em that aren't flying pigs sending me letters."

"Is that the Mississippian way of saying you're getting back together with your ex, or do you mean Captain Catapult sent you a letter?"

She tore into the envelope. "No, and maybe. Yes, I mean. No, I'm not getting back together with Ron, even when pigs fly, which they do, because yes. Yes, Captain Catapult sent me a letter, and he says—"

She gasped as she scanned the letter more closely. "Tara, that man says I owe him and his Wild Hogs squadron two thousand four hundred eighty-six dollars for dumping a pumpkin on their keg."

"That can't be right. The keg couldn't be more than two hundred, tops. Maybe three if it was full of the *good* beer."

Her cheeks were on fire, the left from embarrassment, the right from indignation. "It was moonshine beer. Homemade. And he's claiming I owe four hundred for the keg, plus two hundred for pumpkin cleanup, and the rest is to go for the 'emotional trauma done to highly trained and irreplaceable members of the United States Air Force and their mascot, Gertrude.' Does that man think I'm made of money? I don't mind paying for my messes, but there's no way on God's green earth that keg was worth two thousand dollars. I got me half a mind to march right over there and give him what for."

"Um, Kaci?" Tara made a strangled noise, as if she were emotionally constipated. Or possibly trying not to laugh. "That's a love letter."

She pulled the phone from her ear and looked at the black device on her desk. The cord was plugged in to the unit, and the unit was plugged in to the wall. "Did you just say this here's a *love letter?*"

This time, there was no mistaking the laughter on the other end of the phone. "He's flirting with you."

"That's a bunch of malarkey." Why would the man flirt with her? He hadn't liked her enough to keep kissing her the first night they met, and he definitely hadn't liked her on Saturday.

Either time.

"Well, if he's not flirting, he's trying to push your buttons. Did he put a phone number on it?"

She skimmed the bottom of the page. "Yep."

"Local area code?"

"No."

"Bet you a brand-new slingshot he gave you his cell phone number."

She was getting way too predictable if Tara was betting slingshots.

And life was getting way too weird if Captain Catapult had actually sent her his personal number.

Also, she had research papers to get through, data to analyze in her lab, and a plane ticket to buy for her trip to Germany.

Her heart dipped, her toes tingled, and her chest constricted at the thought of flying.

Which was something *he* must do all the time, being in a flying squadron and all.

"I'll call you right back," she said.

She hung up with Tara and dialed the number.

After five rings, it went to voicemail.

"This is Lance," his voice said, causing an irrepressible shiver that started in her core and flung itself out to her fingertips. Tara was right. He'd written her a letter so he could give her his phone number. And he sounded *good* when there wasn't a sneer in his voice. Friendly. Encouraging. Sexy. "Leave a message."

The phone beeped in her ear, and her mouth engaged, but her brain didn't. "Afternoon, Captain Wheeler. I got your bill, and like I just told my ex-husband, I'm off men. So if you're looking to start a fight, you're gonna have to pick another rock to look under. Toodle-oo!"

She slammed the phone down.

Then she slammed her head on her desk. "P equals V-R-T," she recited. "E equals M-C squared. The speed of light is three times ten to the eighth power meters per second, and the average velocity of an unladen swallow is twenty-four miles an hour."

It was a dang good thing her brain still worked for physics. Because it obviously didn't work for anything else.

*Chapter 5*

A FTER THREE DAYS OF TRAINING missions up and down
the Gulf Coast, Lance was on top of the world. Wasn't any
place he'd rather be than driving his bird halfway between the
ocean and the top of the sky, calling out orders to his crew and
feeling the roar of those engines in his soul. Cheri could have her
fighters. He wouldn't trade his C-130 for anything.

He'd also gotten a message on his phone that shouldn't have
been funny or cute or interesting in the least, but which had
made him grin so hard he laughed.

He'd follow up on that later though. Tonight, he was headed
out with the guys again. Being single was starting to feel almost
natural.

Pony and Juice Box were already at Taps. The local bar and grill
where Lance had had his disaster of a kiss with Dr. Boudreaux
hosted trivia on Thursday nights. Since it was homecoming week
for James Robert College, the bar was featuring beer specials, and
Juice Box had wanted to check out the ladies. Lance was mildly
curious if the students would be the only people out celebrating,
but he'd only admit to being there to keep an eye on Juice Box.
He settled in at the table with his buddies and passed fist-bumps
around.

"Ready for this, Thumper?" Pony said.

"Hell yeah. Got a feeling we're gonna win tonight."

The hairs on his arms went up.

"You boys keep on thinking that," *Dr.* Kaci Boudreaux said. His
stomach tilted when that Southern honey voice hit his ears.

He almost smiled.

She'd shown up.

She didn't look at him, but he knew she knew he was there. "Me and Tara here are gonna whomp your rumps."

Juicy's gaze locked on something below a woman's usual preferred target zone.

Pony glanced between Kaci and her curly-haired friend. "She a doctor too?" he asked Kaci.

"Better. She writes romance novels."

"Aw, man, that's hot," Juicy said.

"Oh, sugar, you have no idea."

Lance tilted his seat back. She still hadn't looked at him. It was like she couldn't see his part of the table.

All the better. This would be fun. "Got your message," he said.

The tendons in her neck tightened. She kept her nose up, without a hint of a blush touching her porcelain skin. "Loud and clear, I hope."

"It was loud," he conceded.

Her companion, the curly-headed Tara, sucked her cheeks in. But she also gave him a second once-over, which she hadn't done with any of the other guys.

"And we're going to kick your ass as soundly at trivia as we did with pumpkin-chucking," he added.

"You wanna put your money where your mouth is?" Kaci's blue eyes darted to him, then away.

He had an insane desire to leave his money out of it and put his mouth somewhere it had no business being.

Getting involved with Kaci Boudreaux was a terrible idea.

But *damn*, was it fun to push her buttons. "No skin off my back. I'll add it to your bill."

This time, her gaze landed hard on him, and she held it steady without blinking or flinching. "Aww, you poor thing. You go on and keep asking, but I'm not giving you my number."

He didn't answer and instead let a wolfish smile creep over his face.

She'd called his cell phone. He already had her number. Which a brilliant physics professor should've realized.

Her poise faltered. "Anyway, good luck to you, gentlemen. And I hope I can still call you gentlemen when the night's over."

She and Tara left, taking seats two tables over. Close enough to watch and see if his table was Googling for trivia answers, far enough away that they could talk about him and his buddies without being overheard.

Much.

"You didn't tell me he was hot," Tara clearly said.

"Honey, the skinny dark-haired one. Not the cute one with the muscles."

"I know, Kaci."

Pony grinned at Lance. "Cute? Girl needs glasses. I ain't cute, and you ain't hot."

"She calling us cheaters again?" Juice Box asked.

Lance watched Kaci and Tara lean closer together, whispering and pretending they weren't watching him back. "Looks like."

"That chick can call me anything she wants. If you don't want her, Thumper, I'll take her."

"She owes me a new keg," Pony said.

"Wouldn't hold your breath," Lance said to both of them. "But we can show 'em who has the brains around here."

Because when it came to this chick, winning was where it was at.

◦২৹

TWO HOURS LATER, KACI WAS drowning in a sea of embarrassment thanks to her mouth being too big for her brain.

Again.

"We have to bet it all," Tara said. Their meals were gone, sweet tea drained, and they were fighting for thirteenth place against Lance's table.

No, he wasn't Lance. That was just what his voicemail wanted her to believe.

He was still Captain Catapult. Captain Kiss-and-Run.

When she'd asked Tara to come out tonight on the pretense of breaking up her routine—and to avoid listening to those hypnosis tapes she'd picked up at the library—she hadn't intended to run into him.

But there they were in all their arrogant flyboy glory, beating Kaci and Tara by one point in a battle not to be last.

She hated losing.

She didn't mind that there were four tables of James Roberts students beating her—none were obnoxiously rowdy or in any of her classes, all had at least one sober driver at each table, and she'd happily give them the high of beating a professor in trivia, if they even knew who she was—but she minded losing to Lance and his flyboy buddies.

"Dollars to donuts those boys are betting it all," she said. "Bet two points. If they've got the answer, they're gonna beat us no matter what. If they don't, two points are all we need."

"You sure?"

"Sugar, math is a third of my life. Trust me on this one."

"Okeydokey." Tara scribbled their final trivia bet on a scrap of paper, then dashed it up to the judge.

Lance was watching Kaci.

*Captain Kiss-and-Run*. Lordy goodness, if she let him have a real name, he'd be a real man, but he couldn't be a real man because there was no way that boy was even flirting with thirty yet.

Which obviously hadn't mattered that night she met him, but one night of making out was far different from whatever *this* was.

Plus, Kaci was off men.

As he'd gotten the message.

Loudly.

The man was a pain in her rear end.

And she wasn't proud of knowing she was probably a pain in his rear end too, but she didn't like the way he rattled her.

Tara slid into her seat as the last question was announced. "Ladies and gentlemen," the announcer called, "your final question: What college football team has won the most national championships?"

Lance's team erupted in cheers.

"Alabama," Kaci whispered. "Write *Alabama*. Freaking ele-phants."

"They're Bama guys?" Tara wrinkled her nose. "Figures. Who's writing these questions? As if half the bar won't know that one."

"Makes up for asking us the pumpkin capital of the US. Who knows that kind of stuff?"

"So you can chuck 'em, but you don't know where they're from?" With a cheeky grin, Tara ran their answer up to the judge. When she plopped back into her seat, her grin had turned grim. "You know he's watching you again."

"He can watch all he wants. I'm done with men."

And fear shot through her belly every time she said it.

She could swing her hips and show her boobs like nobody's business, but if she never had another man in her life, it wasn't the sex she'd miss. Or even having someone reach up to the high cabinets without needing a stepstool, or having a date to faculty functions.

She'd miss the companionship. The safety of knowing there was another person in the world who cared and who wanted to look after her and who would be there.

Sure, she could look after herself just fine. She'd never make a lot of money, but she made enough to take care of herself and Miss Higgs and not have to run home to Momma in Mississippi. She knew how to cook, clean, and brew up a pot of sweet tea. She could make up her face with her eyes shut. She could still balance a book on her head while walking around in heels if the occasion warranted.

She truly didn't need a man.

But there was that lingering shot of panic in her gut again.

"I'd do him," Tara said.

"Hush your tongue," Kaci hissed.

Because that shot of heat rushing through her midsection this time wasn't panic.

It was far uglier.

"As a onetime thing," Tara said. "For research, of course. Maybe

I'll write a pilot one day."

"Tell me you don't sleep with men just for research."

"If I did, at least I'd be sleeping with something. Oh, hey, did I mention that I saw Ol' Grandpappy in the back corner thirty minutes ago?"

"What? *Here?*"

"He looked a little blocked up."

Kaci closed her eyes and blew out a breath.

Ron could go anywhere he wanted. It was a free country. So long as he left her alone and never mentioned counseling or came to visit her at work again, she'd be fine.

They weren't married anymore, and she didn't plan to marry him again. "He always looks blocked up. It's because he puts the *ass* in *academics*."

"There's no ass in academics."

"It's silent until he's involved."

Tara squinted at her. "Why'd you marry him?"

Because he was safe. Calm and rational, competent and lev-elheaded, in a field with low mortality rates, at an age when decreasing testosterone levels would make him less likely to be reckless and wild. Because he could talk to her on an academic level. He understood her love of physics in a way her momma never had, so he'd accepted her as normal in a way Momma never had either. "He said all the right things about my potato gun."

"Is that a euphemism, or do you actually have a potato gun?"

"Do armadillos have armor? Of course I've got a potato gun."

The announcer interrupted them to give the final standings for the night.

And, unfortunately, Kaci and Tara were dead last.

"Better luck next time, Dr. Boudreaux," Captain Kiss-and-Run called.

The guy she'd realized was Pony—whom she owed a new keg—didn't smile. The younger one did, but it held an offer Kaci would never cash.

"Just didn't want all y'all's delicate male egos to take a hit," Kaci called back.

"You ever lose gracefully?"

"Sugar, I don't lose."

"Kaci, we kinda lost tonight," Tara murmured.

"Hush on up. This here's called messing with their minds."

Lance stood, all six-foot-something tall, and sauntered to their table in what looked like two steps.

Primitive interest stirred low in her belly.

Chemical pheromones. Instinctive biological needs designed to ensure continuation of the species. Thank the heavens for evolved brains that were above all that.

Nothing to do with her firsthand carnal knowledge of what he could do with his tongue. Or any curiosity over whether he'd be willing to give her another demonstration.

"You know what's irritating?" he said.

"You talking?" she guessed.

"I was going to say *you* talking."

She pulled herself out of her seat and stared him down. Didn't matter that he had well over half a foot on her and that there was a little voice in her head reminding her she'd been wrong more than she'd been right when it came to this man. She was the daughter of a beauty queen, and beauty queens didn't let anyone see them sweat.

"That's not very gentlemanly of you," she said.

"Your double standards are also irritating."

Holy Moses on a stick, the man was staring at her mouth.

Maybe he *did* want to kiss her again. "Oh, *I* have double standards? Excuse me, Captain Make-The-Lady-Think-His-Grandmomma's-Dying. And don't get me started on what else you've done wrong."

"And you're changing the subject. You lost, fair and square. Say it."

"You lost, fair and square," she parroted.

She had, and they both knew it. But his eyes were swirling into matching black holes, and she was too far inside their gravitational pull.

"I'm starting to see why you've got an ex-husband."

Ooh, that was low. "That supposed to be an insult to him or me? Because you're missing the mark on both."

"Do you just talk to hear yourself say words, or do you actually pay attention to what's going on around you?"

"The average wingspan of a camel is cake times force triangulated."

"Well, at least I know you're not an idiot." His sarcasm was lacking, those black holes had practically swallowed his irises, and she had the distinct impression that he could see the list in her soul that was bullet-pointed with every last one of her fears and insecurities.

Which was the only possible explanation for everything that went down next.

"Kaci? This chump bothering you?" Ron asked.

She had to blink twice before she could tear her gaze from the intensity that was Lance's attention on her, and then she had to blink again before her brain processed that her ex-husband had his hand on her elbow.

She yanked her arm away. "Don't touch me."

"If he's a problem—" Ron started.

If *he* was a problem? There was a problem all right. Her ex-husband wouldn't leave her alone, and she was having irrationally pornographic thoughts about a freaking irritating, arrogant military pilot.

"He ain't a problem," she said. "He's my new boy toy, and this here's called foreplay."

And before her brain could catch up, she yanked a fistful of Lance's polo, went up on her tiptoes, and pulled him down to lay a smacker on his lips.

Except somehow, that smacker turned into something more than just lips smeared together.

Somehow, his hand cupped her neck.

Somehow, his mouth parted over hers.

And somehow, his teeth scraped over her lower lip, and then his tongue licked the sting away, and then a surge of primal lust made her want to wrap her thighs around his hips and see how much cowboy this flyboy had in him.

"Move along, folks," Tara said somewhere in the hazy distance. "Nothing to see here."

She wrenched her mouth free, immediately wishing she could put it back while simultaneously wondering if she shouldn't have gone into researching time travel so she could rewind the past ten minutes to before she got a wild hair to make Ron jealous with Lance.

Again.

Ron was still there, waving his grumpies like a flag in a hurricane, his scowl so big it needed its own ZIP code. "Was that really necessary?"

"No, but it was damn fun," Lance said. He had one hand on her ass, and though he'd answered Ron, he was staring at her.

As though he couldn't decide if he'd lost his marbles or if he'd found the next best thing to chucking pumpkins.

Her belly quivered.

This man wasn't safe. Or reliable. Or even nice.

At least, not in her experience.

"You go on home," she said to Ron. "My business isn't your business anymore."

Ron turned the colonel stare on Lance. "If you hurt her—"

"Sugar, my momma's got me covered," Kaci interrupted. "And she don't get him till after I'm done, and I know you know how I handle men who hurt me."

Ol' Grandpappy gave a heavy sigh, but he moseyed away with a parting, "We'll talk more tomorrow."

Kaci swallowed hard, then put on her daughter-of-a-beauty-queen posture and peered down her nose at Lance, even though she had to look way up to do it. "I do believe you can consider that debt paid in full. I trust we won't have any reason for further communication after this."

"Sure," he said. "We can do that."

She blinked. Seriously? It was that easy? "So glad you—"

"*If* you can convince me that kiss didn't make you feel anything."

Lordy goodness, that kiss made her feel something. That kiss made her feel *everything*.

And that was terrifying. "Anything good, I assume you mean? Because I'm gonna tell you right now, you're not backing out of this deal when I tell you that—that *kiss*, as you call it, made me feel bored."

Those black holes in his eyes were using their gravitational force to suck away her defenses.

"It turned you on," he murmured.

She swallowed. "You being turned on ain't the same as me being turned on. That's called projecting, and you slobbering all over me didn't even register with my lady bits."

She was such a liar.

But the alternative was admitting this man got to her. And she was in a no-men zone. She had to be. Her research, her job, getting to Germany all took priority. "Tara, let's get out of here."

"You talk a good talk, Pixie-lou," he said, "but you felt something. Can't deny it."

"Can and did." She faked a yawn. "Y'all enjoy your night."

"You afraid to feel?" he asked. "Or are you afraid to feel with me?"

"Wow, how much did you have to drink tonight?" Tara gripped Kaci's arm and tugged. "Hope one of your buddies is driving you home, Captain."

Breaking eye contact physically hurt. Like plucking a suction cup off the inside of her elbow. But Kaci tore her gaze away anyway, then turned to follow Tara.

"Still expect payment on that bill," Lance called.

Kaci kept her head high, but she couldn't find the *oomph* to put a swing in her step too.

That man was downright terrifying.

Not because she felt violated by his kiss.

If Ol' Grandpappy could've kissed her like that, they might still be married.

No, she felt violated by his insight into her psyche.

"He's so dadgum full of himself," she said to Tara. "I got me half a mind to make him pay for putting me in a spot like that."

"For kissing you like that?" Tara said dryly. "Because I'm not sure *that* deserves vengeance so much as it deserves an encore. At least, if it were me, I'd be going for the encore."

"For teasing me," she said. "And sending me that ridiculous bill."

Tara slid her a sideways glance. "You want war?"

Kaci sagged against her Jeep. Did she want war? Or was she already at war? "What're you proposing?"

"I know a guy who used to be in the 946th, and I also know where they keep their mascot. If you ask me, the captain's good for a battle."

"Tara Shivers, you are a terrible influence on me." But, oh, did taking his mascot sound tempting. He wanted her to feel something? He wanted her to pay a big bill? She'd dang well get her money's worth.

"You can thank me later," Tara said.

Kaci grinned at her. "You bet your britches I will."

## Chapter 6

IF ANY OF KACI'S STUDENTS had told her that they were considering sneaking into a rival fraternity house to steal a mascot, she would've threatened to call their mommas and have the police waiting for them.

But the beautiful thing about being a full-fledged grown-up was that she didn't have to make the same threats against herself that she did to her students. Which was why, Saturday night, she and Tara were decked out in black, creeping along the edge of a cornfield and heading toward a shed at the very edge of town limits.

"This is great research," Tara whispered. "I need inspiration for writing a man cave."

"But remember—no pictures, no fingerprints, and no vague-booking on social media. Even a little," Kaci whispered back.

"They're going to know it was you."

"Don't mean I have to make it easy for them to prove." A felony breaking-and-entering charge on her record would probably cause some issues with her dean, among other hoity-toities at James Robert. Not to mention the ammunition it would give the sexist pigs on the tenure committee. But she still remembered her daddy laughing over stories of stealing rival squadrons' mascots and the pranks that had been pulled in retribution.

This here was good old-fashioned fun.

"Remember, if we get caught, run."

"And if we get caught again, embellish our stories enough that they don't sound rehearsed." Tara giggled. "I knew all those episodes of *NCIS* would come in handy one day."

"Girl, no more military shows. We're over military men, remember?"

"Ssh. Was that a dog?"

Kaci stopped. She strained to listen, but all she heard were crickets and other night insects.

"I guess not," Tara whispered. "C'mon. Let's go."

They crept up to the corner of the shed, squatting closer and closer to the ground as they went, Kaci clutching a pink stuffed pig from one of those kids' shows she'd heard the department secretary moaning about. They passed evidence of a bonfire, along with a decomposing pile of pumpkin guts.

This looked like the place. According to Tara's friend, one of the guys in the squadron owned the land out here, and he'd converted the back-lot toolshed to a bar that all the guys could hang out at. A house was visible in the distance, barely outlined in the light from the waning moon. The house's windows were all dark, as were the windows in the shed.

"You know how to pick a lock?" Tara whispered.

"I'm a physicist, not a criminal," she whispered back. "But if lots of these guys use this place, there has to be a key hidden somewhere."

"Like in a flowerpot?" Tara deadpanned.

"More like under a fake dead skunk, from what I've seen of these boys."

They crept about the edges of the building, checking beneath windows and on top of the doorframe. On the second pass around, Kaci almost tripped over a rock. "Huh."

She knelt on the ground and felt beneath it. "Bingo."

Tara crept back to join her. "What if they have an alarm system?"

"Sugar, they got at least a dozen dumb flyer jocks who know where this key is. You think they're gonna ask 'em to remember an alarm code to get in here?"

"Pilots have really good memories for stuff that's important," Tara whispered back. "I dated this guy in college who used to recite emergency procedures in his sleep."

Kaci slid the key into the lock. "Guess we'll find out the hard way." She had to jiggle it, but eventually, the lock turned. She twisted the knob, and it released with a *click* that echoed through the night.

"Ssh!" Tara hissed.

No lights flipped on, no security systems beeped, no lasers lit the night—not that lasers worked the way Hollywood said, and Kaci would know—and no masked ninjas leapt out to stop them. "Your flashlight ready?" she asked.

"Ten-four, good buddy."

They slipped into the dark shed. Tara hit the switch on her flashlight, and both of them gasped.

The planked oak floor wasn't unusual. The bearskin rug wasn't unexpected. The bar running the length of the back wall, big-screen TV, pool table, and man-couches were requisite.

But the centerpiece of the room was a taxidermied wild boar, complete with tusks, Mardi Gras beads, and a maid's cap. Its gray-black fur had patches of wear, as though it had once been used for target practice, or maybe as though the guys in the squadron had rubbed the thing's lucky shoulder one too many times. Beneath its marble eyes, proud snout, and curved tusks, its mouth was split in a goofy grin.

"Sweet baby Jeremiah the bullfrog," she whispered.

"This is *so* going in a book," Tara whispered. "I've only ever heard rumors of her existence. That *has* to be Gertrude. Bet she weighs two hundred pounds if she weighs an ounce."

"Nah, they took out her innards." They were probably still looking at dragging forty to fifty pounds of stuffed boar across a cornfield though.

Her pulse amped up, and she grinned. She'd have to drive her Jeep out here, and they had to do it without being heard or seen, and somehow cover up the boar for the ride home.

If she was taking this thing home. It was a beaut, but even Kaci's redneck had a limit.

She plopped the twelve-inch pink stuffed pig onto the bar,

right next to the pumpkin-chuckin' trophy that should've gone to her girls, then circled back around the boar. "Gertrude, sugar, we're fixin' to take you joyriding."

"Kaci, I don't think we can—"

"Don't you be doubting us now. We came, we saw, and we're gonna conquer."

"Before or after we get caught?"

That was the real question of the night, wasn't it?

⁂

SUNDAY AFTERNOONS WERE SUPPOSED TO be for watching football games.

Instead, Lance was standing in the middle of Pony's man cave with half the squadron, stone-cold sober and honestly more pissed than he'd been when Allison called off the wedding.

"What kind of fucker would steal Gertrude?" Pony snarled.

"Could've been the fighter jocks," Juice Box said.

Lance eyed the pink stuffed pig sitting right where Gertrude was supposed to be, and his brain flashed back to a sassy blonde.

She wouldn't have.

She *couldn't* have.

Could she?

"No ransom note?" he asked.

"Just the fucking pink cartoon animal."

Was that something Kaci Boudreaux would do?

And what was with hoping it was? Chick was trouble with a capital W-O-M-A-N. But worse because she was smart, and she knew it. She was also a walking wet dream, and she knew it. And she was dangerous, which she honestly might not know.

"Your sister got any friends in the fighter squadron here?" Pony asked Lance.

Odds were good. She'd either know somebody, or she'd know somebody who knew somebody.

How things worked in their world. "Probably be quicker to go pay them a visit than to wait for Cheri to call around."

"Got footprints out back," somebody called.

"We reporting this to the cops?" Juice Box said.

Lance and Pony shared a look.

None of them had been at Gellings when Gertrude became the mascot for the 946th, but they both knew the story. There had been a refueler squadron here several years back, and the flying hogs had relieved them of *their* mascot not long before they went inactive and transferred to other bases.

So while the unofficial story was that they'd given Gertrude a new home, the real version might call into question the boar's true ownership.

And nobody wanted the squadron to look bad.

"We didn't sign up for the military to hand our problems off to the local LEOs," he said.

"And this here, Juicy, is called tradition," Pony added. "We'll get her back. Question is, how much are the tiny dicks gonna pay first?"

A rumble of agreement went through the room.

"You sure it's not that hot professor chick?" Juice Box said.

A few of the guys snorted.

He had an inexplicable desire to shove Juicy up against a wall and tell him to permanently remove Dr. Kaci Boudreaux from his brain and vocabulary.

Kid was sniffing around something that'd get him in trouble.

Never mind Lance wanted a little more of that trouble for himself.

"That professor chick couldn't have done this," Pony said. "She throws. She doesn't carry."

More laughs bounced around the party room.

But Pony had said the exact wrong thing.

That Kaci couldn't have done it.

Kaci could do any fucking thing she put her mind to.

She was like Allison that way.

That was the *only* way she was like Allison, though. Kaci didn't seem the type to put on dinners or volunteer to teach Sunday school or to wear a dress.

"Besides, how would she know Gertrude exists?" Pony added.
Because Lance told her.

That should've prompted a shitstorm of expletives in his head,
but instead, he caught himself smiling again.

*Would* she have?

Undoubtedly.

And the *would* removed any doubt about the *could*, because if
he had learned anything about Dr. Kaci Boudreaux, he'd learned
she never stopped.

⁓

K ACI WAS HEADED UP TO her apartment late Sunday afternoon after a Physics Club meeting when none other than
Captain Lance Kiss-and-Run Wheeler strolled around the corner
on her floor.

Her heart did a somersault and her ovaries sat up and sniffed,
but the rest of her went on high alert.

Was he here for her?

And if so, because of the kiss, or because of the boar?

"Evenin', Captain," she said. "Fancy meeting you here."

He crossed his arms and took up a position holding the wall
up. "Is it?"

"My momma always taught me to look on the bright side. Fancy's all I got."

Those talented—erm, devilish—lips spread in a smile. "Feeling
something again, aren't you?"

She was feeling a need for a hole in her head. Be more useful
than feeling intrigued by him. "Nausea, but I'm sure it'll pass
before you're out of the parking lot."

"Been thinking about you." He leaned closer. "Imagine you
hear that all the time though. Might even be good sometimes.
Like when it's someone other than your momma, your boss, or
your parole officer."

Dollars to dandelions, the man was sniffing around for his boar.
"Or my ex-husband. Let's not leave him out."

"Has anyone ever told you you're fascinating?"

His voice was too heavy on the sincerity and too light on the sarcasm. She didn't like it.

"If you want something, go on and spit it out." She lifted the grocery bag in her left hand. "I got milk spoiling here."

"You have a bag of okra and squash." He pushed off the wall. "But I'd be happy to walk you home to see to it that your groceries get put away."

He'd be happy to snoop around her apartment, looking for Gertrude.

As if she'd be stupid enough to put the boar in her apartment. And even if she'd had temporary insanity, Tara wouldn't have let her. "Aw, that's just too kind. But I wouldn't want you getting any ideas about my intentions toward you if I let you in my apartment. I know how you boys get confused when the kissing starts. If you can call that kissing."

His gaze went smoky as it dipped to her lips. "No, kissing wasn't the right word for it, was it?"

She hated when he agreed with her. "Definitely not."

"More like making love with our mouths, wasn't it?"

*Zing!* There went her panties, melting themselves off. "You are just too precious for words, bless your heart." She patted his cheek.

Huge mistake.

His skin was hot and stubbled, and getting close enough to touch meant close enough to smell. He carried a scent of pine and pool water over something earthy and male, and her primitive urges made her gaze snag on his lips.

His cocky, smirking, outrageously shapely lips.

He angled his body so she was half-trapped against the wall. "No shame in admitting you're attracted to me."

"My momma taught me not to lie." And if her momma were in her grave, she'd be rolling over. As it was, she probably already had a long list of reasons she'd roll over when she got there.

"Are you fighting this because we got off on the wrong foot? Or is it because you're insane?"

"Don't make me bless your heart twice."

He wasn't touching her, but he wasn't leaving much room for the Holy Ghost either. "What are you afraid of, Kaci?"

Nothing she'd admit to him. She barely liked to admit any of her fears to herself. "Not a danged thing."

He held her gaze without blinking. "Besides losing?"

"I never lose. And what are you afraid of?"

Where his eyes had been dark magnets a moment before, they were doors now. "Not a danged thing," he parroted.

"Oh, sugar," Kaci breathed, "you're as much a liar as I am."

His cheek twitched. "I don't know if anyone's as much a liar as you are."

He might have a point. But the man was hiding something. "You got a secret, Captain Wheeler. And I'm fixin' to find out what it is."

"Get ready to lose, Dr. Boudreaux. I know what you did. And I won't stop until I prove it."

A good shiver tickled her backbone. "You have fun with that."

His lips tipped up, and that shiver went straight to her core.

"I will, Dr. Boudreaux. Have no doubt, I will."

He flashed a cocky smile and left, and she sagged against her door.

The apartment door across the way popped open half an inch. "That boy giving you trouble?" Mrs. Hamm whispered.

"No trouble," Kaci assured her neighbor. "He's just flirting because I'm irresistible."

The door opened wider, and the sweet new grandmother winked. "That's how Gerald and I started too. You let us know if he gets to be trouble, and we'll take care of him."

"Thank you, Mrs. Hamm."

Lance was trouble all right.

But he was exactly the kind of trouble she needed to handle herself.

L ANCE STEPPED OUT INTO THE sunshine, wondering if he was thinking with his brain or his other head.

He wanted to kiss her again.

He was single. If he wanted to kiss a woman, even a hillbilly physics professor in a porn star's body, who would stop him?

Just one kiss. Maybe a roll between the sheets.

He'd been with the same woman for three years. Looking back, those were three long years when he'd forgotten his own favorite hobbies and sacrificed more and more time with his buddies to set himself up with the perfect wife, who, he'd come to realize, had actually been pretty boring.

Wasn't wrong to want something else to jump-start his new single life.

But it was probably wrong to want it with this woman.

She'd stolen Gertrude, he was almost certain.

And *that* was what he needed to focus on.

Not on the wariness lurking behind her bravado. Not on the way he wanted to kiss the sass right out of her. Not on the way she smelled like whiskey and lemon drops, or how he never knew what would come out of her mouth next.

He needed to get a grip and focus on what was important.

On what was real.

On what he could fix.

And Gertrude was what he could fix.

He'd seen Kaci drive into the parking lot in a red Jeep, so he started there. Not that he expected to find anything.

That woman was physically incapable of making anything easy.

He smiled.

He got part of why she kept pushing him away. He'd left her in a bar after one of the most intense kisses he could ever remember having. He could've explained it to her in two simple sentences. *I was supposed to get married that day. But I don't make out with women, especially women whose names I don't know, to get over other women.*

But Kaci?

She struck him as the type who'd appreciate earning that knowledge more than she'd appreciate having it spoon-fed to her. As the type who appreciated the mystery and the unknown. The puzzle. He'd let her play with that for a while.

In the meantime, he'd learn what he could about her.

The first thing he discovered in the parking lot was that her Jeep seemed pristine. No tufts of Gertrude's fur in the back, no indents of her body, no stray Mardi Gras beads or her maid's cap.

But the Jeep's tires were muddy.

Conclusive?

Nope.

But he was just getting warmed up.

"I'll figure you out yet, Dr. Kaci Boudreaux."

And he was looking forward to every minute of the game.

*Chapter 7*

BY THE TIME KACI LEFT her office Monday, her nerves were shot. She needed to go set off a few bottle rockets. Or fling a pumpkin. Or set off fireworks.

Something.

Going into her lab would probably be the wisest course of action, but she didn't like her grad students to see her flustered.

She didn't like anyone to see her flustered.

Ron had taken to emailing her daily. Easy enough to ignore at first. She filed his messages away in her Trash folder.

It wasn't that she was angry with him. She was simply done with that part of her life, and they both needed to move on.

But today's subject line had gotten her attention.

*Suggestion for your next paper,* he'd written.

And like a dingbat, she'd clicked.

He'd been very complimentary.

At first.

So proud of her for being selected to give a keynote address at the Stuttgart conference. Really impressed with her papers and articles and also that she'd managed to get both into such prestigious publications.

But he was concerned she'd overestimated a key compression ratio, and his research proved it. They needed to talk before she went to Germany.

Preferably sooner, so she didn't embarrass herself and James Robert College in the process. He knew how hard it was to be a woman in a technical field—ha!—and he was simply looking out for her best interest if she wanted to make tenure.

*Hey, Kaci. You're wrong, and you're about to make a fool of all of us. Let me hold your hand and patronize you.*

Ron's research was still hypothetical. Yes, he'd earned his doctorate before she had, but he was only beginning to get his first real research lab up and running, with most of his time before this summer occupied with other academic pursuits in his military career. Kaci had hard numbers and a year's worth of experimentation and data to back her up, with three years of preliminary work before that.

Her results had been replicated in two other universities since her paper was published, including in Stuttgart, and she was in contact with chemists at another university who had been integrating her research with theirs.

She didn't mind collaboration.

She *liked* collaboration. If she'd done something wrong, she wanted to know, and she wanted to fix it. Make it better. Stronger.

But Ron didn't have any evidence to back up his assertions. Just theories based on incomplete data sets.

He might've read her papers, but he didn't have day-to-day access to her work.

All he had was his own arrogance.

But she was putting him behind her. Moving forward. Getting out of the office for the day so she could answer him in a dignified manner tomorrow.

She pushed out of the physics building and into the bright fall sunshine. The leaves on the southern maple and pecan trees hadn't yet turned their fall colors, but the green wasn't as lush as it had been a month ago. A cool breeze hinted that the best summer days had already passed.

The cracks in the sidewalk passed in a blur as she charged toward the parking lot, alternately composing a response to Ron in her head and ordering herself to forget about him. She was halfway across the lot before she realized something wasn't right.

And all of that not-rightness simultaneously flooded her veins with panic and made her heart do a swoony number no self-respecting physics professor would ever admit to.

Before she could fully process what she was—and wasn't—seeing, Zada waved from the other side of the parking lot and jogged toward her. "Dr. Boudreaux!" Her chin trembled when she drew to a stop beside Kaci. "Dr. Boudreaux, did the Gellings Fall Fest pumpkin-chucking organizers disqualify that other team?"

Kaci eyed the lone man sitting in the bed of a truck where she swore she'd left her Jeep this morning, then angled away from him and lowered her voice. "Not that I've heard. Their webpage say something?"

"No, but..." Zada lifted a delicate finger and pointed toward the student center down the way. "The bookstore has credit for all of us on the catapult team. The exact amount of the prize money."

Kaci opened her mouth.

Then closed it.

A foreign heat warmed her cheeks.

With all the distractions from Ron, Lance, and Gertrude, she'd forgotten about the bookstore.

"Don't know anything about it, but I know y'all did an amazing job with Ichabod. My momma would say the angels were watching." She steered Zada back toward the building. Because even if she wanted to discuss this—which she didn't—she didn't want to do it with an audience.

While her Jeep was missing.

And with Lance in the bed of his truck right in the very spot where she'd parked this morning.

"Did y'all get my message about setting up a booth for the Physics Club at Spirit Week?" she asked Zada.

"Yes, but—"

"Great. Let me know what you want to do for demonstrations, or if you need ideas."

"Dr. Boudreaux—"

"You don't want to do Spirit Week?"

"We do, but—"

"Oh, good. Y'all will have fun with it. How about you bring a sign-up sheet to our meeting tomorrow, and I'll bring that binder of ideas we put together for our high school visits last year. Bound to have something good in there."

Zada stood there a moment longer as though she were debating pressing for more information about the bookstore.

But Kaci needed her game face.

Because her brain was coming up with all kinds of ugly reasons why her car was missing and why Lance Wheeler was parked in her spot, and she needed to find out the truth before she panicked for no good reason.

Or before her redneck side paired up with her feminine side and overruled her common sense. Because if that happened, she'd be offering to mud wrestle him for her Jeep.

And even with her car missing, she couldn't deny the thrill of anticipation at the prospect of touching the man again.

As far as pranks went, she was facing the losing side this time.

"Okay, Dr. Boudreaux," Zada finally said. She pushed her wispy bangs out of her eyes while her gaze darted quickly toward Lance. "But if you hear who we can thank for the bookstore credit, can you let them know how grateful we are? I—it's going to be a lot easier to buy books next semester."

"I'll keep an ear out, sugar."

Zada went back the way she came, curiosity lingering in the long look she cast at Lance while she walked away.

He nodded to her, and she put her head down and kept walking.

But Kaci wouldn't be running away.

She never did.

※

LANCE WAS EITHER IN FOR one hell of a good time, or he'd be leaving here in handcuffs.

His squadron buddies weren't always right, but they were damn certain they'd always win.

So here he was, in the bed of his truck in a staff parking spot, ready to play mediator since he hadn't been able to stop his buddies' version of vengeance.

And if he happened to enjoy himself in the process, that was the price he'd have to pay.

He was crunching on corn chips with a six-pack of diet soda and a pack of Mentos beside him, debating breaking into the soda when she finally marched up to him.

Not that he'd minded the delay. Listening in on her conversation had been interesting.

Borderline enlightening even.

And watching her process exactly what had happened to her Jeep had been entertaining.

To say the least.

"Captain Wheeler," she said when she stopped beside his truck, arms crossed, and some *where the hell is my car?* warring with some *you're gonna pay for this* in her murderous glare.

He suppressed a grin. "Dr. Boudreaux."

Her nostrils quivered. "There's a line, and I'm standing here hoping to sweet baby Jolene y'all didn't cross it."

Did she know how funny she was, or did she think she was projecting hard-ass? Either way, he gave her credit for not pitching a hissy fit.

"Gertrude is part of our family," he said. "I'm here to negotiate."

"This here doesn't call for negotiation. This here calls for war. And you're gonna have more luck defying physics than you'll have proving I have anything that belongs to you."

"Sweetheart, I defy physics every day."

Something twisted in her expression, but she straightened it out before he could read her. "There's no sweetheartin' in my line of work."

"Maybe not, but we have security tapes from your apartment building. I know you have what I want."

A blush flooded her round cheeks. Her pulse visibly fluttered at the base of her throat. "Rather extreme escalation, Captain Wheeler. If your *Gertrude* is worth a car, she must be practically priceless."

"She's very near and dear to our hearts."

"If you ever want to see her again, you better be fixin' to offer something better than just returning my Jeep. I can get another one of those."

He had to swallow a smile again. She might not have twelve guys behind her strong enough to lift a Jeep onto a flatbed, but she carried herself as though she did.

Would've been disappointing if she hadn't.

He lifted the soda and Mentos. "How about this? Got a feeling you're the type to get a kick out of watching a bottle of pop explode. If that suits your fancy, I can probably find something more too."

She cocked a brow at him. Her blond hair shimmered in the sunlight, and those perfect tits sat up straighter. "More? Or bigger?"

"Define more and bigger."

"I've never fired a cannon."

"Cannon authorizations are above my pay grade."

"Humph." She swung her hips back into motion and turned around as though she were headed back to the physics building.

Where she could make a phone call that would land *all* of them in a hell of a lot of trouble.

Car theft almost certainly carried a higher penalty than boar theft.

And he hadn't been able to convince Pony—or anyone else— that they'd be giving her the upper hand if they took her wheels.

He wanted the hell out of Georgia. Criminal charges would not only keep him here longer, he'd miss his deployment.

"Ever ride in a Cessna?" he heard himself ask.

She visibly shuddered but snapped her spine straight and tossed a coy smile over her shoulder. "Sugar, unless you're getting me in the backseat of an F-15, I don't have much use for talking about airplanes."

"Give me two days."

The blood drained from her face as though someone were sucking it out of her toes—forehead to chin, then her neck went pale as milk too. Her voice was still strong and sassy though. "Heard that one before."

"My sister flies fifteens. She has a hookup for incentive rides."

Kaci swayed. "Sure you got a sister. You kiss her before you go to bed every night?"

Her tone didn't match the sass in her words.

And even Lance's ego wasn't big enough to convince himself that Kaci was bothered because he'd mentioned another woman.

No, she was—holy shit. "You're afraid to fly."

She sniffed. "You been sitting out here all afternoon? The sunshine's gone to your brain." But her knuckles were white while she held herself straight as a lightning rod.

He scooted to the edge of his own tailgate. "You know airflow. Lift. Drag. All that science shit. Statistically, you're safer in an airplane than—"

"I said I ain't afraid to fly," she snapped.

"But you're lying."

"No wonder even your own sister won't kiss you if this is how you do your negotiating."

"You ever been in an airplane?"

She had to have flown somewhere in her life.

Hadn't she?

"This conversation is over. I want my car in its place at my apartment within an hour, or I'm calling the police."

She marched away, and this time, he didn't try to stop her.

As far as negotiations went, that had been an epic fail.

But as far as gathering useful intel went, he'd hit the gold mine. Dr. Kaci Boudreaux was afraid to fly. Hadn't seen that coming.

That fear was the chink in her armor.

She was suddenly more than brains and sass wrapped in a killer body.

She was human.

Which only made her more intriguing.

KACI COLLAPSED INTO HER CHAIR and grabbed her phone.

She should be furious. She should be horrified. She should be plotting something bigger than that hot-sauce-and-bottle-rockets incident of her sophomore year of high school.

Instead, she was mortified. And on the verge of hyperventilating.

He'd threatened to put her in an F-15. Yet she *still* nearly hadn't been able to walk away from him.

She was going to puke.

And that hog had to go.

As long as she had Gertrude hidden in her apartment's storage unit, she'd never be rid of him.

Even when she was so furious with him she couldn't think straight, even when he was threatening to take her airborne, she loved the thrill of being near him.

Not even seeing her Jeep missing had been enough to squelch her absurd attraction to him.

Sooner or later, he'd break her. She'd give in to the temptation to kiss him again. And then she'd want to touch him.

Closely.

Intimately.

Repeatedly.

But she didn't do flyers. She didn't date military men, especially car-stealing, F-15-threatening military men, no matter how much healthy respect she had for their style of escalation. She didn't even want to date men who loved her brain.

She wanted…to simply be loved by someone safe who wouldn't leave her too young.

Like Daddy had left Momma.

She wouldn't find that with Lance Wheeler, and she shouldn't want it.

She pounded in her home phone number. Tara had been working last night, so she hadn't yet filled her in on yesterday. "We have to get rid of Notorious P-I-G," she whispered when Tara picked up.

"They're onto us?" Tara whispered back.

"Oh, yeah."

"Crap. Okay. Meet me at home. I have an idea."

Kaci did too, but much as she was intrigued at wondering how high they could take Gertrude in a makeshift low-altitude space-ship—and what those danged flyers would do if they saw the pictures—she'd never be rid of Lance if she didn't hand over the hog.

"Can you pick me up? Those dang flyers stole my car."

"They *stole your car?*"

"Like I said, we have to get rid of that boar."

And then she'd get her head screwed back on right.

⁂

TEN MINUTES LATER, TARA'S LITTLE red coupe careened to a stop near where Lance had been parked. "Whoa, hey, what's wrong?"

Kaci scrambled into the car. "Let's get that boar loaded up and dropped off."

"I brought a friend." Tara hooked a thumb behind her. "Mrs. Sheridan stops in at Jimmy Beans, and she got us visitor passes for the base and permission to put the boar under that big fighter jet on a stick right inside the main gate. Isn't that fabulous?"

Kaci blinked at the other woman behind her.

Mrs. Sheridan. She'd come to a few events at James Robert. Always very nice. Always very official.

"You brought the base commander's wife?" she hissed. Mrs. Sheridan's husband oversaw *all* operations on the base, for all the squadrons and units and departments. Everyone could be in serious trouble, from Kaci to Lance's squadron to who knew who else?

"Bob was in the refueler squadron who owned that boar once upon a time," the older woman offered. "He's highly amused. Unofficially, of course."

Oh, lordy. This was getting bad. "So we're gonna let the whole world know their mascot got stolen by some girls?" Kaci said. Oh, no. No, nope, not gonna happen.

Lance won.

She was done playing with that man. He had the royal flush, and all she had left in her hand was a pair of twos.

Forget her Jeep. If he wanted to, he could tell the whole world she was afraid to fly.

And then her trip to Germany would be under even more scrutiny.

"Kaci? They won't seriously hurt your car. They can't. Even they have to know how much trouble they'd be in."

"Your *car*?" Mrs. Sheridan said. "They took your *car*?"

"Probably just took it out for a car wash." Kaci had started this. She could own the consequences.

"Or they're boxing it up to drop it off a ramp next time they're in the air over the Eglin range," Mrs. Sheridan said.

Kaci's already overworked heart gave a whimper. Surely they wouldn't...would they?

She knew about the range at Eglin. Down in the Florida Panhandle, probably not even an hour away by air, hundreds of square miles for nothing but target practice by big flying gunships.

If they dropped her car over the range, she'd *never* see it again.

But...this *was* just a prank.

Wasn't it?

"If you girls got this covered, I'll just help you get Gertrude out of storage, and then I'm gonna wait for those boys to bring back my car. Been a doozy of a day with the ex too."

"You're not seriously backing out, are you?" Tara asked.

Was she?

Her pride yelled no, but her inner redneck had gone in hiding. "Not enough room for the three of us and the boar on the way to the base." She bit her lip. "And it won't exactly look good to *my* boss if he hears I've been fighting with the local military men."

Twenty minutes and a helping hand from two neighbors later, she waved as Tara and Mrs. Sheridan headed to the base without her.

Was she a chicken?

Hell yeah.

But she needed Lance Wheeler out of her life more than she needed fun.

Besides, that was her pink lipstick that Gertrude was sporting. She'd gotten her last bit of fun.

Now she was getting back to her normal. Waiting for her car to come back. Convincing herself she was done with Lance Wheeler forever.

And listening to hypnosis tapes in the meantime.

Her only real priority needed to be getting to Germany.

⋐∖⊙

THE SUN WAS SINKING IN the sky when Lance pulled through the gate to the base, then promptly parked beside Pony's truck. "Lipstick?" he said.

"Shut up and help me get her in the truck."

Lance stepped onto the grass beneath the life-size F-16 mounted on a stick at the entrance to the base. "How'd you hear she's back?"

He snorted and pointed to the gate. "Half the base saw two women dragging her out here while they were headed home for the day. Who *didn't* call is a better idea. By the way, the colonel wants to see us in the morning."

No doubt. "About Gertrude, or about our extracurricular activities out at the campus?"

"Better be about Gertrude, or I'm stringing Juice Box up by his toes."

They squatted on either side of the stuffed boar, then lifted her and carried her to Pony's truck.

"You boys need any help?" one of the security forces cops at the gate called.

"We got it," Pony called back.

Gertrude wasn't heavy. She was just *big*.

"Hope so, since Mrs. Sheridan and her girlfriend didn't have any problems with it."

Lance and Pony shared a look.

"Dr. Blondie knows the base commander's wife?" Pony said.

"We're fucked."

"No shit."

"You tell the guys to deliver her Jeep?"

Gertrude wobbled between them. Probably would've withered under the weight of Pony's glare if she'd still been alive. "Boar first. Then the Jeep." He swore under his breath. "If she told Mrs. Sheridan…"

"Let's get the hell out of here," Lance said.

"And then let's stay the hell away from that fucking nuisance of a physics professor," Pony said pointedly.

Lance ignored him.

Didn't need Pony telling him who he could and couldn't hang out with. And he damn well knew for himself that he needed to walk away.

Didn't mean he wanted to though.

Kaci Boudreaux was a pumpkin-sized boulder dropped into the placid lake of Lance's life, and he wasn't ready to let go.

She was unexpected. She was funny. And there was something about her—a puzzle, a mystery, or maybe just the fact that she was crazy—that had him hooked.

He'd wanted a distraction.

Looked like he had her.

## Chapter 8

TUESDAY MORNING, KACI CAREENED INTO her office thirty minutes early. In her Jeep, thank you very much.

She hadn't been entirely convinced Lance's squadron would bring it back, and she'd been on the verge of reminding him she knew the number to the police station when they'd shown up. She'd watched from the window while they pulled it off a flatbed trailer and delivered it safely into her normal parking spot, and now she was done with Lance forever.

To compensate for the weird feelings in her heart and belly, she'd had two brownies from Jimmy Beans for breakfast with her coffee, and she was bound and determined to do some research on overcoming phobias before she was due for any meetings or lectures.

Her phone was blinking, so while she waited for her computer to boot up, she checked the voicemail.

And all the fizzing in her veins from the caffeine and brownies instantly turned to flat-out jitters.

Except the jitters were eighty percent hormonal and twenty percent scaredy-cat.

"Hey there, Dr. Kaci," Lance's voice drawled in that subtle twang of his. "Just wanted to thank you for making sure Gertrude was safely guarded until we could get there to pick her up yesterday. If she had to be kidnapped, we're all relieved she was with someone who had her best interests at heart. Hope you found your Jeep without any trouble this morning. But there's still that matter of Pony's keg to settle. Appreciate if you'll give me a call."

That arrogant, muscle-headed son of a cow's uncle. She didn't want to call him. She didn't want to hear his voice. He was nothing more than a—

"And in case you're wondering," his message continued, "I *did* feel something when I kissed you. Both times."

All the jitters in her veins swirled together and her heart gave a big ol' *thump*.

This man was dangerous.

And lately, danger was exactly what she wanted.

❧

KACI COULD FIRE A POTATO gun without flinching, even if she could never aim the darn thing straight. She could set off fireworks with her eyes closed. And she could stare down a uniformed military man without so much as a twitch.

But she wasn't sure she had it in her to knock on the door of the gray brick cookie-cutter mini-mansion where she had it on good authority that Lance lived.

If he rejected her proposal, she might just crawl into a hole and never come out again.

Not that she *liked* him.

Not like that. Why would she? First of all, she didn't date flyers. Secondly, he was entirely too young for her. She liked her men with some experience under their belts.

But having a...a *friend* was never a bad thing. Right?

Of course, *friends* probably didn't need to call in favors to figure out where their *friends* lived. But he'd found her apartment—and temporarily commandeered her Jeep—so turnabout was fair play.

Or she could leave.

Nobody had to know she'd been here.

This was a stupid idea anyway.

James Robert College had a perfectly good psychology department. She'd go talk to an acquaintance or two over there, and—

"Huh. Am I supposed to be surprised or terrified?"

So much for the chicken way out. She lifted her eyes to look at the man who had just opened the door. "Honored, sugar."

His eyes went smoky and black holey, sucking her in while his lips curved in that maybe-I'll-smile, maybe-I'll-smirk kind of way he'd apparently mastered. "Don't hold your breath."

His green flight suit shouldn't have been sexy, but something about the way it hung off his broad shoulders all the way down to his boots was doing weird things to her belly.

Like the suit said *I am man and I can fly.*

Like men and flying were suddenly sexy.

"I assume since my door isn't smoking and hanging off its hinges that this is a friendly visit," he said.

The man knew her too well. "Doesn't have to stay that way."

His pearly whites flashed, and there went her femininity swooning. "I'm not here to do anything I wouldn't do in front of my momma. Just so you know."

"Or your ex-husband?"

She had a sudden flash of Lance's hands on her rear, his tongue in her mouth, his heady male scent enveloping her while his surprisingly strong body pressed against her, and she had to remind herself she was the daughter of a fighter pilot and a beauty queen before she felt her chin lift and her spine straighten. "You like sleeping with roadkill? Because I know where you live, which means I know where you sleep."

He chuckled and held the door open wide. "You coming in?"

Her pulse ricocheted.

She'd been alone with him, but never *this* alone.

But she wasn't here for his killer smile or his lean strength or even his suck-her-in bedroom eyes.

She was here to improve herself.

So she marched inside. "Hope you got sweet tea."

"Pretty sure I need mine leaded," he muttered.

But when she arched a look back at him, he was grinning.

She flipped her hair and faced forward again, then stopped flat out.

His living room was a shrine to the unholy Crimson Tide. A

University of Alabama blanket was tossed over the brown leather couch, and Bama bobbleheads lined a shelf beneath the big-screen TV on the wall. Surrounding the TV were Bama football and Air Force airplane posters tossed in for what was undoubtedly his idea of balance. Strikes eight and nine against any possibility of this man being good dating material. Though she'd bet that TV was fabulous for watching Ole Miss football. "You shouldn't let your frat buddies decorate your house. It's unbecoming."

He snorted. "And your apartment doesn't have Razorback crap and Albert Einstein posters all over?"

Only because Tara had threatened to call and invite her momma to do some more redecorating if Kaci didn't relinquish that job to her. Also, she was a Mississippian through and through, and not a single soul from her bloodline had ever come from Arkansas. "I'm a Rebel, not a pig, thank you very much. You gonna offer me something to drink, or just stand there acting like you've never had company before?"

"Depends on why you're here." He dropped onto his couch and propped his boots up on an ottoman, watching her.

She blew out a short breath and took a stiff position in his matching recliner, idly wondering if he had any tequila in those cabinets she could see behind the half wall separating the living room from the kitchen.

He was right. Might as well get to it.

"What we have here is a classic problem," she said. "You got a buddy with a blown keg, and I've got this little discomfort with being airborne. So I'll go flying with you, and you'll let this whole bill-over-the-keg thing drop."

He didn't blink. "And I get what out of this bargain?"

"You get to watch me be miserable. There's nothing good about me being in an airplane. But if you can fly it low enough and slow enough—but not too slow, we don't want to negate Bernoulli's principle here—then we might could both survive. Trust me, sugar, we both live through that, you're gonna be begging me to never get within three states of you again."

"Huh." He stroked his chin, lazy eyes watching her. "Still not seeing what's in it for me."

"You get to get rid of me."

"Why would I want to do that?"

He'd gone and popped a button in his brain. "You hit your head somewhere today?"

His wolfish grin made her ovaries stand up and do a striptease. "If I say yes, you gonna check me out, Dr. Nurse?"

She'd known he wouldn't cooperate easily. But did he have to go and torture her with his nurse fantasies? "If you hit your head, there's no way I'm flying with you, no matter how hard you beg."

"Won't be me doing the begging, Pixie-lou."

"So I could walk right on out of here this minute, and you'd never wonder what it would've been like to have me at your mercy in a—an airplane?"

In an airplane.

Thousands and thousands of feet above ground.

Oxygen so thin a gnat couldn't survive.

Temperatures so cold a polar bear would freeze.

If a plane busted up there, she'd turn into a popsicle in four-point-three seconds.

And then there would be the descent.

All her blood rushed to her toes.

She'd be falling.

Down, down, *down*. No net. No hope.

Her head went woozy.

Her bones turned to fluff.

She knew everything there was to know about forces, about statics and dynamics, fluids and pressure and airflow, but the safety and security of physics only went so far when the contraptions were built and flown by man and still subjected to Mother Nature's whims.

Lance's brows knitted together. "Okay there, Dr. Boudreaux?"

"You bet your britches," she gritted out. "So. When we going flying?"

Lordy Jezebel.

Flying.

Her feet off the ground. A plane off the ground. Soaring at unnatural speeds. The world shrinking. Until the plane stalled out and went into a tailspin, hurtling faster and faster, the wind ripping her hair out, slicing her skin off her bones—

His boots thumped to the ground while black spots danced in her vision. Her head felt funny, like someone was churning butter out of her brains, and she suddenly realized she couldn't feel her fingertips.

Did she even have fingertips?

A solid, warm hand settled on her neck and pushed. "Head between your knees," he said. "Breathe."

Breathing.

That was what she was missing.

Once she found it again, she'd kick his ass for seeing her like this.

She couldn't feel her lips either, but she thought she parted them. She could hear something that sounded like a dog panting. Heat flushed her skin. A rush of sensations swirled where his hand touched her neck.

"C'mon, Kaci," he said. "Slow down. Close your mouth. Breathe in slowly."

She latched onto his voice, and her body instinctively reacted to his orders. Her lips sealed. Her nose quivered. Fresh oxygen channeled to her lungs while the churning in her head slowed.

"There you go," he murmured. His thumb brushed her hairline, and she gasped out a mouthful of air.

She was sweating like a hog in August and her limbs were heavy as lead pipes, but the tingling in her fingers and toes receded. She squeezed her eyelids tight for three more long breaths.

It was time to go. Time to stand up, tuck her pride away, slink out, and never come back here again.

Shouldn't have come in the first place.

She lifted her head, and her eyes connected with two big ol' black holes of compassion.

He was right there, inches from her face, drawing her into his orbit with silent false promises of safety and security. His thumb rubbed a slow circle at the base of her skull. If she leaned forward, if she moved barely two degrees, her nose would touch his. She'd be close enough to taste him.

Close enough to tug down the zipper on his flight suit. To push the fabric off his shoulders, to see if he still felt as hot and solid and potent as she remembered. She usually preferred a man's brain to be his biggest muscle, but holy sweet jingle bells, she wanted this man's body.

"Better?" he murmured.

She licked her lips. "Oh, sugar, that was just a test." Her words were shaky, and so was the hand she tried to flutter. "I'll be sure to tell your commander you passed with flying colors."

He smirked. "*Flying* colors?"

The man was trying to kill her. "Flying colors," she repeated, though her tongue tripped over *flying*.

He tucked an errant strand of her hair back behind her ear. "Why would you trust me to take you flying?"

Why, indeed? "Seems to me you want to live through it as badly as I do."

"Not so sure anybody wants to live half as badly as you do."

"I'm gonna assume that was a compliment."

"Do you really want to go flying, or is this your way of trying to get into my pants?"

"Aww, your ego is too precious. Captain, if I wanted in your pants, I'd already be handing them back to—*mmph!*"

His mouth covered hers, his fingers tangling in her hair, his tongue making a slow stroke of her lower lip. She latched onto the rough green fabric of his flight suit, and though her pride said she should push him away, she spread her knees and tugged him closer, his hips between her thighs. She parted her lips and touched her tongue to his. A primal male rumble came from his chest, rattling beneath her grip over his heart.

And Kaci fell.

Under his spell, into his gravitational pull, with no safety net.

She was sitting on a chair, but she was soaring, unrestrained, *alive*, her heart dancing, her skin tingling, her body pulsing.

His hands slid down her neck, down her back, then under her shirt, his fingers hot and hungry on her skin, pulling her closer to him, spreading her legs wider, the ache at the core of her begging to feel him *there*. His nimble fingers reached her bra strap.

She scooted closer. *Closer.* Almost—

*Whoosh.*

The chair beneath her backside was suddenly gone. Her shoes slipped on the rug. Her feet shot forward. His arms tightened under her armpits, but she slid right out of his grasp, hands in the air, tailbone thumping to the ground. Her shirt was half up, and she was face-to-face with the tent in his flight suit, her rear end throbbing.

She'd slipped off the danged chair.

And she wanted to launch herself at him, kiss him again, peel his clothes off and ride him like she'd just gotten out of a convent.

"Aw, *shit*, Thumper? The blonde? Really?"

At the second voice in the room, she shoved at Lance.

A young pup who looked vaguely familiar was gawking at them from the door.

"Shove it, Juicy," Lance said. He untangled himself and pushed back on his heels, eyeing her as though *she* were the problem here.

She was, wasn't she?

"You okay?" he asked.

She scrambled to her feet, but had to grip the dang chair behind her for balance. "Getting sloppier, Captain. If that's how you fly a plane, I changed my mind. Hope you wear a parachute."

And before she could do something stupid—more stupid than coming here in the first place—she darted past the kid and out the door.

Maybe Lance was capable of helping her get over her fear of flying, but he wasn't capable of helping her get over her fear of him.

～

L ANCE HAD EIGHT HUNDRED MILLION reasons why continuing his fascination with Kaci Boudreaux was a bad idea. It was a wide-ranging list, starting with *she's two figs short of a fruitcake* and ending with *she'll make your life hell.*

Right in the middle of that list was the fact that she was a walking disaster.

But Wednesday morning, instead of hanging with Pony or the guys before their scheduled night flights, he hopped in his truck and drove over to James Robert College.

But unlike Kaci, when Lance went somewhere, he went with a plan.

Which was how he'd managed to get himself sitting in her office, feet propped on her desk, with a dozen red roses in hand when she unlocked the door and stepped inside.

"*Holy sweet jumping jacks!*" she screeched. "Who let you in here?"

He held out the flowers. "Gentlemen don't kiss and tell. Hope you like red. Blood-colored struck me as something you'd go for."

She was in jeans and a pink T-shirt with the speed of light equation stretched across her breasts. Her hair was tied back in some kind of knot. And she had a wild look in her blue eyes like she wanted to strap him to a catapult and see how far she could fling him.

He wanted to muss her hair, kiss her until neither of them could breathe, and learn every curve of that body.

Not because her body oozed sex appeal and her craziness promised an unforgettable time between the sheets, but because she was a walking contradiction. Spunky. Smart. Headstrong. Impulsive.

Still a mystery, but less so by the day.

She talked tough, but she hadn't ratted them out to the base commander. She was afraid to fly. She loved her students.

He wanted to know what other secrets she had.

She eyed the flowers but didn't take them. "This college is private property."

"I'm going." He swung his feet off her desk and set the bouquet on her keyboard. "My offer's in the card." He crossed around toward the door, taking grim satisfaction in the way her eyes darted over his body and lingered on his lips before her expression settled into a scowl.

"Pretty sure you'll like it," he murmured.

"If that there's got an offer of a striptease in it, I'm gonna aim my catapult at your house next time I get a wild hair."

"I'll warn the neighbors."

Did she realize she'd stomped her foot along with dialing up her glower? "Shouldn't you be at work?" she said.

"I'm flying tonight."

Her cheeks went the shade of her shirt.

He grinned. "Probably see me if you look out your window just after nine. I'll wave."

"I won't be watching."

"I'll wave anyway."

"You go on and do whatever you think you need to do. But you can do it outside of my office."

He sauntered two more steps to the door and caught sight of a familiar figure lingering in the hallway. "Sitting okay today?" he asked her.

"Doing better'n you will be if you don't get your rear end on out of here."

"I'll miss you too, Pixie-lou." He pulled her door shut behind him, then came to a stop before her ex-husband.

Lance didn't say anything.

The older man pointed a finger at his chest. "Leave her alone."

He didn't know the details—who'd left whom, why, or when—but he'd picked up enough that he was reasonably certain Kaci didn't want the guy.

Not when she'd kissed Lance the way she did.

"You hear me?" her ex said.

"You want her back?"

"Point is, she doesn't want you."

That was a *yes*.

"Word of advice, man?" Lance said. "You want her back, don't go threatening the competition. Lady likes to do that herself."

He clapped the older guy on the back, then headed out of the building.

He wasn't worried she would choose her ex over him.

He was worried about what it meant that he wanted to be one of her choices.

Short-term, this was fun.

But if she went wiggling into parts of his psyche where she didn't belong, this distraction would turn into a catastrophe.

⸙

KACI LOCKED HER DOOR AND pressed her ear to it, listening to Lance and Ron's short conversation. Her heart bounced like a rubber ball against a paddle.

She shouldn't want either one of them. Ron was a mess she would never touch again, and Lance was too heavy on the sexy to be good for her long-term.

But he knew her pretty dang well, didn't he?

The voices stopped, and an authoritative knock rang in her ear. She yanked the door open. "What?"

"Can I come in?" Ron said.

"No."

His chest puffed up, then deflated with his nose-sigh. "I have a therapy appointment tonight. I was hoping you'd go with me."

"You can keep hoping, but that won't turn a butterfly into a fish." She slid a glance down the hallway.

No Lance.

Not that she should care one way or another. The man had seen her at her worst. She didn't need a man like that in her life.

Ron looked down the hallway too. "He's not good for you, Kaci."

"Not your call."

"You're still ignoring my emails."

"Don't have anything to talk to you about."

"I'm trying to help you here—"

"Dr. Kelly, when and if I need help from a chemist, I'll seek out a chemist based on his or her résumé, background, and standing in the professional community. Not on who I know personally. If you'll excuse me—"

"There's an opening on my research team. I want you to fill it."

Her jaw flapped open.

"We're working toward a similar goal," he said. "A hybrid project makes sense. You're among the best physicists here, and with the funding I'm working on, I think I could help you really take off."

"Who's helping *who* to take off?" Of the two of them, *he* hadn't been invited to speak at a major international symposium on the next generation of efficient combustion technology.

"Think about it. My experience—"

She shut the door in his face.

And when she turned around, Lance's roses leered at her.

"Good *gravy*," she muttered.

Ron knocked again.

She locked the door.

There were too many things red roses could mean. And by *too many things*, she meant *one bad thing*.

That the man was falling in love with her.

Why else did men bring red roses?

She plucked the card out of the plastic lining and settled into her desk chair, refusing to contemplate if it was still warm from Lance's recent occupation of it.

He'd brought her flowers.

To work.

And then left nearly as soon as she asked him to.

*Was* the man falling for her?

She pulled the note out of the white envelope.

His handwriting was strong and dark, in black ink.

*Kaci,*

*Hope the flowers don't give you the wrong idea. Figured it was the easiest way to get help getting into your office.*

She let out an indignant squeak.

What kind of man all but said *I don't like you like these flowers say I like you* in a note?

Whatever his offer, she was saying no.

*I'll make you a deal. Three hours of flight-prep training and one hour in the air, plus I'll give you an entire day alone to do whatever you want with my catapult.*

*In exchange, you go on a date with me.*

*One date.*

*My choice.*

*Final offer.*

*You have until five o'clock Friday night to decide.*

*—Lance*

Her belly defied gravity.

Flying for a date would've been an easy no. She could easily accuse him of getting the better end of the bargain on both of those, though she knew full well she'd be lying.

But the catapult.

Ooh, the man played dirty.

She lifted a rose and rubbed the petals over her lips. The floral scent invaded her senses, the silk tickling her skin.

She liked dirty.

She had healthy respect for dirty.

And she wanted to know just how dirty he could get.

KACI WAS USUALLY IN BED before Tara got home from her evening shifts at Jimmy Beans, but tonight, she was too wound up for sleep.

She'd tucked Miss Higgs in on her bed, and now she was sitting cross-legged on her couch, making notes for her speech and trying not to listen for the sound of a C-130 overhead.

She could've gone back to campus. Her lab was nearly soundproof.

But Tara wouldn't be there.

The door clicked open just after ten thirty. "Oh, hey," Tara said. Her keys clinked on the kitchen counter, and a *thump* suggested she'd dumped her bag on the floor. "We had leftover brownies tonight. Want one?"

"That's the best idea I've heard all day." Kaci set her notes aside and patted the couch. "How was class?"

"Boring as usual, but hey, in another six months or so, I might be able to apply for real jobs again." She plopped onto the couch. "I got some writing done though. Bubba's having trouble accepting that he's just met his soul mate. She's way too hoity-toity for him. Super fun."

"You got a hero named Bubba?"

"Romance novels are all trends and cycles. I need to be ready for when redneck comes back in style. Then I'm gonna make a million dollars and retire to Destin. If I can ever finish one of these and get it out, anyway."

"Haven't ever known a Bubba I'd date, but then, I'm done with men. Period. But I'll still read your books when they come out, sugar."

Tara passed over a brownie. "Ol' Grandpappy?"

Kaci's nose wrinkled. He'd emailed her a bullet-pointed list of all the reasons she should join his team. And all of his reasons meant that, as lead researcher, Ron would get credit for anything she did.

Still, she'd emailed her own dean about setting up a meeting to discuss expanding her own project to include consultation from the chemistry department.

"Oh, no. Kaci. Are you *speechless?*"

"Near about."

Tara pulled her legs to her chest and released her hair tie. Her dark curls tumbled free. "You didn't go launching more pumpkins without me, did you? Did you hit his house? Or were you facing the wrong way again?"

"No, I...I got another problem."

"You found out one of those sexist bastards on the tenure committee is actually a cross-dresser, and you're not sure if you should expose her or not?"

A smile tugged at her lips. "No."

"A billionaire farmer with a tractor problem stopped in to see you today and offered to fund your research personally if you'll come be his concubine?"

"You know you're the best roommate I've ever had?"

"Considering Ol' Grandpappy was your last roommate, that's not really saying much." But Tara's bright eyes twinkled, and she leaned over to shoulder-bump Kaci. "But you're the best roommate I've ever had too. And considering Brandon was deployed well over half our marriage, that *is* saying something. So. Is this about Captain Kissy-Pants?"

Kaci took a bite of her brownie to stall.

"It *is*," Tara said. "Kaci, he's not a good idea.

"The man brought me roses and offered to let me at his catapult if I go on a date with him."

"Isn't that moving kinda fast?"

"He didn't ask me to *marry* him. Besides, he doesn't like me. He's one of those masochistic types."

"Hmm. Maybe you should go. Then tell me if he does anything weird. He looks like he could be into some freaky stuff."

"*Lance?* He's a stubborn billy goat, but other than wanting to take me out, he's not freaky."

"Ooh, he has a name." Tara whipped a notebook out of her back pocket. "And such a great one at that. *Lance*. Short for Lancelot? Or short for *look at this lance in my pants?*"

"Seriously?"

"Hey, *I'm* not the one contemplating going on a date so I can touch his catapult."

Or so she could see him again.

Because that was what she'd been thinking about.

All day.

Lance wanted to see her again. And despite the million reasons she shouldn't have wanted to see him again, she wasn't strong enough to resist. "We're not picking out china patterns here," she said. "We're just…having some fun."

Tara pinned her with a *don't bullshit me* stare. "Does the name *Gertrude* ring any bells? Kaci, the man could've gotten you in serious trouble at work. And then he *stole your car*. And you're going to freaking *Germany*. I'd give my left nut to go to Germany. I'm all about having fun with a guy, but this guy? It's not a good idea."

Kaci bit into her brownie.

"You do *want* to go to Germany, don't you?" Tara said.

Of course she did.

She didn't want to get on a stinking airplane, but she'd do it to get to Germany.

"You're not secretly banned from going to Germany because of any potato gun or catapult mishaps, are you?" Tara whispered.

"That's only one county in Mississippi, and I never wanted to go back there again anyway."

"So why bother with the captain? Plenty of other men you could have fun with."

Kaci twisted the tassels on her chenille blanket. "So I can touch his catapult."

"Is that a euphemism? Because…" Tara frowned at her hand, lifting her index finger to simulate the motion of a catapult.

Her mind went back to making out with Lance yesterday— his capable hands on her skin, his tongue gliding against hers, that ache in her core—and she straightened. "I mean his pumpkin-chucking catapult. Ain't got no other use for him. He's barely more than a boy."

"He has a job, the government lets him fly multimillion-dollar airplanes, and he doesn't live with his momma," Tara said. "How much more grown-up can you get?"

"The young bucks are too reckless," she said.

Tara lifted a dark brow.

"What?" Kaci said. "Somebody's gotta be the responsible one."

"So long as you know what you're doing," Tara said on a sigh.

She didn't. Not by a long shot.

But if she were ever going to make it to big conferences overseas for herself, she had to start somewhere.

And that somewhere—or some*one*—had fallen in her lap.

If Lance could help her get comfortable enough that she didn't have to go to her doctor for antianxiety medicine, then she was willing to give it a shot.

## Chapter 9

WHILE KACI'S WARDROBE WAS EQUIPPED for every-thing from fancy galas to tromping through the mud, she wasn't sure which outfit would handle it best if she tossed her cookies because of her new agreement with Lance.

She settled for jeans and her favorite Ole Miss T-shirt. For cour-age, she told herself. Not to provoke Mr. Alabama.

And even though she would've liked a shot or two of vodka, she settled for picking up a cup of tea from Jimmy Beans on her way to Lance's place Saturday morning. Probably a good thing Tara had gone to visit her folks in north Georgia this weekend. Because if she'd known where Kaci was headed, there would've been questions.

And advice.

And probably too much overthinking what to wear.

She'd overthought enough as it was.

When Lance opened his door, she decided the man himself was more terrifying than the flight training he'd promised to give her.

He had a five o'clock shadow going on at nine in the morning, jeans that looked buttery soft over his long, lean legs, and all kinds of delicious mischief written in the curve of his smile. "You made it."

"Didn't think I'd chicken out, did you?"

"Not you." He pulled the door wider, and she stepped past him. The living room was dark.

Blinds down, sheets-over-the-windows dark.

Kaci's steps faltered. "We doing some kind of trust exercise, or are you about to go axe murderer on me?"

He pointed to the TV with a remote, and it flashed on. "Somewhere in between."

"We closer to the trust side or the axe-murderer side?"

"Takes all the fun out of it if I tell you." He took her by the shoulders and nudged her toward the couch. "Sit. Get comfy. I have to go find my axe. And don't worry—I made my roommate disappear so he won't hear your screams."

"That young buck's really your roommate?"

"He rents a room. I keep him out of trouble."

"That what you're doing with me too?"

"There's not a force strong enough in the world to keep you out of trouble."

He had a point. She sipped her tea while he snagged two video game controllers from beneath the nearest end table.

He sat beside her, his hard thigh and arm lined up against hers. "Here. This one's for you."

"A video game? Sugar, you done lost your mind."

"Deal's a deal. Sit back down, Dr. Boudreaux. We're just getting started." He grinned again, but it was the dare lurking in his dark eyes that gave her pause.

*Chicken*, that look said.

*I knew you couldn't do it*, it said.

*No skin off my back, Dr. Boudreaux. I'm not the one afraid to fly*, it said.

She slowly lowered herself back to the couch.

With a full cushion-width between her and *Captain* Wheeler.

Because there was also some *you can trust me* lingering in his authoritative gaze.

She set her tea aside and gripped the controller with both hands. "How old are you?"

"How old should I be?"

Huh. Good question. "Old enough to know you can't just pick how old you get to be."

The TV screen flickered again. Her stomach hit the pavement.

"Ah, good. Here we go," he said.

A simulated but highly realistic-looking cockpit appeared on the screen, with windshields looking out over a runway.

Her pulse roared through her veins, and her fingers went tingly again. She knew it was a game, but the graphics were incredible, and her brain kept tripping at the idea that she was actually sitting in a real airplane.

"What's this supposed to do?" she scoffed.

Or tried to.

Lance leaned over, his head angled against her shoulder, while he pointed to the controller. "This is your throttle. It's going to make the engine go faster or slower if you pull it this way or that way. Control your rudders here and here, and the aileron here. Stabilizers here. Brakes here."

She nodded as if she had half a clue what he was talking about.

He lifted his head and grinned at her. "Won't work in flight though. You're copiloting, so anything you mess up, I'll fix."

A sexy woman's voice announced they were cleared for takeoff.

"Ready?" he said.

*Ready?*

Hell no, she wasn't *ready*.

"Great," he said. "Let's go fly."

This wasn't real.

It was just a game.

She was safe on the ground, letting her mind think it was rolling down a runway in an airplane.

Huh. Maybe this *was* a good idea.

"Wanna give her some power?" he said.

She licked her lips. "Which way do I push the thingie?"

"My thingie, or *the* thingie?"

"That date isn't until after I see your catapult, *Captain*. And even then, I'm not making any promises about touching *your* thingie."

"We both know you won't be able to keep your hands off." His skin brushed hers while she breathed in the scent of shampoo and coffee.

The man was right.

He'd have to beat her off with a stick.

"This one," he said. "Push the throttle up."

Kaci thumbed the controller forward, but her hands wobbled. He was so close. So relaxed. So confident.

"There you go," he said. "Just like that."

The white dashed lines on the TV screen sped by faster until, suddenly, they drifted lower. "Oh!"

"You're flying," he said.

Her heart was still pounding, but he was right.

She was flying.

A click sounded on the screen. "What was that? Did the wing fall off?"

"I put the landing gear up."

"Oh. Right." To minimize drag. She stared at the screen, watching the view of the land below shift and change. Trees faded into little green specks, and the horizon changed with a dark mass rising up before them. "What's that? What's going on?"

"Thunderstorm. We can go around it. You're going to lift your right aileron—no, the aileron—"

The plane suddenly pitched forward, and she saw the ground coming to meet them. "Oh, sweet Jesus, we're gonna die!"

"No, we're—yep. Yep, we died."

Orange flames overtook the screen.

She tossed her controller down and stood. "Well, that was fun. Maybe we can do it again sometime never."

"Kaci."

Shivers tickled her spine.

He sounded so much older when he said her name that way.

"I know what you're doing," she said. "But it's not working."

"It won't if you don't give it a chance."

"I'm giving it a chance."

He didn't contradict her or try to stop her. Instead, he lounged deeper into his couch. "Why are you so afraid to fly?"

In all her life, no one else had ever figured out that she was frightened to be airborne. But she was. Deathly terrified, to be blunt about it.

There weren't any answers for why her daddy's plane had gone down in the first Gulf War. Pilot error, enemy fire, or a mechanical malfunction—the government had never been able to give Momma a definitive cause. Probably because Daddy had crashed into the Persian Gulf, and all of the pieces of his plane had never been fully recovered. Kaci had been old enough when Daddy died to lie in bed at night and wonder if he'd known his plane was going down. If he'd seen the water rising up to meet him. If he'd tried to eject.

If he'd thought about her and Momma in his last moments.

She'd been old enough to have nightmares, but young enough to be unable to separate the nightmares from reality.

Old enough to understand that what went up had to come down.

Old enough to decide she'd never, ever voluntarily put herself at the mercy of an airplane.

Even Momma wouldn't fly, and Momma wasn't afraid of anything. She was going on sixty, and she hadn't been on an airplane since before Daddy died. If ever.

So why was the idea of confessing all this to Lance even more terrifying than the idea of flying?

"Why do you kiss women in bars and then run away?" she blurted.

Best she could do.

"I don't make a habit of kissing women when I don't know their names," he said. "It was a bad day."

She didn't say anything.

Because she'd had a bad day that day too.

"Can't say I'm sorry I met you though, which probably makes me crazier than you are," he continued. "And speaking of you, it's not uncommon to be afraid to fly. People aren't born with wings. Weren't meant to fly. Course, neither were pumpkins. Or BCGs."

Kaci stifled a groan.

She'd forgotten about Ron's military-issue glasses. Lance had probably found the medal too. And possibly the sock.

"Or don't you want to go wherever it is you're supposed to fly to?" he said.

"I want to go."

She wanted to go to Stuttgart badly enough to get on an airplane, didn't she? She wanted to rub elbows with famous physicists. She wanted to see the wind tunnels at the university. She wanted to stand up and present her research as the featured keynote guest and make connections with people who were brilliant and creative and driven.

She wanted to prove she was every bit as smart as every man who had ever taught in the James Robert Physics Department.

As the first female professor in the history of the department, she had a lot to prove.

Lance dangled his hands off his knees. "Where?"

"Germany. I was invited to speak at a symposium in Germany."

He tilted his head toward her vacated seat. "Then let's go to Germany."

She'd been showing her crazy since the moment they met, but here he was, offering to stay by her side and help her overcome her fears.

And for what?

To spend *more* time in her company.

Was it possible he was simply one of the good guys? That he'd simply had an off day the day they met, and this was his way of making up for it?

He pulled himself out of his seat, and once more he put his hands on her shoulders to steer her. Except this time, he guided her away from the couch, then pulled her to the floor. He sat behind her, straddling her, and wrapped his arms around her front, game controller firmly in hand.

"One more time," he said, his breath hot on her ear.

He hit two buttons. The screen flashed back to the opening sequence again. Two big windows overlooking a runway, with a control panel holding more buttons and levers and displays than any single human being could possibly monitor at one time.

That sexy woman's voice cleared them for takeoff again.

Lance's arms flexed around her. He tilted the controller, and the dashed white lines on the screen flew past quicker until the plane left the ground.

Her breath came in shallow bursts. She'd never been a snuggler—when she was married to Ron, she'd never wanted him to hug her after a bad day. She'd slept on her side of the bed, and he stayed on his side.

She'd also never told Ron she was afraid to fly.

"You know how lift works," Lance said. "Flying's just a matter of keeping the wings and tail in order."

The ominous thunderclouds rose up again, but he tilted the controller, his fingers doing something to the right buttons. The view of the world angled and the thunderstorm disappeared in the bottom right corner while his body leaned left, pulling her left along with him.

His fingers shifted again, and the view lazily returned to a normal bearing lined up with a big body of water on the horizon.

Kaci slowly eased back until she was resting against his solid chest while they straightened as well. The water wasn't real. She couldn't get hurt. "You play this game a lot?"

"I fly a lot."

She tried to suppress a shiver, but she didn't quite manage it.

"Got a real good crew," he said while he turned the plane on the screen to bring a distant island into view. "They keep the aircraft in top-notch shape. I test everything before I take any bird up in the air. Rather be grounded for nothing than up in the air with something, and I've never known a pilot who felt different."

"Have you…" She shook her head.

She didn't want to know. Not if he'd ever had engine trouble. Not if he'd ever done an emergency landing. Not if he'd ever lost a friend.

"You sure you want to go to Germany?" he said. "This island looks pretty damn nice to me."

Didn't look to be many places a girl could get in trouble on an island.

Her momma would like that, but Kaci might get bored.

"We could see who could build a better slingshot for all those coconuts," he continued.

Her lips parted, and she felt a pang, but this one wasn't in her heart.

It was much lower.

"Make a bet. Could probably come up with some pretty good stakes." His breath tickled the hair behind her ear while he steered the plane around the island, giving her a better view of the impressive graphics of the tropical paradise. "Whoever flings the coconut farthest gets a...*favor* from the loser."

"Ain't so sure I trust you not to cheat."

"Might lose on purpose just so I owe you a favor."

If he was half as capable with a woman's body as he was with a video game controller...

"You wouldn't do that."

His chuckle rumbled across her back. "Probably not."

He leveled the plane and pointed it out toward the open sea. His arms tightened against her, and his breath tickled her hair.

He had nice arms. Lean and long and defined as though he spent as many hours swimming and slicing through water as he did flying planes.

He took one hand off the controller. She flinched.

"Here." He palmed her hand and guided it to the controller. "You can fly."

Could she?

The view out the window on the TV wobbled, but Lance's hand was sure and solid around hers.

He guided her other hand to the controller too. His skin was hot, his legs propped on either side of her, his chest pressed against her back. Her belly quivered.

She needed to focus. She was here for help getting over a little discomfort flying so she could go to Germany. Not for a tumble with a flyboy.

But he was obviously interested.

What was the harm in having some fun on the side?

"Little more speed," he murmured.

His thumb pressed hers against the thrust button. The view on the TV became nothing but blue sky. Her belly dipped.

His arms tightened at her sides. "Beautiful."

"This supposed to teach me how to fly that dang plane when my pilot has a heart attack?"

"You'll be telling people you defied death and landed that bird even though it's all autopilot these days. Don't pretend you won't."

"Says you." The man had figured her out. And she couldn't decide if that was comforting or terrifying.

Most days, even her own momma didn't understand her. Kaci understood herself. Since her second semester of college, when she'd finally stood up for what she wanted to do with her life, she was the only person she'd ever truly counted on.

"You're all talk, Dr. Boudreaux."

"And fire and catapults. You forgot that part."

"And hog thief." He chuckled again, that warm, delicious sound going straight to her core.

"Now you're making stuff up." She felt a smile growing.

Huh. Smiling while her body and mind were half-convinced she was flying. No small miracle there.

"Level her off." He touched her thumb again, and she released the pressure on her throttle control. Spots of land appeared in the distance.

"That doesn't look like Germany."

"All right, smarty pants. You take us to Germany." Lance released her hands.

She shrieked. She jerked the controller, and the view pitched and wobbled. A giant mass of sea loomed beyond the plane's nose.

"Making it too easy, Dr. Boudreaux." He covered her hands again, and with three easy flicks of his thumbs, the screen righted itself again.

Her heart flung itself against her ribs as though it had been launched out of a cannon. "*Don't do that again.*"

His chest shook against her back.

"Are you laughing at me?"

"No." But there it was again. That vibration. Along with a suspicious cough-snort.

She twisted around.

He dropped his gaze, but not before she caught the amusement dancing in his dark eyes. His lips wobbled, and he seemed to be sucking in his cheeks.

Kaci launched to her feet.

He *was* laughing at her. She was getting all hot and bothered, and he was just playing. "Thank you for your time, Captain Wheeler. Obviously, this isn't gonna work."

"It's fine and dandy for you to give me shit over geography and who can fling a coconut farther, but I can't give it back? Sit down and get over yourself, Miss Know-It-All. Turbulence happens, and the plane keeps flying. Did I let you crash? No. And you know what? The pilot flying a commercial jet won't crash either. You're in more danger in a car than you are in the air. You're not going to crash."

Ice crystallized over her skin, and her lungs couldn't take in enough air. "Tell that to my daddy."

She didn't wait for understanding to dawn.

She couldn't.

She needed fresh air, and then she needed to go blow something up.

# Chapter 10

L ANCE'S PLANS FOR SATURDAY MORNING had been to ease into putting more moves on Kaci and play a few video games.

Instead, he'd gone and done something he was kicking himself for—he'd found the tough-as-nails, redneck physics professor's supersecret soft underbelly.

If the woman would've told him who her father was, he might've gone easier on her.

Maybe.

He still would've let her take the controller, but he wouldn't have told her planes don't crash. After spending the morning following a hunch and hitting pay dirt on Google, he knew he'd fucked up.

Plain and simple.

She was supposed to be a fun distraction.

She'd just become something more.

Which was why on Saturday night he found himself squatting outside her apartment with two melting hot fudge sundaes when he would rather be hanging out at Pony's place with the guys.

There weren't any pumpkin-chucking contests going on in the area or any hog wrestling or pyrotechnic displays, so he assumed she'd be home sooner or later. She hadn't answered her office phone number, and he didn't have her personal number.

He'd barely settled on the floor, though, when he felt an ominous presence.

Kaci stopped against the opposite wall, arms folded over the dirt streaks on her Ole Miss T-shirt.

He squinted.

Looked almost like soot. So did the streaks on her tight jeans and her left cheek.

"You lost?" she said.

He'd had a speech planned. Something about pushing too hard. About being sorry about her dad. About...something.

But there was danger written in those sparking blue eyes. As though she were daring him to suggest she'd been a chicken. Or that she needed to be handled with kid gloves.

This woman had been through something. Possibly more than losing her father at a young age.

And he wanted to tear down every last brick in those walls she'd put up, to discover what made Kaci Boudreaux tick.

What made her happy.

What made her sad.

What motivated her. What inspired her. What she'd seen in her ex-husband.

In other words, the woman who was supposed to be his distraction was rapidly becoming a fascination.

And he wasn't entirely certain that was a bad thing.

Good thing he was leaving in four weeks.

He slowly climbed to his feet, watching every nuance of her stance and expression. There were tight cords in her neck, a slender but defined bulge to her biceps, and a sweet heat rolling off her.

He held out a sundae. "Nuts?"

She eyed the sundae toppings with a flat, blue-flame gaze that he guessed probably left some of her male students more than a little uncomfortable from time to time. "You're pushing it, sugar."

"Got one without nuts too." He lifted the other sundae. "Take your pick."

She shifted those baby blues between his eyes and the ice cream. Just when he thought she would give him the boot, she plucked the sundae with nuts out of his hand and pushed past him to unlock her door. Without a word, she held it open for him.

Kaci being quiet—this was borderline terrifying.

Lance stepped into her apartment and followed her to the small kitchen. He caught a whiff of something girly, along with something that almost smelled like sulfur.

No telling if that was a good or bad sign.

He popped the plastic top off his sundae and settled on a stool at the countertop separating her kitchen from her living room. She slid him another unreadable look before digging into her own ice cream while she leaned back against her white cabinets.

Based on what he'd learned sniffing around the internet today, Kaci was about six years older than he was. She'd been in grade school when her father sank his F-15 in the Persian Gulf during the first Gulf War. She'd graduated as valedictorian from her high school in Cotton Blossom, Mississippi. And she was one of the featured speakers scheduled at a conference in Germany, presenting her breakthroughs in her research on efficient combustion.

But that wasn't all he'd discovered.

He took a slow lick of hot fudge and melted ice cream, watching her eyes narrow and those tendons in her neck stiffen tighter.

"You come here to talk, or you one of those horn-dogs who gets off on watching a woman eat ice cream?" she said.

"Some of both."

The corners of her lips flicked upward as though she were amused by his honesty.

He dipped his spoon back into the soupy mess of his sundae. "So, Miss Grits, huh?"

"You might want to switch back to just the ogling. Safer that way."

He grinned. "How's a beauty queen go from planning on majoring in English to being asked to fly across the Atlantic as the smartest professor at a physics conference?"

"The question you need to be asking yourself is how dumb you're fixin' to look when you walk out of here with your rear end where your face goes."

God, this was fun. "Just saying, English to physics is a big leap."

"And I'm just saying it's none of your business."

He stirred his melted ice cream and watched the fudge swirl into the milky substance. "Went through pilot training with my sister," he said. "Watching the shit they put her through for being a woman made me wonder what year we were living in. And she wouldn't let me fight her battles for her, because she needed to prove herself to them. Not a single one of them's laughing now, because she schooled *all* our asses. She had to. Nobody thought a woman could keep up. Changed her. And she loves flying fighters, but I still wonder how much she had to give up that I'll never know about."

She was poking her sundae but watching him closely as though she were puzzling him out.

He lifted a shoulder in a casual shrug. "Going out to Jim-Bob reminded me of how few female professors I had in college. Thought maybe you and Cheri had something in common."

She slid the spoon into her mouth, and his groin twitched at the sight of her tongue. Behind him, something snuffled.

"Oh, Miss Higgs, I know." Kaci set her ice cream down and crossed to the living room, where she picked up a massive white ball of fluff. "But you can't have ice cream. Doctor's orders." She carried the thing—an oversized ferret? A mutant lab rat?—to the kitchen, then deposited it next to the fridge. "How about some kibble, kitty cat?"

Ah.

She had a cat.

A cat that needed a full minute to lower itself to the ground and roll onto its side while it made the snuffling noise again.

He shoveled a scoop of ice cream into his mouth, because if he didn't, he was afraid he'd ask what was wrong with the thing.

And he had a feeling Kaci wouldn't much appreciate that.

She pulled out a can of cat food and a can opener. "My momma wanted me to major in English," she said to the can. "Thought my prospects would be better that way. She's a strong believer in the power of making a good home to make a good life."

He shoveled another spoonful of melted ice cream into his mouth to keep from insulting her momma.

Not that there was anything wrong with a woman wanting to be a homemaker—that was half of what he'd found attractive in Allison, if he were being honest with himself—but Kaci didn't fit the homemaker mold.

"And you're right," she said. "Not many people switch from English to physics. Weren't many who thought I could do it. But if you're fixin' to—"

"It's impressive," he said before she could get back on the war-path.

She slid him a suspicious eyeball.

He didn't blink.

Had a feeling blinking would be a bad thing.

The cat snuffled again. Kaci set its food bowl on the floor, right next to its head.

"I have to go to Germany." Her words held a ferocity that Lance recognized too well. "If I let being afraid of flying stop me from going to Germany, I'm missing a chance to show young girls everywhere that they're smart enough to study science, technology, engineering, and math too. What good does it do me to be a good physicist if I can't help pave the way for more women like me who are being told girls aren't smart enough for math and science?"

"So let's get you on that plane."

She bit down on her lower lip.

"Come over tomorrow." On second thought, Juice Box would probably be at home tomorrow. "Or I can bring the game over here. You can play it anytime you want."

"Why are you being so nice to me?"

"I'm a nice guy."

Her eyes narrowed, and he swallowed a chuckle.

She stalked to the counter between them. "Why did you quit kissing me that night we met?"

This was getting too personal. "Why did you let me kiss you in the first place?"

"I found out I had to get on a plane to Germany, then my ex-husband came sniffing around, and I was out of tequila at home. I needed a distraction. Your turn. Why did you really quit kissing me?"

He swallowed. "I didn't know your name."

Any other woman might've given him credit for his gallant chivalry.

Not Kaci.

"Then why did you start kissing me?" she said.

"I can't tell you that."

"Why?"

"Because if I do, it'll change the way you're looking at me, and honestly, I'd much rather have you sassing me and being a bulldog. You're a sexy bulldog."

"That's the most insulting compliment I've ever gotten."

"Mission accomplished."

"Oh, no, sugar. Not that easy. I know a deflection when I see one. And that was a bad one."

She had a point.

But she was also close enough for his favorite kind of distraction.

The *good* kind of distraction.

He brushed his thumb over the tip of her ear. She sucked in a surprised breath. He pushed up on his stool and touched his lips to hers, a soft whisper of a touch, and added the slightest flick of his tongue across her ripe lower lip.

"You're cheating," she whispered.

But she didn't pull away.

He tugged her hair tie loose. The silky strands of her hair cascaded over his fingers while he angled his head and went in for a long, slow, deep kiss. She whimpered in his mouth and gripped his T-shirt, holding him in place while he tickled and teased her mouth with his tongue.

*This* was where they should've ended up last month.

Except tonight, he knew exactly who she was, and she was the only woman on his mind.

And tonight, she was letting him kiss her. Not only letting him, but kissing him right back. Her sassy tongue darted into his mouth. A low, throaty growl purred out of her. All rational thought fled his brain.

More.

He needed more of this woman.

His hands trailed down the soft skin of her neck to the curve of her shoulders. Too much fabric. Too many clothes.

She tightened her grip on his shirt. His hard-on bumped the underside of the counter, and he had to push up on the stool rungs to get close enough to her.

He wanted to feel the skin on her elbows. Taste her nipples. Lose himself between her legs.

And he wanted her *now*.

"Kaci—"

"No talking."

She sealed her mouth back over his, and with one more tug, she had him crawling over the counter.

Crawling.

For *this* woman.

She gripped the back of his head with one hand while the other trailed down his shirt, igniting a sizzle on his skin that short-circuited the few brain cells he had left.

He landed on her side of the counter and suckled his way along her jawbone, each of her pants and moans making his groin throb harder.

She was crazy.

But she was also shoving her hands under his shirt while he bent her over the counter, wrapping her legs around his waist and thrusting against him while keeping up a running list of demands and instructions.

"Don't stop."

"There."

"Sweet baby Jenga, that's the spot."

"More."

"I hope you don't kiss your momma with that—*oooh*, yes. Yes. More."

She tweaked his nipples. She pushed his shirt off and nipped his shoulder. And that sweet core of hers rocking against him had him about to explode through his jeans. "Kaci—"

"*No talking*," she said again. "Oh, my holy sweet heavens, who taught you to—*yes*."

"You need to get naked," he murmured into her elbow. He flicked his tongue over the silky skin.

She arched into him, her legs a vise grip on his hips. "If you think I'm taking orders from—"

Kissing her was remarkably effective.

But if he didn't get both of them out of their clothes, his main event would be over before it started.

He lifted her shirt, letting his knuckles brush her ribs and lacy bra.

Something furry brushed his leg, and a long, snuffly wheeze broke through Kaci's gasps and whimpers.

Lance pushed the cat away and pulled Kaci's shirt over her head. She wrapped her arms around his shoulders and planted those sweet lips back on his mouth.

The cat hacked out another wheeze. It yowled an unholy sound, as if it had a hairball from hell stuck in its throat.

"*Miss Higgs.*" Kaci shoved him away and dropped to the ground.

Her cat's frosted eyes bulged out and its tongue hung limp. Its chest heaved, but the rest of it twitched and spasmed, its paws stretching and contracting involuntarily.

Kaci pulled the cat into her lap. "Oh, no, baby girl, don't you do this. You're gonna be okay. You're gonna be fine, sweet kitty. You just hang on."

Shivers went down Lance's spine.

The yowl dropped off and the twitching stopped, and the cat seemed to melt into Kaci's lap. Its foggy eyes drifted shut, chest still heaving, but the rest of it—the thing looked dead.

She leapt to her feet, cradling the cat, and pushed past him.

She didn't look at him, but he could see the gloss in her eyes and the fluttering of her pulse in her neck while she spun until she found her keys. "Sorry I can't see you out, sugar."

"Kaci—"

"I gotta get Miss Higgs to the doctor."

The cat wheezed a desperate, gasping breath. Its front legs went stiff again, paws stretched out as though it were reaching for the doors to heaven.

Kaci sucked in a breath that would've sounded like a sob coming from any other woman. "Hold *on*, Miss Higgs. Just hold on, baby."

"Kaci, your shirt."

She whirled around, eyes wide, lips parted. She glanced frantically at the moaning cat in her arms, then at the shirt Lance held out.

His hard-on whimpered in frustration. And if the cat hadn't looked about three centuries old, Lance might've suspected it was playing him.

"Here." He gingerly reached for the furball, surprised to find it lighter than a six-pack under all its white fur and scarily stiff. "Let me take you to the vet."

She had her shirt on and was reaching for the cat before he finished asking. "I got this. Thanks for—" Her chin wobbled, and this time, when she looked at him, there was an uncertainty he wouldn't have expected from her a week ago. "Just...thanks."

She ducked her head again and barreled for the door. The cat let out one last whimpery yowl.

Lance was right on her heels. "Kaci, you can't drive and hold a cat. Let me take you."

"You're not dressed." She banged on the door across the way. "Mrs. Hamm? Mr. Hamm?"

The door flew open, and a kindly older gentleman swept one gaze over Kaci before springing into action. "Wanda, hon, I'm runnin' Kaci and Miss Higgs to the vet," he called.

"Door locks on its own," Kaci said to Lance.

And then she was gone with her neighbor, leaving him with a half-mast erection and the growing suspicion that his little post-being-left-at-the-altar, pre-deployment fling was doomed.

FOUR HOURS LATER, AFTER RACKING up an emergency vet bill Kaci didn't want to think about, Miss Higgs was resting comfortably.

Given her age, there wasn't much the vet could do for her, but she'd stopped having seizures and was drinking water, so that was something.

She wasn't gone.

Yet.

Kaci would've stayed all night with her cat, but the vet ordered her to go home. If Miss Higgs was supposed to go tonight, she'd be gone already, the vet had said. Kaci needed sleep so she could take care of Miss Higgs when she came home tomorrow.

So once Miss Higgs was comfortably asleep, Kaci left the vet and climbed into her Jeep.

Mrs. Hamm had picked up Mr. Hamm after Kaci had assured him that Miss Higgs would be fine and then threatened to call a cab for him. So it was just her.

Going home would be the easy thing to do.

It would also be the chicken thing to do.

Tara wasn't there. If she wanted to crawl into bed and cry herself to sleep, no one would ever know.

But she wanted a friend more than she needed her pride. A friend who apparently understood more about her than she would've thought possible.

She fired up her engine and headed to Lance's house.

He'd been sweet to offer to go with her. She wasn't used to accepting help. She wasn't used to having help available. Even when she'd been married, she'd been independent.

She wouldn't have asked the Hamms for help tonight, except Lance had been right. She shouldn't have driven herself.

And she hadn't wanted him to go with her. She hadn't wanted him to see her if Miss Higgs didn't make it.

So who was she doing the greater disservice? Herself, in denying herself a friend?

Or Lance, in denying him her trust?

It was approaching midnight when she reached his house. Lights glowed in his windows, so she climbed out and knocked.

But it wasn't Lance who stared back at her from the other side of the doorway.

It was one of his little flyer buddies.

His roommate, apparently, who still couldn't stop his eager-beaver eyes from drifting toward her chest. "Looking for round two with Thumper?"

"You old enough to shave on your own? Or does your momma still do that for you?" She squeezed her eyes shut. Probably not the fastest way to get to Lance, but she couldn't help herself. Her mouth did most of its own thinking when she wasn't in a classroom. "Is he here?"

"Nah. But I'm starting to wonder about his taste in women," the kid said.

That got her attention. "Excuse me?"

"Don't get me wrong. I wouldn't turn you down either. But then, I didn't just get rid of a crazy ex-fiancée."

A cold jolt shot through her stomach. She'd been showing her own crazy lately. Waving it like a flag. Might as well have tattooed it to her forehead.

But she and Lance—they weren't serious.

This was about lust.

Lust and flying and catapults.

With a side of quasi-friendship.

Right?

Still, if he was into crazy, that explained why he kept coming around.

"You wanna come in?" the kid said.

She didn't answer. Instead, she marched herself back to her Jeep. She had a friend to track down.

## Chapter 11

KACI FOUND LANCE IN THE last place she would've thought to look, but in retrospect, it made perfect sense.

He'd stayed at her apartment.

Waiting for her.

He'd been snoozing on her blue-checkered couch, as evidenced by the heavy eyes and sudden bolting when she walked through her door. He scrubbed a hand over his stubble. "How's your cat?"

"Fine."

Lordy, she was a mess. She opened her mouth to say more, but before she could get it out, he grinned.

"Good. Wanna get back to making out?"

She sucked in a gasp as realization settled in.

The man *wanted* her to give him a good what for.

Still, heat flooded her cheeks, and it took effort not to fly off on her broomstick. She turned her back on him and stalked to the kitchen. "It's getting real clear why your ex-fiancée's crazy. Was she your ex before or after the night we met?"

She grabbed three bottles from the cabinet over her sink.

Lance was eyeballing her as though he couldn't decide the right answer.

She cocked a hip. "Well?"

"Before." He visibly swallowed. "And she wasn't crazy."

"Huh."

He stood and stretched, pulling his polo tight over his hard abs "Just wanted to make sure your cat was okay. More flight prep tomorrow?"

"Sit on down." She snagged a stack of shot glasses, then carried the lot to her coffee table. "Pick your poison. You've been so nice helping me get over my little phobia, least I can do is fix your girl troubles."

He grimaced and stepped around her.

"Sit," she said again, gentler this time. "Don't have to say a word. I'll do all the talking. You grunt once for yes, twice for no, and I'll keep the Jack coming as long as you need it."

He stopped.

"Don't bother me a bit to be your rebound." Bold, even for her, but he kept coming back. Touching her. Kissing her. Even talking to her. Until this exact minute, anyway. "You're forgetting I've been there. But I wasn't so lucky as you—I actually married him."

His gaze shifted to the table, where she'd laid out her tequila, a fifth of Jack Daniels, and a bottle of cheap vodka she'd confiscated from an underage student.

"Don't leave me hanging. My cat's holding on by a thread and I'm still facing too many hours on an airplane in less than two months." She poured herself a shot of tequila and tossed it back.

Lance threw himself onto the couch beside her, arms crossed, still silent.

She took a guess and poured him a shot of the whiskey. "She break up with you that day we met?"

He grunted twice, then downed his whiskey.

"Was she the reason you were in the bar?"

One grunt, and he held his glass out for a refill.

Kaci topped them both off.

She didn't remember much about him clearly from the night they'd met. He'd been handsome. Sexy in a broody kind of way, surprisingly so. Something to take her mind off that phone call about going to Germany.

What would've put Lance in the bar that night?

"Oh," she whispered. "Did she leave you at the altar?"

He didn't answer, but instead tipped his glass back and swallowed his whiskey in one gulp. His throat worked, and she was suddenly struck by how rugged he looked when he didn't have to shave.

Weekends looked damn fine on Lance Wheeler.

She patted his thigh, which was a mistake, because his muscles were solid beneath the warm denim, and she knew firsthand that he was capable of being solid elsewhere in a matter of moments.

Not that she'd yet learned if he was proficient with his equipment, but hope sprang eternal.

She cleared her throat, and her voice came out softer than she meant it to. "Sugar, you don't know it yet, but meeting me is the best dang thing you've ever done for yourself."

He held his glass out for another refill. "Your humility is so inspiring."

"Gotta toot my own horn. Nobody else is gonna do it. Especially in academia. But the important part is, I know exactly how to get a woman out of your life."

"This isn't where we light a bonfire and set her pictures on fire, is it?"

"Bless your heart. That what that little kid at your house told you to do?"

He squeezed his eyes shut. "Juice Box."

"You need a juice box?" Weird, but okay. "I got some orange—"

"The kid. Juice Box. He told you about Allison."

Military men and their nicknames. "So that's her name."

"You went to my house."

"I—"

"You went to my house, and you're being nice to me," he accused.

"Most folks would take that as an honor."

"I'm not most folks."

"And I'm starting to believe that part about her not being the crazy one in your relationship."

"Not here looking for sympathy," he growled.

"Pish. If I was giving you sympathy, I'd be spoon-feeding you ice cream and complimenting your manhood. No, this here's me offering to help you move on with your life for real when you're done rebounding with me."

He scratched his chin and regarded her with a healthy mix of distrust, suspicion, and curiosity.

"You still got anything of hers?" she prompted.

"Got the rings." His lip curled.

"Good. After we torture me with your video game tomorrow, we'll go blow 'em up."

His lips parted.

"That Juice Box kid gonna be at your house tomorrow?"

"The United States government trusts *that kid* to fly multimillion-dollar airplanes."

"Shoot, three universities have trusted me to cause molecular explosions. Don't mean the whole world wants to spend time with me." She grinned at him. "But I'm right honored that you do."

He grunted twice and reached for the Jack.

Kaci stood and stretched, and she didn't miss the way his sleepy eyes lifted to roam her body.

But the man was headed toward a hangover, and she wasn't as steady on her feet as she should've been.

Dang tequila.

She bent over, leaning into his space, her head in a swirl-a-whirl. His eyes went dark as night, inviting her in, commanding her to come closer. "Glad you stayed, sugar," she whispered. She touched her lips to his and let her fingers drift down the hard planes of his chest. His capable hands cupped her breasts, and he suckled her lower lip into his mouth. Even with her head starting its swim in the drunk tank, a jolt of electric need shot through her bones.

When she found his jeans, she tucked her fingers into the pockets, drawing circles with her thumbs over his shirt while she went fishing.

She could've found what she wanted in seconds, but sweet holy jumping jacks, the man's mouth and his hands and his very essence were more intoxicating than any tequila she'd ever met. So she let him kiss her, indulging in the feeling of being wanted. Of being desired. Of being womanly and powerful and seductive, and in womanly, powerful, and seductive being *good* things.

But while this magnetic attraction to Lance might make her nipples ache and her inner core throb, she knew she wasn't the woman he really wanted. Whether his ex was that woman or not, Kaci would never be.

So why couldn't she let herself sink into him, to straddle him on her couch, unzip his jeans, and enjoy a night of drunken, no-strings sex that neither of them would have to regret in the morning?

Her left fingers connected with a metal ring. She tugged his keys out of his pocket, then slowly pulled out of his kiss. "Sleep well. I'll see you in the morning."

And even though her swollen breasts and her needy core groaned and protested, she tossed him an Ole Miss blanket and retreated to her bedroom.

---

LANCE BANGED AROUND KACI'S KITCHEN, his skull pounding almost as hard as his nutsack.

He shouldn't have stayed.

He shouldn't have taken that sixth shot of Jack.

And he shouldn't be clanging metal pots together if he didn't want his head to split open.

But his head splitting open was preferable to the sinking knowledge that he couldn't shake Kaci Boudreaux from his life.

He'd had his chance to score with her three times in the past twenty-four hours, and every last time she'd walked away.

She was out. Three strikes. So it wasn't anyone's fault her cat almost died the second time, but as far as he was concerned, that was a foul ball. Still counted as a strike.

So why, instead of banging down her door and reclaiming his keys, was he toasting bagels, fixing a fucking fruit salad, and looking for a pan to fry eggs, hoping she'd get up before he couldn't make any more excuses to stay here?

He slammed the door shut on her pots and pans.

Eggs were too much work, especially with the racket threatening to slice his brain open. If she'd had bacon in her fridge, that would've been one thing. Or if the noise of him *thinking* about making eggs would've gotten her out of bed.

But no.

She was in her room, probably on her back with her hair all spread out, her chest rising and falling, her covers pristine over her body as though she were Sleeping fucking Beauty.

And now he had a hard-on.

Again.

"*Dammit.*"

A burnt bagel popped out of the toaster.

Lance grabbed it and ate the damn thing anyway. He poured himself a second cup of coffee and nearly burned himself on his first gulp.

"Morning," Kaci chirped.

He spun, sloshing coffee onto his hand. He slammed the mug down and grabbed a towel.

"Hope you slept well and dreamed of Bama getting their rumps whomped by my Rebels," she said cheerfully. "Thanks for the coffee, sugar."

She helped herself to the mug he'd just set down, then took the second half of the burnt bagel and carried it into the living room. "Love me some charcoal in the morning."

Her hair was in a messy knot, her face scrubbed clean of makeup. Her baggy pajama pants and oversized Ole Miss T-shirt shouldn't have been sexy, but Lance was beginning to suspect the woman could make a garbage sack sexy.

He had a problem.

And it was called *Kaci Boudreaux*.

"Your keys are on my dresser. I gotta run out and check on Miss Higgs. Vet said she didn't have any more seizures last night, so I'll probably get to bring her home. Ain't like they can do much for a cat her age anyway. But don't you worry. She can come with us when we go take care of your wedding rings. You mind bringing your game thingie over here? Wouldn't want to have to break one of the military's finest if your roommate can't figure out where my eyes are."

Her ramblings should be annoying.

Her bravado should've gotten old before he'd stepped off the grounds of the pumpkin-chucking contest two weeks ago.

And her assumption that she could help him by doing something with his wedding rings should be insulting. Not just crossing the line, but fucking obliterating it.

But the part of him that had stood over a pair of pumpkin-gut-coated birth control glasses was insanely curious about what this woman would do with the band that could've been suffocating his finger now.

*Did* she have a magic formula to lift the odd guilt he still felt at being relieved his wedding had been canceled? At ignoring all the signs that while Allison would've made a damn fine officer's wife, she'd never really been the woman of his dreams?

"Oh, and you might want to wear something you don't mind getting dirty," she said. "By the way, no more kissing until that date you're making me go on. Just so you know."

That did it.

Lance stalked out of the kitchen and around the couch. He snagged the bagel from her hand and tossed it over his shoulder. The coffee mug went on the coffee table.

He thought.

It was possible she'd have a mess to clean up when he left.

But he didn't care.

Because Kaci had just dared him not to kiss her. As if she didn't want to kiss him.

He damn well knew better.

He cupped her head in his hands and slammed his mouth over hers. The vixen parted her lips, clenched his shirt, and slid her tongue against his.

He was already stiff as a pipe, but that sassy mouth and her assertive grip on his clothes made him harder than he'd ever been. His shaft pulsed against the restrictive hold of his jeans, his balls ached, and he felt the pain all the way up in his stomach.

He needed to be inside this woman.

He needed to strip her down, bust through her defenses, and lose himself in her essence. Where she was simply a woman who wanted him, and he was a man going mad over needing her.

But what he really needed was to get a fucking grip.

He wrenched himself free. "No kissing. Right."

While she sat sputtering on the couch, he retrieved his keys, marched out of her apartment, and let the door slam shut behind him.

Wasn't sure how he'd explain it to his throbbing dick, but he was almost certain he'd done the right thing.

Almost.

◈

IF KACI THOUGHT LAST NIGHT'S tequila had made her light-headed, the alcohol was nothing compared to Lance's goodbye kiss.

Her head was woozy, her knees jelly, and her ovaries might've exploded, by the way they were aching.

Telling Lance he couldn't kiss her?

She might as well have dressed herself all in red and jumped in a pen full of angry bulls.

Her legs had almost quit shaking by the time she stepped out of the shower, but her lips could still feel his, and she could still taste him on her tongue.

She needed to call him.

Find out if he ever wanted to see her again, or if she'd pushed him too far.

Pushing was what she did.

She'd pushed back against Momma putting her in beauty pageants in high school. She'd pushed back against sitting in the back row in pre-calculus and chemistry. She'd pushed back against advisors who'd laughed when she'd wanted to switch majors and study physics.

And she'd never stopped pushing.

Because there was always one more person telling her she

couldn't do it.

Ever since her daddy died.

Now, she was the one standing in her own way.

She was the one afraid to fly.

She was the one who had overreacted to not winning a pumpkin-chucking contest.

She was the one who kept pushing people away.

All the way to the vet, she couldn't stop thinking about Lance. She was hardly looking for husband number two, but she wasn't planning on being celibate the rest of her life either.

Seeing Miss Higgs was a good distraction. The poor kitty was moving slowly, but she hadn't had any more episodes, and her blood work was as good as it got for an elderly cat. Given her age, the vet saw no reason to keep her any longer, so Kaci brought her home.

Where she found Lance waiting in the hallway.

"We're kissing," he said.

Miss Higgs let out a pitiful meow.

And Kaci's inner vixen jumped up and did a happy butt-wiggle. She swallowed down her instinctive *says you* and instead unlocked the door.

Inside the apartment, Lance went straight to the TV with his game system. Kaci cuddled Miss Higgs and scratched her under the chin, alternately making sure her cat was okay and watching him maneuver wires and cords with long, nimble fingers. Too soon, her screen flickered with the familiar cockpit view.

Her stomach dropped.

Lance shoved a controller at her. Her grip tightened on Miss Higgs.

His dark features were set in granite. Not a flicker of a smile, not a hint of amusement.

"Happy to see you too," she muttered.

Because she was.

He tossed his own controller on the couch and yanked his shirt off. His long biceps bulged, his sun-kissed shoulders took up half the width of the room, and the light dusting of dark hair over his solid pecs made her mouth go dry.

Her eyes flared wide and every muscle in her body clenched.

Miss Higgs yowled and crawled off her lap.

Lance plopped down beside her, all taut muscle, tan skin, and testosterone. "Say another word and I'm taking my pants off."

Dear sweet baby Jesus, she could already see his erection outlined in his jeans.

Had she done that to him?

And if so, *when?*

He hit two buttons, and light flickered in her peripheral vision. "Pay attention," he ordered.

She blinked and forced herself to look at the screen. The woman's voice cleared them for takeoff.

"Push your throttle up," he said.

Her thumbs fumbled with the knob she remembered from yesterday, and the plane picked up speed.

"By the way, if you crash, *you* have to take something off."

"Don't come in here thinking you can—"

He reached for the button on his jeans.

Kaci snapped her mouth shut.

And a smug, satisfied smile crossed his lips.

It should've been ugly. Taunting. Demeaning.

Instead, she felt an intrigued pull deep in her core.

He was playing strip airplane with her.

And dang if it didn't give her a rush heady enough to make her forget why she was pretending to fly in a video game.

She glanced at the screen.

Back at Lance.

And back to the screen.

The runway disappeared. Blue sky and fluffy clouds appeared out the front of the cockpit.

She studied her controller. Which button had he said was the aileron?

No matter.

She hit four or five buttons in a row, some short, some long, then pushed down on the throttle.

The view on the TV wobbled, the ground came into view, and everything on-screen exploded into an orange mess.

"Oops," she said.

Lance tilted his head toward her.

Miss Higgs *harrumphed* and demanded to be let off the couch.

Kaci obliged the cat, then flicked a button on her blouse. Another button. A third.

She should probably call Tara and tell her not to hurry home.

His eyes went darker than midnight. His crotch visibly moved and his biceps bulged, but the rest of him held perfectly still.

She popped the last button and let her blouse hang open, her pink lace bra peeking through the gap. "Go on and be a gentleman and help me get this thing off."

His lips tightened. When he reached up with both hands, his fingers brushed her neck and shoulders with featherlight touches. Goose bumps skittered over her skin. Cool air swirled around her back and belly.

And when Lance had her shirt off, he picked his controller back up, hit two more buttons, and once again they were cleared for takeoff.

She could've pointed out that she'd spoken and he hadn't taken his pants off, but the thrill of anticipation was more exhilarating than chucking pumpkins.

"Go on," Lance said. "Take off."

She bit her lip to keep from asking *what* he wanted her to take off, and instead pushed up on the throttle knob.

The plane rolled down the runway, then went airborne.

Unlike yesterday, a storm didn't appear in the corner of the screen, and they were flying over land instead of water. Lance pointed to a button on her controller. "Raise your landing gear."

She hit the button and heard a *click*.

He pointed to a second set of buttons, his bare arm brushing hers. His hair had a clean shampoo scent, but the rest of him was all sexy, earthy male.

"Left rudder, right rudder." He indicated the top buttons next. "Left aileron, right aileron. We're coming up on wind shear. You're gonna need these."

Before she could ask how he knew, the view on the TV screen shifted violently.

She shrieked.

"Left aileron, right rudder," he said.

She hit a string of buttons, but she had no idea if they were the right ones. Her heart leapt into her throat, and the plane pitched forward. Miss Higgs yowled. Ground rushed toward the cockpit windows. "OhmysweetbabyJesus, we're gonna *die!*"

She tossed the controller and covered her face with her hands.

Maybe with two fingers spread so she could watch.

In case he was serious about taking off more clothes if she kept talking.

He snorted a disgusted, manly grunt of irritation, and moved his fingers over his own controller. The tendons in his neck were strung taut, that muscle visibly clenched in his jaw, and he radiated controlled, powerful focus.

She spread her fingers wider and glanced at the screen.

The horizon came back into view at the top of the screen, a strip of blue over the massive green forests on the ground. Slowly but surely, Lance righted the plane.

And he hadn't even broken a sweat.

She couldn't say the same.

"Pick up your damn controller and *fly*," he said.

Her hands mindlessly followed his orders, fumbling for the controller until she had her thumb back on the throttle, blinking at the various knobs and buttons and trying to remember which ones were rudders and ailerons and the tail.

"More thrust," he ordered.

Her thumb pressed upward.

"Good. Now ease off—that's enough—and hold it there."

He tossed his controller aside. She forced air into her nose while he stood and unhooked the button on his jeans.

Her nipples went painfully hard.

In one swift motion, he had his pants down at his ankles. He sat on her couch in his black boxer briefs and tugged the jeans the rest of the way off, tossed them onto her coffee table, then lounged back. His legs were long, lean, sculpted perfection, and his white gym socks added an odd, almost cozy sexiness to him. She had an inexplicable desire to lick his kneecaps.

But what truly had her heart sputtering was the thick bulge in his boxer briefs.

If he could use *that* joystick half as well as he righted video game airplanes…

"Left rudder," he said. "You're veering off course."

Was he kidding?

She couldn't have operated a door handle, much less control a video game airplane.

And he hadn't yet picked his controller back up.

"Pay attention to the screen." He was still using that *I am a pilot god* voice, but this time, instead of her body instantly snapping to attention and taking orders, her rebellious streak roared back to life.

She let her gaze linger over his body. The sinewy muscles in his forearms. The flat copper nipples on his hard pecs. His stubble. His treasure trail. His erection.

"No reward until you land the bird," he said.

"Oh, sugar, you sure you want to do that?"

He reached down and whipped off one sock.

She dropped her controller on the floor, stood, and slowly popped her button and slid down her zipper.

Miss Higgs crawled into her cat bed with a sigh and turned her back on them.

Kaci arched her back, tucked her thumbs in the waistband of her jeans, and took her time pushing them down first one hip, then the other.

Lance's eyes went coal black. His boxer briefs visibly strained, and his biceps bunched again.

She stepped out of her jeans.

His lips parted.

Apparently he liked her matching pink lace boy shorts.

"Your plane's crashing." His voice was low and husky, his eyes on her.

And a remarkable thing happened.

Kaci didn't panic at his words. She didn't go light-headed. She didn't hyperventilate.

Instead, she straddled him on the couch, put her hands to his face, and hovered with her lips a whisper from his. "We're doing this."

"Damn well better be good."

"That's supposed to be my line."

He snorted again. "You're not making the rules on my time, Dr. Boudreaux."

She'd let him believe that.

For now.

Because much as she enjoyed a good debate with Lance, she liked his lips on her more.

She licked his lower lip.

His eyes slid shut. He gripped her hair, thrust his hips against hers, and claimed her mouth.

She forgot everything except her desperate, driving need for release.

He pushed her onto her back, kissing her, stroking her, igniting every nerve ending she possessed, from her roots to her toes. Her skin was too tight, her muscles clenched too hard, her burning desire too big.

She was going to explode.

She shoved at his boxer briefs until she'd freed his erection and held him, hot and silky and heavy. He yanked on her panties. Something ripped and cool air rushed around her most sensitive parts. Her breasts ached in her bra, but it was a good ache. A needy ache. An *I'm ready* ache. Lance's hot body and his wicked-talented mouth and hands swirled in one big, chaotic jumble of feelings over her body, in her brain, burrowing into her heart and soul.

"I need—" she started.

"No talking."

She caught a flash of silver. He guided her hands, still holding his cock, and she helped him roll on a condom.

And then finally—*finally*—he pushed at her entrance and slid into her, filling her, stroking her, thrusting into her. Her feet dug into the cushions and she lifted her hips to take him in deeper, fuller, closer. She couldn't tell if that was his ragged breathing or hers, and she didn't care. That sweet wave was building deep inside her, bigger, stronger, closer—

The world exploded around her, and suddenly she was falling, sparks erupting behind her eyes, her body pulsing out of control in the most intense climax she'd ever felt.

He moaned, and she felt him coming inside her, his shaft pulsing against her inner walls.

He dropped his head to the crook of her neck, his chest heaving against hers, his breath hot on her skin.

She couldn't speak.

Because that wave inside her had carried beyond the basics of coupling. It made her chest squeeze, her heart spin as though it were locked in a centrifuge, and put a big ol' lump at the base of her throat. Her stomach rolled. Her eyes stung.

Never had she felt so powerful yet so helpless.

Because this hadn't just been sex.

That hadn't been a normal orgasm.

It had been more.

She'd wanted sex with Lance to take the edge off. To work out this weird attraction. The tension.

Instead, she wanted more.

More talking. More understanding. More accepting.

More Lance.

And she wanted more without fighting. Without orders. Without pretense.

But as far as she could tell, the pretenses were exactly what he liked about her.

L ANCE'S EYES WERE SO CROSSED he was honestly concerned he wouldn't be able to fly for a week. His sated limbs were heavy, and he had his nose buried in the sweet smell of satisfied woman.

*Firecracker* was an understatement.

And that was before she'd gotten all the way out of her clothes.

The woman rose to every challenge and left him struggling to keep up.

She took a shuddery breath beneath him. He struggled to lift his head, which felt like an anvil on his neck. About as useful too.

"Are you—" he started, but before he could finish, Kaci grunted and rolled.

While he was still on top of her.

His limp arms refused his commands to move. His body shifted. She gave him one last shove, and he tumbled off the couch and landed ass-first on the carpet. "What the hell?"

The last thing he saw was her wiping her nose on her way to grab her cat and shut both of them into her bedroom.

He gaped at the plain wood door.

On the screen, the plane was still burning.

Maybe ordering her out of her clothes had been an asshole move.

But Kaci Boudreaux didn't take orders unless she wanted to. She'd crashed the plane on purpose.

Twice.

She'd wanted to play along.

So what the hell was her problem? She'd gotten off just as much as he had.

Unless she'd been faking.

Would she…?

No, he decided. Not Kaci.

She'd much rather give him shit for *not* getting her off than fake her way through it for the sake of his ego.

And she'd initiated the kissing.

She'd wanted this.

Hadn't she? Had he missed some signal? Some sign?

He rose to his feet and tugged his underwear back up. "Kaci?" he called through her bedroom door.

She didn't answer.

He knocked. "Kaci?" he called again.

"Thanks for a nice time, sugar," came the response, albeit more strained than her normal flippant sass. "Turns out I got something to do, so we'll have to take care of your rings some other time. I'll call you later."

"Still owe you twenty minutes of flight prep for our hour today."

"We'll call it good enough."

The hell they would.

He twisted the doorknob, but it was locked. "Kaci—"

"Don't worry about locking the door on your way out. It's automatic."

Leaving would be smart. This thing with her wasn't about a relationship. It was about mutual sexual attraction. Her emotional state over their grown-up decisions wasn't his responsibility.

But he liked her. As a friend. She amused the hell out of him, and he had a lot of respect for what she'd obviously accomplished professionally.

Plus, he knew if he walked out her door, he wouldn't be coming back.

Did he care if she got on her plane to Germany? Sure, he cared.

But one woman had already screwed him up enough for his commander to worry over him. With Lance leaving for a deployment in a month?

No way in hell could he keep coming back for a woman who wouldn't even look at him after sex. She was either in this friendship, or he was done.

He yanked on his clothes and stalked to the door. And when it shut, he let it slam good and hard.

She wanted to make a statement?

He'd damn well make one too.

# Chapter 12

KACI'S WINDOWS RATTLED WHEN THE door slammed. She suppressed a shiver and nuzzled Miss Higgs's head while she choked out the teary gasp she'd been holding in.

There was a nice guy, a patient guy, a decent guy who had bent over backward to spend time with her and help her get over her fear of flying.

He'd tolerated everything she'd thrown at him, and then told her he understood.

He'd come back time and again.

And now he'd given her an earth-shattering orgasm, and she couldn't stop crying.

Kaci Boudreaux did *not* cry.

Crying was a sign of weakness. And she wasn't weak, dammit.

But she also wasn't used to *feeling*.

And she didn't know what to do with all of the feelings coursing through her body.

The elation. The satisfaction. The comfort. The intimacy. The vulnerability. The joy.

There was too much emotion for her to handle.

She settled Miss Higgs on the bed, then stepped into the bathroom for a good, long shower. By the time she was out and dressed, she almost felt Kaci-ish again.

Not exactly normal, but not drowning in emotions either.

Miss Higgs was sleeping peacefully on the quilt. Tara had texted—she was heading back from her parents' place and would be home sometime after dinner.

Kaci left the bedroom, intent on finding a sandwich in the kitchen.

Instead, her heart went into overdrive, adrenaline crashed through her veins, and she yelped. "How in the Sam Hill did you get back in here?"

Lance tossed his phone aside, but he didn't rise from his perch on the couch. "Never left."

Her eyes flew to the door, then back to him. "You fake-left."

"You for real ran away."

"I…" She trailed off. Because "I can't handle my feelings for you" wasn't something she could admit to him.

Not to a military pilot.

Not to a man just off a breakup.

Not to anyone, really.

Feelings didn't solve physics equations. Feelings wouldn't get her tenure. Feelings didn't improve her research habits or lecture style.

Lance sat there, leaning over with his elbows on his knees, and waited.

He'd tossed his clothes back on, though his T-shirt wasn't tucked in. His video game system was still hooked up to her TV. And his dark brown eyes were twin orbs of interested, nonjudgmental questions.

Unwelcome moisture stung her eyes again.

"Did I do something wrong?" he asked.

The arrogant flyboy was gone, and in his place was a simple man asking an honest question.

She shook her head.

He watched her, but for once, she couldn't find the words she wanted.

Or maybe she simply couldn't find the courage.

"Do you want me to leave?" he asked.

She shook her head again.

"No more rules, Kaci. You can talk. I won't take my clothes off."

She couldn't decide if she was relieved or disappointed.

The wise answer was probably neither, but she was leaning

more toward both.

He patted the couch. "Up for some Bama football?"

The man was brilliant.

Kaci tried to affect a snooty sniff. "Neither of our teams are playing today, and we both know it."

He flashed a grin, and the tension in her neck and shoulders eased. "Might catch some highlights."

She slowly approached the couch and curled into the opposite end. "Suppose I can watch some TV with you. Seeing as how you'd have to put up with your roommate if you went home."

He nodded gravely. "Nice of you to let me stay."

He didn't push for more on why she'd run away, but he was doing that *Lance* thing again.

Just being there.

Accepting her.

Acting like he still wanted to know her.

Kaci didn't have room in her life for a relationship, and sweet baby gingerbread knew Lance probably wasn't in a love-and-commitment place either, but that just made them fit better.

For now.

❧

LANCE SHOWED UP IN THE squadron room Monday morning feeling off-center. He hadn't slept well, and he didn't want to pinpoint why.

"Colonel's looking for you," Pony said when Lance dropped his bag at his desk.

The commander's door was closed, so Lance flung himself into his seat and took a minute to log in to his email. "Say why?"

"Need to know, and apparently I don't." Pony's chair squeaked when he swung it around to face Lance. "Heard you got some arrangement with the blond professor chick."

"Jealous?"

"Want my keg, dude." He swung back to his own desk. "And your head better be in the game when we leave."

Lance had four weeks. By then, he would've seen Kaci through her fear of flying, let her touch his catapult, they'd have had their date, had sex a few more times, and he'd be fine.

"Wheeler." Lieutenant Colonel Santiago stuck his head out of his office. "Got a minute?"

Lance dutifully followed him into the standard-issue seventies-style office. Award plaques, signed squadron photos, and a military coin rack hung on the fabric-covered walls. Lance sat on the flat-cushioned chair across from the colonel and propped his flight boot over his knee.

The colonel's desk chair squeaked when the man sat. He pushed his keyboard out of the way, then kicked his feet up on the desk. "Ready for deployment?"

"Yes, sir."

"Nice of you to step in for Flincher."

"Like to think he'd do the same for any one of us."

Colonel Santiago inclined his head. "Juice Box working out?"

Lance almost smiled. He'd discovered his roommate wasn't so much horny as eager to fit in, and he thought being a *man* would get him there faster. "At home or here?"

"Both."

"He's figuring it all out. He'll be fine."

"Seems you're a good influence on him."

"Kid just needs a friend."

The colonel smiled a shark's grin. The hairs on Lance's arms stood up.

"You heard we're looking for a few good IPs," Colonel Santiago said.

Oh, hell no. Lance's bags were packed. He wasn't staying here to babysit kids younger than Juice Box while the rest of the guys went out on the mission.

Hell, he wasn't staying here *period.* "Sir, with all due respect, I've done my time in the South. Like to see the rest of the country. The rest of the *world.*"

"You want to run away."

"I want the experience I signed up for."

"Since the fiancée's out of the picture."

"Life changes. Have to change with it."

"You're a damn fine officer and an even better pilot. That hasn't changed. So what are you going to do for your country?"

Aw, *fuck*.

"Been watching you with the young guys," Lieutenant Colonel Santiago continued. "They look up to you."

"So I need to be out there doing my job."

"Your job could be here, making sure the guys you'll be flying with for the next fifteen years are getting the best training they can get. Spend three years in the training squadron, you'll get your pick of assignments after. Italy, Germany, Hawaii...anywhere."

Lance swallowed the "no fucking thank you" trying to make its way out.

Two problems with the colonel's scenario.

First, it would take him off the mission. No deployments. No front line.

More time stuck here in that house he'd bought for Allison, three hours from home, six hours from his first squadron. Much as he still loved Bama football, he was ready to see something new, to *be* somewhere new. Maybe to be *someone* new.

Second, the colonel said *fifteen years* as though that was as long as Lance would last.

Wasn't any way in hell he was planning on serving his twenty and getting out. He'd damn well stay in until he had as many stars on his shoulders as the Air Force would give him, and the stars wouldn't come until he'd been in at least twenty-five.

But that was only if he was out there, on the front line, doing the mission year in and year out.

Three years here in the training squadron?

Might not be career suicide, but it was damn close.

And a cushy overseas or tropical follow-on assignment wouldn't change that.

"With all due respect, sir—"

"Think it over, Captain. Got a couple weeks to get your paperwork in if you want to volunteer."

"I don't need a couple weeks."

"Take them anyway."

Lance might be stubborn, but he wasn't stupid, and the colonel didn't want to hear no this morning.

Fine.

Lance could tell him no just as easily next week.

And because the Air Force was the Air Force, they could just as easily tell him too bad, he had to do it anyway.

The colonel dismissed him with a twinkle in his eye. "And go see your girlfriend," he said. "I hear she's an inspiring teacher."

He was going to break Juice Box's neck. "Don't have a girl-friend, sir."

"Then go see whoever she is." He flicked a hand toward the door.

Conversation over.

Out in the squadron room, he got a few curious stares, but he ignored them all.

He needed to call Cheri. She'd done a stint as an instructor pilot right out of undergrad flight training, and she'd gotten her choice of airplanes afterward and a near-guarantee of a thirty-year career. Being offered an IP job now, as opposed to right out of pilot training, apparently implied a cushy chance to kick back and count on retiring ten years earlier than planned.

The Air Force might still tap him to do IP duty, but damn if he'd volunteer for it.

Still, later that afternoon, he still found himself on the James Robert campus, strolling through the main physics building to the musty lecture hall.

He slipped into the back of the room unnoticed.

Odd. When he was an undergrad, the back rows had always had a smattering of people in them.

In Kaci's lecture, the whole class was no farther back than half-way.

She stood down front, facing the side wall while she hung a stuffed pink pig on a string connected to a pulley. Her voice carried without the aid of a microphone. In fact, he wasn't certain the room was even equipped for a microphone. They were old-school here.

Instead of her usual sassy twang, she spoke with a confident authority. Still Southern, but not redneck. He'd noticed the same authority, though her voice had been more relaxed when she'd been with her student last week. And though Lance couldn't see her students' faces today, he recognized the posture.

Leaning in. Interested. Not sleeping.

Some took notes, mostly on their electronic devices but a few on paper notepads.

Kaci was making gravity the most fascinating concept in the world.

Impressive skill.

Too bad she was afraid to fly. Half the guys who showed up for C-130 training were disappointed they hadn't gotten fighters. Needed that fire lit under them to love their birds the way Lance did.

He tugged at his collar and sank lower in his seat, letting Kaci pull him out of his own thoughts.

She yanked the pig up until it was at the top of the pulley, about twenty feet in the air, with a red laser dot centered on it.

The dot, he realized, was coming from the laser scope mounted on a crossbow on the table. He smothered a grin behind his hand.

She was going to shoot a stuffed pink pig in her classroom. A pink pig identical to the one sitting on the bar at Pony's man cave.

"Who wants to tell me what's going to happen when we fire this crossbow?" she said.

"It'll miss," said a girl up front.

"Why?"

"Gravity."

The door opened behind him. Three older men in slacks and button-downs entered and took seats across the aisle. Two women hovered in the doorway. "Has she shot it yet?" one whispered.

"I don't think so," the other whispered back.

The dark-haired one was vaguely familiar—had she been with Kaci on trivia night?—and he was almost certain the short-haired one was the department secretary. She'd helped him get into Kaci's office to deliver his offer.

"She's insane," one of the men across the aisle muttered to his colleagues.

"Can't believe she's going to Germany," another added. "What the hell were they thinking?"

Lance curled his fingers around the armrests. He'd endured years of lectures from Cheri about letting her fight her own battles since they both signed up for ROTC in college. About letting her earn her respect without interference.

Still, he glared at the three dudes until the chubby, balding one who'd called Kaci insane noticed him. "She's fucking brilliant," Lance said.

The older man gave him a once-over. "Who are you?"

"Just a guy interested in basic physics." He jerked his head toward Kaci. "Best lecture I've ever seen."

"You enrolled here?" the second dude said.

"He's here on a cooperative effort with the base, working to bring attention to STEM careers," the secretary interjected. "It's a community outreach project."

First Lance had heard of it, but sure. "Heard this was the best lecture to get started with," he said.

"If you like train wrecks," the third muttered.

"Wasn't a train wreck until you walked in," Lance muttered back.

Assholes.

Kaci pointed to the girl who'd said the crossbow wouldn't hit the pig. "Jess, come on up and do the honors."

The girl jumped up. She had her hair tucked into a baseball cap, and she was wearing a Dr. Who T-shirt. Kaci leaned into her, pointing to various things on the crossbow, then stepped back.

Jess fired.

The arrow thudded into a strip of Styrofoam on the wall four feet below the stuffed pig.

Several students clapped. A few groaned. Some kid called out, "You shoot like a girl."

Kaci strung the crossbow and pointed. "All right, Blake. You come do better."

Lance picked the kid out by the way his friends jostled him and jeered.

But Blake didn't move.

"Come on up," Kaci said again.

"I was just kidding, Dr. Boudreaux."

Kaci took up a perch on the table, ankles crossed, legs swinging. "It's funny to mock your classmates for their gender?"

The room went deadly silent.

"I'm a physicist, not a biologist," she continued, "but above all, I'm a scientist. And this idea of gender differences fascinates me. Scientifically, can you elaborate on why having a penis might make a person better able to shoot a crossbow?"

The kid shook his head.

"Sounds like some interesting research, doesn't it?"

A muffled groan went up among the students.

"Anyone who can scientifically prove to me that having a penis directly correlates to superior crossbow proficiency gets an A for the semester," Kaci said. "In the meantime, this classroom will be a safe and welcoming learning environment for everyone who enters that door regardless of age, race, gender, religion, sexuality, or any other discriminatory factor. Understood?"

Murmurs of, "Yes, Dr. Boudreaux," echoed off the walls.

She hopped off the table. "Can someone tell me how we're going to impale this pig today?"

"This is way better than last year's pig-impaling day," the secretary whispered.

"Y'all must like this lecture," Lance said to the three men across the aisle. "You come every year too?"

None of them acknowledged him, but the loudest of the group left.

The dark-haired woman took the seat beside him. She leaned in to whisper softly so only he could hear. "Dr. Asshole is on the tenure committee."

Lance didn't know much about academics, but he figured that

was a bad sign for Kaci.

"If she makes it to Germany for this conference, she'd basically have to be tossed in jail for some kind of heinous crime before they could deny her tenure. She's eligible to go before the board in another two years." She leaned back and crossed her arms. "So make sure she goes," she said softly.

He nodded.

Wasn't his fight.

But he liked Kaci. And she was good at her job. Also, considering *his* job depended on the laws of physics, it was technically in his best interest to make sure the people designing those planes had the best education possible.

Just as it was in Uncle Sam's best interest to make sure every pilot flying one of his birds was as well-trained and motivated as he or she could be.

Lance's gut tightened.

He didn't want to stay in Georgia. Didn't want to give up his deployments.

He shouldn't have come here this afternoon.

Up front, Kaci moved to the whiteboard. "Okay, we'll try it this way," she said. "How are we going to calculate where to aim to compensate for gravity?"

The second man across the aisle left.

Kaci flicked a glance in their direction when she turned to face her students, and a glimmer of a smug smile crossed her features.

The third older dude across the aisle looked at Lance. "You're right," he said. "She's damn good."

"And he's *not* on the tenure committee," Kaci's friend murmured.

Twenty minutes later, the kids had figured out a better way to impale the pig that didn't involve any equations at all, and Jess walked away with a holey pig as a souvenir.

The last dude left along with the two women. Kaci stuck around answering individual questions, but eventually, the last student hightailed it out of the lecture hall too.

Kaci leaned back against her table, arms crossed, and waited until Lance reached the front of the lecture hall. "If you're fixin' to start a fight, I don't have a lick of care left in me," she said.

He pulled a small box from his pocket and popped it open. "Still owe me some ring disposal."

She eyed the box with Allison's one-point-five carat, princess-cut diamond engagement ring and the two simple his-and-hers wedding bands that went with it, then lifted her gaze to his face.

"That's all you want?"

Not nearly. But it was all he could ask for. And if he had to be stuck here at Gellings, shutting a few more doors on what should've been his life with Allison was a good step. "Yep."

"Huh." Her redneck side visibly glimmered to life in that smile. "Let me get all this cleaned up. If Miss Higgs is doing okay, I got an idea where we can go."

God help him, he was irrationally excited to find out what she had in store. "Great lecture," he said while she shooed him away from the crossbow.

"More fun than cherry bombs in a barrel of fish guts," she said.

Had any other woman said that, he might've laughed. But this was Kaci, and the probability that she'd actually done it was too high. "Have you tossed cherry bombs in a barrel of fish guts?"

"Sugar, if you don't know the answer to that question, you ain't half as observant as I give you credit for."

He was ninety percent sure that was a yes. "Was this sometime in the last few months, or were you significantly younger?"

She grinned. "Bless your heart, you don't really think I'm gonna tell you all my secrets, do you?"

"Your mother drank a lot, didn't she?"

"Beauty queens don't drink. They sip." She dropped the crossbow in a box behind the table and gathered the rest of her things. "But this former Miss Grits is getting ready to school you in something called closure. You ready?"

He honestly didn't think he needed closure, but if Kaci was taking him on a field trip to redneck land, he was all in. "Absolutely."

# Chapter 13

KACI TOLD LANCE TO MEET her at her place in half an hour. When she got home, her first stop was to check in with Wanda Hamm across the hall. Her sweet neighbor had taken Miss Higgs while Kaci was at work and Tara was in class, since Kaci hadn't wanted to leave her cat alone. "How was she?" she whispered.

"Happy as can be," Wanda replied. "She slept most of the day, but she ate the tuna you left."

Miss Higgs was snore-purring on the Hamms' flowered couch, but she opened one frosted eyeball and stretched a paw in greeting before drifting back to sleep.

"Do you mind keeping her for a few more hours?" Kaci asked. "I have a friend who needs some help with something, and Tara's working tonight."

"Of course. She's welcome here anytime. Poor girl shouldn't be alone at her age."

She kissed the kitty's head and thanked Wanda again. She darted to her own apartment, dug out a box from beneath her bed, grabbed a few supplies from the kitchen, and was back down in the parking lot as quickly as she could get there.

She'd just shut her tailgate when Lance pulled up beside her. He hopped down from his truck and eyed the back end of her Jeep. "Tell me you have a license for that."

So he'd noticed what she was carrying. "Ain't doubting me now, are you?"

"You didn't say 'ain't' once in your lecture."

"Duh."

He grinned at her, and she couldn't help smiling back.

Things had been odd between them when he left her apartment last night—she'd kicked him out before Tara got home so she wouldn't be subjected to any eye rolls or lectures from her roommate—but the minute he'd walked into her classroom, her heart had kicked into overdrive and launched itself against her ribs like it'd been shot out of a cannon.

He'd come all the way from the base to see her in the middle of the afternoon.

And she was irrationally happy to see him. She hadn't gotten heart flutters over a boy since high school.

Temporary insanity, she told herself.

Otherwise, she'd worry what it meant for her long-term emotional health.

Because Kaci wanted to make tenure. She wanted to stay at James Robert. She wanted to keep doing her research, keep volunteering with the Physics Club and other kids, and keep teaching students, both about physics and about life.

And Lance would get orders and leave one day.

Simple as that.

Her brain knew it. Her heart needed to remember it.

"So where are we going?" he asked.

"Little spot I know."

After the pumpkin-chucking disaster, she wasn't risking open fields anymore, even known open fields in the daylight. Instead, she steered her Jeep out of town, pointed it south, and kept going through pine forests and pecan orchards with the help of her phone for directions. With the windows down, talking was impossible.

After about an hour, she pulled onto a gravel road. Lance had been leaning back in his seat, but he sat straighter, his dark eyes going more alert. "Where are we?"

She flashed him a smile. "Somewhere we can't hit a darn thing for miles."

They bumped along the road for several minutes before she

stopped in a little clearing that would've been fantastic for camping. She killed the engine, hopped out, and grabbed the case from
the back. "Before we go, you sure you don't want to keep those?
Looks like you could get a pretty penny for the sparkly one."

He shook his head. "Wasn't money I ever planned on getting
back."

"Completely positive?"

"One hundred percent sure." His talented lips quirked up in a
grin, and she had an overwhelming desire to yank a fistful of his
shirt and pull him down for a kiss.

She had to remind her libido that they were here to help him
blast his past out of his life, not to go for a roll in the hay.

Besides, there wasn't any hay out here. Just pine needles and last
year's fallen live oak leaves. "Then grab that bag and follow me."

He snagged her purse as ordered and followed her to a small
trail in the woods that led down to a creek. "Nice place," he said.

"Great fishing."

"We feeding my rings to the fish?"

"Wouldn't make nearly a big enough bang to make you feel
better."

"Should I have brought some whiskey?"

"I don't know what y'all do in Alabama, but I practice safe
rednecking."

He made a noise in his throat, and even though she knew he
was laughing at her, she had to squeeze her thighs together.

Later, she reminded herself.

The man still owed her a date. She'd get him naked again. But
today, she'd be good and respectful.

Even if it killed her.

She squatted along the creek bank and unbuckled her case.
Lance leaned over her while she opened the lid.

And there it was.

Gleaming pink with a six-foot barrel, a built-in propane tank,
and electric igniter. Complete with a shoulder strap and custom
grip. Built with love by her own two hands, swabbed clean after
her divorce.

"Is that a potato gun?"

"Sugar, this is *the* potato gun. This potato gun puts every other potato gun to shame. This potato gun spits on your momma's potato gun. This is the potato gun to end all potato guns."

He swiped his hand over his mouth, but his dark eyes were dancing with amusement.

"Won't be laughing when my potato gun puts your rings into orbit," she said cheerfully.

"Into orbit," he repeated.

"Yep."

"That a promise or a threat?"

"You doubt my potato gun?"

There went that amused gleam again. The man packed more sexy into a simple smile than she'd ever encountered in all the men she'd met in her life combined.

"You *do* doubt my potato gun!" she exclaimed.

"Sweetheart, I know better than to underestimate *anything* you do."

"Then what's that smile for?"

"Anticipation."

"Hmm."

He squatted beside her. "And the joy of an afternoon in your company."

"Pushing it, Captain. Get your mitts off my potato gun."

Dang man.

When he grinned at her like that, as though he could see right through her bluster, she wanted to kiss him again.

She made quick work of checking that everything was in working order, then reached for her purse and pulled out a sack of potatoes. "Let's get to it."

"You're not serious about orbit, are you? The FAA doesn't like foreign objects in their airspace."

"You going prissy on me, Captain Chicken Pants?"

"I'm going *adult* on you."

"No need to get your flight suit all tied up in a twist. We'll keep it below the radar." She cocked her head at him. "But I *could* put it in orbit."

"I have every faith in you. Not so sure the dudes in the back row did though."

The *dudes in the back*, her fellow professors in the Physics Department, were no better or worse than any other set of men she'd worked with. "They think I'm biding my time until I get knocked up with a few kids and decide to stay home instead of playing at being a scientist."

"My sister gets that a lot too." He grinned. "But she's trained to fire real rockets. None of this homemade stuff."

"You keep talking, I won't let you do the firing."

"It's all my pent-up anger and frustration with women. I can't help myself."

She eyed him. He didn't *sound* pent-up and frustrated.

In fact, he sounded downright happy.

Those brown eyes went puppy-dog pathetic. "I'm sure I'll be better after I fire your potato gun."

"How long were y'all together?"

A muscle strained in his neck, and he shifted his attention to the burbling creek. "Three years."

"Long time."

"She was in school half of it. Getting a master's in education. She took a 'starter job' with a high school in Atlanta last year, so I asked to be assigned here. Wasn't my first choice, but it was the closest I could get."

"And she didn't want to move."

His lips straightened into a grim line. "Couldn't find a job here this fall. Should've known something was up when she wouldn't move here and let me take care of her."

"I liked moving when I was a kid," Kaci said.

Lance turned a surprised look on her. "You did?"

She nodded. "I liked going where nobody knew me. Starting over. I'd always try to be someone else, tell the other kids I was secretly a princess in hiding, that sort of thing. After Momma settled us back home in Mississippi, I wished we could move again. I didn't like my classmates and they didn't like me."

"That seems so unlikely."

She shoved his arm, but despite all his valid reasons for not liking her, he was still here, egging her on. "My daddy understood me better than Momma ever has. I always knew he'd forgive me for whatever stories I made up, and then probably take me out to have some fun setting off bottle rockets or launching produce. But once he was gone, I had to try harder to fit in. I just—oh, listen to me. This here's about *you*." She stood and dusted her pants, then grabbed her potato gun. "You're gonna have to point it down the creek that way—that's west, right?"

"That's west," he agreed. "How far does that thing shoot?"

"It'll go half a mile if it goes an inch."

He looked at her, then shielded his eyes and peered down the creek. "What's down there?"

"Miles and miles of pine trees, all the way to the Alabama border."

Which he probably knew, because he seemed the responsible type who wouldn't shoot a projectile without having an idea where it would land.

Still, she wasn't surprised when he took off, his long stride eating up the ground.

Of course he didn't believe her that they were clear to launch.

After the pumpkin-chucking disaster, she couldn't entirely blame him.

She jogged after him, her legs pumping double time to keep up. "See, you don't trust me," she said with a fake sniff. "Suppose you didn't trust your ex either. Maybe that's why she left."

He slid her one of those *I see you right through your baloney* smiles. "When we got engaged, she kept saying she couldn't wait to see the world. But when it came down to the wire, she didn't want to go. Likes being close to her family, doesn't like being alone, and military life isn't good for that."

"You miss her?"

He kept his gaze straight ahead as though the forest might give him the right answer. "I miss what I thought we had," he finally said. "But I miss the idea of her more than I miss the reality of her."

She had to stifle a snort. "Oh, sugar, been there."

"You get married so you could keep moving?"

"Probably some of it," she conceded.

"Still want to move?"

"No."

"Give it another year."

She understood his theory—wanderlust happened—but in the past year or so, especially with Ron following her here to Georgia, she'd begun to understand she hadn't liked moving for the change in scenery or the challenge or even because she got bored.

She'd liked moving for the chance at a fresh start. To try to be someone else for a while.

"I don't want to start over anymore," she said. "I am who I am, and I'm about done looking for a place I fit better. I fit how I fit. And there's not a place in the world that's gonna bend to fit me any better than I can fit myself."

He grinned at her. "You're one of a kind, Dr. Boudreaux."

"And I'm sure the world's grateful."

Thirty minutes later, Lance had agreed that it was safe to shoot the potato gun. They hiked back to where they'd left the equipment, and Kaci handed him her pink pride and joy. "Stuff one of those potatoes into the top of the barrel, but don't push it all the way down yet. You got a knife?"

He pulled a four-inch folding pocketknife from his back pocket.

"Once you get the potato in up top, we're gonna cut a slit for the ring," she explained. "Then you can finish loading it and fire it off."

"You're going to let me fire your potato gun."

She dug a foot into the sandy ground. "I have this little problem with aim…"

He snorted. "No way."

"Hush up. It's not because I'm a girl. If my daddy hadn't left us too soon, he would've had me out at the firing range every Saturday afternoon. But my momma kept stuffing me in dresses and making me do all those dang beauty pageants. I snuck out and had my fun where I could, but you ain't met the woman. She could've been a drill sergeant."

He was still grinning as he inspected the potato gun. "You want, I can take you out to the shooting range sometime. Teach you a few tricks."

"Don't you go teasing me like that. You ever shot a spud gun before?"

His wide grin answered the mating call in her pure redneck heart. "Never one like this."

"You're in for a treat."

"For once, I just might agree with you."

***

THE WOMAN WAS NUTS, BUT Lance liked her craziness more with every passing day.

Did he honestly need to shoot off his wedding set to get over Allison? Hell no. And his own momma would probably have a heart attack at the idea. But when he twisted a potato into the barrel and dug out a channel in the spud to shove in what should've been his wedding ring, he felt an anticipation stronger than the anticipation he'd had in the weeks leading up to his wedding.

Might be some appreciation growing for being here in Georgia too.

Not enough to stay—he still wanted to see the world—but enough to make it tolerable for the next year and a half until he could hopefully get an early assignment anywhere else.

"Shove that ring in there good," she said. "Don't want it to come out on launch. But not too deep—don't want the potato to explode either."

"Yes, Dr. Boudreaux."

She humphed. "Or maybe you do want the potato to explode."

He sucked in another grin. Too easy to get her goat.

Once he had the potato loaded with his ring, he took the broomstick handle from her and shoved the spud all the way down the barrel.

"Put the strap over your shoulder and aim it from your hip," she said. "You put that puppy to your shoulder, you'll land on your ass and probably have to see a doctor about your rotator cuff."

"Lesson learned the hard way?"

"By a man who didn't listen to me."

He tucked in another grin. "He deserved it, then."

"Dang right. This here's the fuel control. Watch the pressure gauge when you're filling it—that's good right there." Her arm brushed his, and the contact sent warm shivers over his skin. She eyed him, then stepped back. "Let her rip whenever you're ready."

He glanced down the way at the canopy of green over the lively creek. Patches of orange and yellow were finally peeking through after a long, lingering summer that had lasted most of October. If he'd been married now, he'd probably be headed home to a discussion of what had gone on at the Officers' Spouses Club meeting, which vegetables had been on sale at Winn-Dixie, and if the chicken was too dry. He'd probably be tired and half-bored, but attentive because that was what husbands were supposed to be.

And he wouldn't have ever met Kaci Boudreaux.

The brilliant beauty queen who made redneck sexy as hell.

He hit the switch to fire the igniter. On the third try, it lit.

A swift *shoomp* sent reverberations up his arms. The potato sailed over the leafy canopy, a spud rocket racing toward infinity.

Kaci whooped. "Beautiful shot!"

He lost sight of it beyond the trees. The thing had to have gone four or five hundred yards.

Lighthearted peace took up residence in his chest.

"Feel better?" she asked with a broad grin that lit her blue eyes and put a shade of pink in her round cheeks.

Damn. She was right.

He *did* feel better.

"Hate to tell you, but I think you're wrong," he said.

One hand went to her hip, and that stubborn pout took up residence on her lips. "I don't mind being wrong when I'm wrong, but—"

"This isn't a potato gun. It's a freaking cannon."

She blinked. "Hush on up and reload. I got midterm reports to work on and I miss my cat."

Yeah, that was totally worth risking getting a potato chucked at his head. He set the spud launcher on the ground and went back for a second potato.

No hesitation, he loaded it up and carved a notch to shove in Allison's diamond ring. "You do this after your divorce?"

She laughed. "And more, sugar. And more."

"How long ago did you leave him?"

"Little over two years." She settled onto the creek bank, no obvious worries over getting her jeans dirty or mud under her fingernails. "And he left me."

"He—"

"Yes, yes, he left me. And I can admit it."

He shoved the diamond-laden potato down the barrel. "Must've been some damn good revenge you got."

"By the time I moved here, it wasn't about revenge. It was about settling where I belonged and taking care of me and Miss Higgs." She grinned. "But now you can say you know someone legally banned from using a blowtorch in Colorado."

As if he needed another warning about getting on her bad side.

But the funny thing was, he wasn't worried about Kaci and revenge.

He was more worried about why he couldn't stay away. "Think I can hit that tree with this one?"

"I sure as heck couldn't." She tucked her legs up to her chest. "And I never would've admitted that to Ol' Grandpappy."

He did a double take.

Was she talking about—

She grinned wide. "Not too much fuel there or you'll have French fries."

He switched off the fuel valve and checked the pressure gauge. Higher, but not dangerously so. "Does your ex-husband know you call him *Ol' Grandpappy?*"

"He knows I think he's an old geezer."

"And he still gets jealous over you being with other men."

"The man has issues."

He didn't bother holding in a laugh.

"And I'm one to talk," she said cheerfully. "Go on, plant that diamond in that tree up there."

He slid the strap over his head and pointed the cannon toward a towering pine fifty yards down the way. Firing from the hip made it hard to know for sure if he was lined up, but it felt right.

He hit the igniter three times.

The force of a giant *THWOMP* from the end of the barrel pushed him back a step. There was a *crack*, and the top of the straggly pine shook.

A primal surge of satisfaction flowed through his veins.

Kaci jumped up beside him. "Uh-oh."

"Uh-oh?"

He glanced down at the potato gun.

Still pink, still in one piece.

She pointed. "You done took off the top of that tree."

As they watched, the top fifteen feet or so of the pine wobbled, then slowly toppled, crashing end over end into the forest below with a rustling, muted crash.

"Who'd you say owns this land?"

"It's the backside of a national forest," she whispered.

He scooped up a third potato and shoved it into the barrel. "So I should hurry?"

"Might not be a bad idea."

It took less than thirty seconds for him to shove Allison's wedding band into the potato and finish loading the gun.

And the satisfaction that came from shooting it far, far over the trees wasn't something he could've gotten from flying a plane, drinking with his buddies, or even getting laid.

It was a farewell. A farewell, and a true welcome to Georgia.

And he felt lighter than he'd ever thought he could be here.

They packed up the potato gun and hustled back to Kaci's Jeep.

"So," she said once they were safely back on the road, "you have dinner plans?"

He let his hand slide down her thigh and squeezed the firm muscle. "Hope so."

She flashed that impish grin his way, complete with a promise of what she wanted to do to him once they were off the road, and for that moment—and several hours afterward—all was right in his world.

## Chapter 14

TUESDAY MORNING, WHILE MISS HIGGS was home with Tara and while Kaci *could've* been in her lab running numbers, she booked her airplane ticket to Germany.

Her stomach knotted so hard she almost had to bend over, but it was done.

She was going to Stuttgart. She'd present her research and subsequent hypotheses to some of the world's most brilliant minds. The stuffy old billy goats who had run the Physics Department here at James Robert for decades wouldn't be able to keep her out.

Because after she did Stuttgart, she'd apply to go to other conferences. She'd put on her professor face, and she'd show them all that she could do it.

And no one else would ever have to know she'd been afraid to get on an airplane.

She was still perspiring, though, when someone knocked on her office door. She fanned her blouse and took a slow, even breath. "It's open," she called.

And dang if Ron Kelly himself didn't walk in.

She barely kept herself from rolling her eyes. "Dr. Kelly."

"Great news," he said. "I'm going with you to Stuttgart."

"The hell you say."

"My department chair saw your planned topic, and he thought it would be good for me to be there in case you need backup."

She didn't realize she'd risen to her feet until her chair crashed into the metal blinds on the window behind her desk. "I. Do.

Not. Need. Backup."

He held his hands out. "Support," he amended. "For your first conference. And since we're both working on efficient combustion—"

"Out." She should've let Lance fire *him* out of that potato gun last night. "Get. Out."

"Kaci, if you'll think about it a minute, you'll understand that this is good for—"

"*You*," she spat. "This is good for *you*."

"The benefits of the combination of physical and chemical combustion—"

"Is covered in six research papers I've had published in *Physics Today* and is a concept I fully support. I *will* find a chemist to work with, and when I do, Dr. Kelly, it will be a chemist selected for his or her knowledge, intelligence, and capability to fit within my team." She pointed so hard, her knuckle throbbed. "Once more, Dr. Kelly, remove yourself from my office."

He ran a hand over his graying hair. "I don't know what I've done to offend you—"

"Dr. Kelly," a smooth voice interjected from the hallway, "I believe you're keeping Dr. Boudreaux from her work."

Dr. Kwami, her dean, folded his arms over his massive chest and stared down his nose at Ron.

Ron gave her one last glance, then muttered something to himself while he left her office.

Letting a man tell him to leave when Kaci herself telling him to leave hadn't worked.

"My research belongs *here*," she said to her dean.

Dr. Kwami settled into the plastic chair on the other side of her desk and pushed the door closed. He propped a dress shoe over one knee. "You've been having troubles."

She pinched her lips together.

"I can't fix issues if I'm unaware of them."

"With all due respect, neither of us can turn me into a man, and I wouldn't let you even if you could."

A glimmer of a smile turned his lips up, but his dark eyes stayed serious. "I agree. Your research needs to stay here in our department."

Her fingers slowly uncurled.

He tugged at the black tie over his crisp white shirt. "A student reported overhearing another professor making derogatory comments about you. Has someone from our department been harassing you?"

"Dr. Kwami, I've lived in this world so long, I wouldn't recognize harassment if it walked up behind me and licked my ass." And if he wanted to fire her for saying *ass*, so be it.

She'd build a shack out in the woods and sell potato guns out of her garage.

"I don't tolerate harassment, Kaci. Nor do I tolerate my professors undermining one another, especially to the students. You belong here. You're making a difference. If you have issues, give them to me. We need you inspiring these kids and working in your lab. Understood?"

"I didn't get where I am by being a tattletale."

"My daughter wants to be an astronaut, Dr. Boudreaux. I'd like to think she'll have a safe place to learn, but that starts with us. With you and me. We can't fix a problem if we don't address it."

"And not every problem has a solution. Not when people get involved."

"Let me try." He stood. "I'll have a talk with the dean of the chemistry department. Dr. Kelly won't be an issue anymore."

Right.

Because Ron's dean would respond to a man, whereas Kaci would just be a hysterical woman who wasn't mature enough to handle working with her ex-husband.

"This is my job as your boss, Kaci. Let me handle the people. You handle the physics." He flashed a rare smile, white teeth glinting against his dark face. "And knock 'em dead in Stuttgart."

"I don't want Dr. Kelly going to Stuttgart. He's going to try to claim my research as his own or at least take credit for some of it."

And there she went, whining to her boss about her ex-husband.

"I won't let that happen. Keep up the good work, Dr. Boudreaux."

She sank back into her chair, hopeful relief making her limbs weary.

Keep up the good work? She'd do her darnedest.

She always did.

❧

KACI'S PLANS FOR SATURDAY MORNING had been to let Lance think he was going to give her another hour of flight-prep training, but seduce him in her living room instead while Tara was working the day shift.

But Lance's plans for Saturday morning turned out to be something different.

"Come with me," he said from her doorway. He had a pair of aviator sunglasses on top of his head and a brown leather jacket over a white thermal T-shirt. She wanted to yank him inside and not even bother with the pretense of doing flight-prep training, but he wouldn't budge. "We're on a timeline. We have to go. *Now.*"

Curiosity got the better of her. "Can Miss Higgs come?"

"Absolutely not."

Since that was his grown-up pilot jock voice, she didn't argue. "How long are we out for?"

"Back by noon."

She arranged an impromptu playdate for Miss Higgs with the Hamms across the hall and squeezed the cat extra tight before she left. Miss Higgs gave her a frosted eye roll, as if to say *Chill, lady. I'm not dying while you're gone today.*

Kaci certainly hoped the cat was telling the truth.

And she owed the Hamms a nice gift certificate to their favorite Southern buffet.

"Where are we going?" she asked while she followed Lance to the parking lot. "Do I need my spud launcher?"

He flipped his glasses over his eyes and gave her an ovary-exploding smile. "Trust me."

"You get a watermelon cannon?" she asked.

He laughed. "No."

"We shooting bottle rockets?"

"Nope."

"Goin' muddin'?"

"I didn't say you were going to *like* it," he said with a cocky grin.

She thought he was kidding.

But ten minutes later, he pulled in front of a metal-sided shed before a tarmac lined with propeller planes.

"Oh, no," she started.

"Trust me?"

"You still owe me another hour on that game thingie."

"You're ready, Kaci." He squeezed her knee. "You can do this."

Her frozen lungs didn't agree.

Neither did the piston firing in her chest.

"It's like a Band-Aid," he said. "Just rip it off."

She was going to hurl.

This wasn't a Band-Aid she was ready to rip off. She needed mental preparation time. She needed a paper bag. She needed a happy pill.

Lance pulled her door open. "Where's that badass pumpkin chucker I know? Come on. It'll be fun."

Somehow she got out of the truck.

Her legs wobbled, but he had a firm grip on her hand.

And he didn't even comment on how ice-cold her fingers were.

"If I die, you damn well better take care of my cat," she forced out.

"You got it, Pixie-lou."

He pushed her into the meatlocker that doubled as the office for the private runway. A dude in a Hawaiian shirt greeted Lance by name, then passed over a clipboard. He didn't seem to notice how frigid the room was. Nor did Lance. Not a goose bump or shiver from either of them.

She sank onto a blue-and-red pinstriped couch that had seen better days and springier cushions. If Lance noticed her head hanging between her knees, he didn't comment.

She didn't think.

She couldn't entirely hear over the roar in her ears.

"C'mon, Kace. We're ready." His hand was hot on the back of her neck. His thumb rubbed into her hairline, and despite herself, a longing pull pulsed deep in her center. His breath tickled her ear. "Got a big reward for anyone brave enough to get in a plane with me today."

"Evil," she gasped out.

"You're going to Germany. We're not letting those fuckers win." That did it.

She was still light-headed, but she shoved to her feet and snapped her spine straight. "Don't make me hate you for this."

He looped an arm around her waist and steered her toward the back door. "You're going to love me for this."

Their plane was a single-propeller Cessna with room for four passengers. It smelled like old sweat and burnt jet fuel. He swung open the passenger-side door, a thin sheet of metal with a flimsy latch.

"Sweet baby jalapeño," she whispered.

He slapped a white paper bag on the blue leather seats covered in sheepskin. "Barf bag," he said. "Just in case. You want to walk around it with me, or you gonna stand here?"

"Stand." Maybe drop to the ground and hug it and ask it not to let her leave. Pray to the flight gods.

Squeeze her eyes shut and pretend her daddy was here to reassure her.

He'd loved flying. Loved being in the air. Her memories had gotten hazier as she'd gotten older, but she still remembered the unique scent of his flight suit, a combination of cotton, grease, and gasoline. The way his smile would light up the whole house when he came in from flying a day mission. The stories he'd tell about bending the laws of physics in his fighter jet.

Too soon, two arms encircled her and pulled her against warm leather. "All good on the outside." Lance pressed a kiss to the top of her hair. "Climb on up. I'll talk you through everything."

Her toes felt as though they were lead bricks, but she let him boost her into the seat. There was a space-age steering wheel sticking out of her side of the dash identical to the one in front of Lance's seat.

She also had pedals at her feet.

He closed her in, and she was suddenly ridiculously aware of how little space there was inside the aircraft.

She was within two inches of being outside.

Which meant she'd be within two inches of being outside once they were airborne.

"Breathe, Kaci," she whispered to herself while she clutched the white barf bag.

The whole aircraft shuddered when Lance climbed inside. He tossed his jacket in the backseat and grinned at her.

She blew another breath out her nose and closed her eyes.

This thing was supposed to survive flying through the air.

Another shudder went through the plane.

He'd turned on the engine.

She was in an airplane. About to leave the ground.

"Here." He passed her a set of headphones with a slender microphone. "Any questions, just ask. And trust me—this will be fun."

Fun.

Right.

She forced a practiced beauty queen smile. She could do this. She could be brave.

He wouldn't take her up in the air in a plane that wasn't airworthy. He wouldn't put her in danger. He wouldn't push her if she couldn't do this.

She could do this.

His lips spread in that heart-stopping grin. "That's my girl."

She clapped the headphones over her ears.

Too few minutes later, after he'd made a thousand notations in a notebook and flipped a half dozen switches and checked every last readout and gauge on the dash—telling her exactly what he was doing each time—they rolled away from the building and across the postage stamp-sized parking area to the edge of the runway.

She was going to be fine. Lance knew what he was doing. They'd both survive.

But her breath rushed in and out too shallow and that pinch in her forehead was spreading into her brain and her fingertips were numb.

"With me, Kaci?" his voice said through the headphones.

She pressed her lips together and nodded.

"Hey."

Black dots danced in her vision.

*No.* No, she wouldn't hyperventilate and pass out. Not again.

She was *doing* this, dammit.

Her nails sliced into her palms.

A solid, steady hand cupped the back of her head.

But instead of pushing her forward, head between her knees in a classic get-over-yourself pose, he pulled her in to his waiting lips and devoured her mouth.

Warmth flooded back into her fingertips. Her breathing evened out, then went ragged again, but this was a *good* ragged. His tongue slid against hers, his fingers kneaded her scalp, and she melted into him.

His rumble of approval sent a jolt of heat straight to her core.

But when she grabbed onto the corded steel of his forearms, he pulled back from the kiss. "That's my girl," he murmured. "Ready?"

She lifted his sunglasses so she could see the smile dancing in his eyes too. "Yes."

"Good."

He gave her seatbelt a tug, adjusted his pants, and clicked a button. He said something into his headpiece that she didn't hear, and a minute later, they were rolling down the runway.

Picking up speed.

Faster.

And faster.

And faster.

Until—

"Oh, my sweet baby Jar Jar Binks, are we flying?"

"You bet your sweet ass we are," came Lance's cocky response.

The plane shuddered and dipped, but he kept smiling.

And the green patch of ground and houses beneath them kept getting farther and farther away.

"Breathe through it, Kace. Don't want you to miss this beautiful view."

Despite the panic dancing at the edges of her brain, she couldn't deny he was right about the view.

She could see so much of the earth from here. Treetops. Roofs. Half the base. "Is that the golf course?"

"Yep. You play?"

"Nah, but I've modified a club or two."

His chuckle chased away the lingering panic.

She was flying. Soaring above the ground. With physics keeping them aloft in a plane Lance had declared airworthy.

"Do all pilots check their planes like you do?"

"Hell yes."

The plane dipped again.

So did Kaci's stomach.

"Normal turbulence," he said. "Like being on a roller coaster."

He was right.

Despite the dips and the way the plane seemed to sway from side to side occasionally, it kept flying straight. He made adjustments with the pedals and the wheel thingie, and soon they were flying over the national forest where Lance had launched his rings, headed toward mostly harvested farmland.

She was flying.

He grinned at her. "Fun, isn't it?"

"If you like defying death," she said.

One eyebrow arched over his sunglasses, and she laughed.

"How fast are we going?"

"Little over a hundred knots."

She did some fast math in her head. "So if we hit something, we'd die."

"We're not going to hit anything."

"You know how to land this?"

His eyebrow was significantly less amused this time, but she felt her own smile growing bigger.

She was freaking *flying*.

And he was right. It was fun. An adrenaline rush she hadn't expected, with the bonus of being personally chauffeured by a capable, highly trained, sexy-as-sin pilot.

He pointed out her window. "You look down, you'll see the Flint River."

Light danced and sparkled off a thin strip of black cutting through the patches of square and round fields.

"And straight ahead is Pickleberry Springs."

She leaned forward and peered at the cluster of buildings and roads on the horizon. "Why do I know that town?"

"Billy Brenton's hometown."

"The hot country music Billy Brenton?"

"That's what they tell me."

"Why do *you* know about Billy Brenton's hometown?"

"I was engaged to his biggest fan."

A voice interrupted their conversation, and Lance talked to another pilot over the radio for a few minutes about the weather and some rough air over in Alabama.

When he was done, he glanced at her again. "Got more than enough fuel to get us to the Gulf and back. Want to see the beach?"

Her fingers twitched.

Daddy had gone down in water.

But, oh, the view from the air would be amazing.

She shook her head. "I'm good."

He squeezed her thigh. "Doing real good."

"Hands on the controls, please." But when they landed, his hands would be *hers* the rest of the day.

The plane banked, and she yelped.

"Just turning," he said. "Let's go tour south Georgia."

❧

FLYING WAS AMAZING. LANCE WAS right—nothing to be afraid of. The plane was shaky, but if it hadn't come apart yet, Kaci could trust it would make it back to the airfield where they'd started. And her redneck heart had come out of hiding and was enjoying the thrill of it.

She would absolutely get on that airplane and go to Germany. And she wouldn't be afraid, and she wouldn't hyperventilate, and she wouldn't cause any international incidents by melting down in any airports. She had her passport, her tickets, and her schedule. Everything would be—

*Crunch.*

The plane swerved and dipped. Feathers plastered the windshield. She gripped her own legs, because there wasn't an armrest. "What was that?"

Lance didn't grin.

Nor did he answer.

One of the readouts on the dash blinked red, and another was flashing something.

"What was that?" she repeated.

He flipped a switch, then tugged at the wheel. "Bird," he said shortly.

"A bird? A bird as in—*wooo.*"

The plane dipped again, but this time, it pitched her sideways toward Lance.

"Kaci," he said, his voice clipped but steady and forceful, "sit still. And trust me."

Oh, god. Sweet baby Jesus and Jehoshaphat and Jim-Bob.

They were going to crash.

A beeping came through her headphones. Lance hit the button to silence her comms, and all she could hear was the irregular whir-sputter-whir of the engine.

The plane tilted sideways.

Lance's lips were set in a straight line. He kept one hand on the wheel, his feet doing something with the pedals, his other hand flipping various knobs and switches. He was talking, but she couldn't hear him.

"Lance?" she said.

He didn't answer.

*"Lance!"*

He flipped the switch to turn her headphones back on. "We hit a bird, and it damaged the propeller," he said.

"Oh, my God."

"Kaci, listen. Are you listening?"

She thought she nodded, but she wasn't sure. The ground was getting closer. Not fast, not like in the video game, but still closer.

"We're going to land on a strip of farmland a little ways up the road, but I need you to keep calm and trust me."

He was using that *I am god of the air* voice. The cocky voice. The *I'm an invincible pilot* voice.

Her daddy had used that voice.

She whimpered.

"Hold tight, Pixie-lou. We're just fine."

All went silent again.

But the plane didn't have to make noise for her to know.

They were in serious trouble.

## Chapter 15

MILLIONS OF CUBIC FEET OF airspace, hundreds of planes in the air, and that fucking buzzard picked Lance's flight path for its suicide run.

Today.

When he had a jumpy passenger.

He could land a Cessna with one eye closed, but landing a Cessna on God only knew what kind of terrain with an engine that kept going out took a bit more concentration.

Hell if he'd let Kaci hear him talking to the nearest air traffic controller about an emergency landing.

He was still two hundred feet up when his suggested makeshift landing strip came into view. The plane was pitching and pulling, dipping and groaning, but he held steady, talking to the machine, manipulating the tail and ailerons and flaps to compensate for the sputtering engine.

The Aero Club guys would never let him live this down.

Hell, neither would anyone in his squadron.

*Nice aim, Thumper. Most people just buy a Thanksgiving turkey at the store.*

Damn bird had been half as big as a turkey. Couldn't have been a sparrow or a robin.

Had to be a fucking vulture.

It was a fucking miracle the bird hadn't taken out the whole engine. Must've just clipped its wing.

But they weren't on the ground yet.

He pulled back on the throttle, breathing a sigh of relief when the damaged propeller gave him all she had. Nose up. Attitude good. Airspeed questionable. Altitude perfect.

Passenger hyperventilating.

Where was a good bottle of Jack when a guy needed one?

Two minutes later, they were on the ground. The plane bounced, but it stayed down, shuddering and jiggling over the uneven plowed dirt until it came to a full stop.

As soon as Lance unbuckled his seatbelt, Kaci lunged for the door.

It didn't open.

She banged on it.

"Kaci."

"*Let. Me. Out.*"

He reached across her and flipped the lock. She tumbled out onto the ground, where she promptly fell face-first into the dirt.

He followed her out her side of the plane, because it was faster than walking around the damn thing. "Kaci," he said again.

She lifted an arm. "Sugar, sometime later, I'm gonna thank you for me being alive. Might be a day, might be a couple weeks. But right now, you need to back off and let me and this ground get reacquainted."

He needed to walk away.

Give her some space. Let her cope.

But—"I landed a fucking airplane *without an engine*, and it was a fucking good landing at that. The ground didn't do a damn thing, you big baby."

She lifted her face. Her nose and forehead were smudged with Georgia clay, but her bright blue eyes glowed as though they'd gone nuclear. "Did you just call me a baby?"

Had he?

Apparently he had.

And he didn't want to take it back. "I signed up to put my life on the line every single fucking day, and you prance around shooting off pumpkins and potatoes and God only knows what else, but someone so much as says the word *airplane* around you and you turn into a Big. Ol'. Baby."

She pushed to her knees, then all the way to standing, her every pore shooting out laser death beams. "I'd rather be a *baby* than an asshole."

"Who was it throwing out cheating accusations? Refusing to admit defeat in trivia? Acting like you're doing *me* the favor in putting up with your crazy-ass redneck shit? And *I'm* the asshole. Right."

"You don't have any idea—"

"Your father died a *hero* so you could pussyfoot around, letting some stupid fear be bigger than all of your brains. I've never lost a parent. You're right. I don't know what that's like. But I lost a buddy in pilot training. I've lost friends in Iraq and Afghanistan. You keep living, Dr. Boudreaux. Because *that's* how you honor someone's memory. So go on. Hug the ground. Skip your damn conference. I'll keep fighting for your right to be a baby."

He turned around with a growl and kicked at the dirt. He had to call the Aero Club. His commander. Someone for a ride. Go talk to the farmer and thank him for use of his field for an emergency landing.

This was a fucking disaster.

Something hit him square in the back.

He twisted around. "Did you just throw a mud ball at me?"

She launched another chunk of Georgia mud at him, but it sailed left and over his head. "I. Am. Not. A. Baby."

He didn't want to care.

He *shouldn't* care.

She was a hot mess. Trouble with a capital everything. A walking catastrophe who couldn't aim for shit.

"The bird throw that first one?" he said.

"Go to hell," she snarled.

And this time, she turned her back on him and marched those sweet hips away.

"Where are you going?" he called.

"Ain't none of your concern, Captain." She punctuated the sentence with a raised middle finger.

Lance growled to himself.

She wouldn't go far.

She couldn't. They were in the middle of fucking nowhere, at least fifty miles from Gellings.

So he'd let her cool off—and he'd do some cooling off himself—and he'd get back to taking care of the damn plane.

∽

KACI HAD NO IDEA HOW far she walked, but thank heavens for GPS on phones. When Tara finally pulled up on a backcountry road two hours later, after leaving work to come rescue her, she had no idea where she was.

"Oh, jeez, you're a mess. Where's Captain Flyboy?" Tara asked.

"Don't ever say that man's name to me *ever* again."

"He didn't push you out of the plane, did he?"

"He crash-landed us in a cornfield."

"Is he okay?"

"Is *he* okay?" She rubbed her dirt-streaked hands down her pants. Her favorite Ole Miss shirt was ruined, her feet had blisters, and her knees and ankles ached almost as much as her calves and thighs. "That man took aim at a mutant flying ostrich, killed the plane's engine, nearly made me have a catatonic stroke, and then he called me a baby. And you want to know if *he's* okay?"

"So that's a no." Tara handed over a bottle of water.

Kaci's phone rang. She pulled it out and glanced at it, and unwelcome tears clogged her throat.

"Um, does he know where you are?" Tara asked.

Kaci shoved the phone at her.

Lance was right.

She was a big ol' baby. And she didn't know how to admit when she was wrong. Or how to say thank you for everything he'd done for her.

"Hi, you've reached Kaci's phone," Tara chirped. "Oh, yes, we've met. I was there that night she kissed you at Taps… Uh-huh. I can—no, no, she's fine. Do you need a ride back home too?"

Kaci flared her eyes wide and made a *what the hell?* gesture at her friend.

Tara ignored her. "Oh, good. Great. Yeah, I imagine that has to be a pain in the ass. Hey, so I know this is awkward, but I write romance novels in my spare time, and I would *love* to pick your brain about—hey!"

Kaci hung up the phone and shoved it back in her pocket. "Bad timing, sugar."

"He's worried about you. And he says to go ahead and take you home. He's making sure the plane gets back to the Aero Club."

Being the responsible one. Cleaning up a mess he wouldn't have been in if it weren't for her. "I think I screwed up," she whispered to Tara.

Tara looped an arm around her for a shoulder hug. "All the best people do from time to time. You hungry? I brought beef jerky and bananas."

She wasn't hungry.

But she was tired of fighting all the time.

And of all the men in the world, Lance deserved to be fought with the least.

"I don't want another military man in my life," she said.

Tara squeezed her again. "Sometimes, we don't get that choice."

A FTER FOUR HOURS TAKING CARE of the plane, another hour and a half drive back home with Juice Box chattering the whole way, and a five-mile run, Lance still wanted to hit something.

Instead, he settled for heading out with the guys to spend some quality time with Gertrude and that bottle of Jack at Pony's man cave. He was tossing darts and riding a buzz when an unexpected knock sounded at the door.

He didn't think much of it until the room went silent behind him.

Slowly, he turned, knowing without looking that he would never be prepared for whatever it was she was up to.

"What the hell do you want?" Pony said to Kaci.

She was in jeans that hugged every curve, shitkicker boots, and a skintight pink cotton shirt that perfectly showed the outline of her bra. Her lips were painted, eye makeup smoky, hair mussed and styled and falling about her shoulders. She lifted her pert little nose, but uncertainty kept her blue eyes dimmer than usual. "Just bringing by what I owe y'all."

She reached over beside her, grunted a little, then lifted a keg into the doorway.

"That filled with cyanide?" Pony asked.

Her nose twitched, and a flash of irritation brought a spark to her eyes, but her voice came out far meeker than Lance would've thought possible. "It's SweetWater IPA."

Five of the guys had gathered around her. Lance had to shift to see her between them. She stood her ground, but for once, she wasn't standing there belligerently, daring any of them to challenge her.

Pony snapped his fingers. "Juicy, get over here and try the beer."

Kaci's gaze dipped to the floor. Her cheeks weren't just pink. They were flaming red.

She was embarrassed.

Her discomfort hit him like a sack of bricks to the gut.

No matter how mad he was with her for walking away today, for leaving him alone wondering if she'd gone and gotten herself run over by a car or a random marauding bull or attacked by a rabid sparrow—which all seemed equally likely, knowing Kaci— he still didn't want her swallowing her pride.

She'd worked damn hard to earn that pride, at least professionally.

And he shouldn't have called her a baby.

"This beer's shit," Juice Box announced.

"Sugar, that's your age talking," Kaci said.

She clamped a hand over her mouth and looked down again.

Pony snickered. He snagged the red Solo cup from Juicy and tipped the beer back. "Lady ain't wrong," he declared. He pulled the keg into the building and gave her a nod. "Good beer. Thanks."

And then he shut the door in her face.

Lance shoved forward. "Dammit, Pony, don't be an asshole."

"What? We're even. Not friends."

He was going to regret this. Even buzzed, he knew it was a bad idea. But he still stepped around his squadron buddies and flung himself out into the night.

Kaci turned back toward him. She bit her lower lip, then looked down again. "Thank you for landing the plane safely this morning."

He stopped and crossed his arms. Chilly tonight. "Like you said. I want to live as much as you do."

"I can be...outspoken sometimes."

"I shouldn't have called you a baby."

"About this deal we made," she said. She shoved her hands in her pockets, then looked up at him. "I need to change the terms."

Hell. He hadn't meant to make her feel bad. "Kaci—"

"I need to take *you* on a date. Not the other way around. Because I—I was getting the better end of everything. So...can I take you out? On a date? And then you never have to see me again."

She was the one putting it all out there, going out on a limb, risking her pride, risking him saying no.

So why were his cheeks warm, and why couldn't he figure out what to do with his hands? "I never said I didn't want to see you again."

"You don't have to. When it comes to me and men, that's just how it ends every time. But you've been really nice to me, and I'd like to be really nice back. I can do it. I promise I can. Well, my mouth might get involved a little, but I'll try to make it behave."

She was adorable. "I like your mouth."

"Even when it's talking?"

"Maybe twenty percent of the time. Just when you're funny."

She barely cracked a smile, and even in the semidarkness, he could tell it didn't reach her eyes. "So I'll call you about setting up a date."

"Kaci—"

"And I'm sorry for having a meltdown on you. All the meltdowns. Have fun with your friends tonight."

"Kaci," he said again.

"Seriously. Go have fun with your friends. Miss Higgs and I have plans tonight, and she gets cranky when I leave her too long."

She faded into the dark night.

But if she thought she was leaving that easily, she could think again.

This wasn't the Kaci he knew.

Which meant something was wrong. She'd hit her head on landing this morning. Or she was still dealing with the trauma. Or not dealing with it at all. He trailed after her, his slow gait turning into a trot as he realized how quickly her shadow was disappearing into the night. "Kaci, you should probably go see your doctor."

"I'm fine. Just trying to be a better person."

"We crash-landed in an airplane this morning."

"Wasn't any crashing, Captain Hot Shot. You put that plane down just like we were on a runway."

"You've never seen a plane land on a runway."

She was almost to her Jeep down the street from Pony's place, still speed-walking as though the devil were on her tail. "True enough, but if we crashed, that plane would've been in pieces."

"Kaci—"

"Go back to your friends. Have a good time. You and me? We need a little breathing room. My head's not on straight, and you just make it more muddled."

He could relate.

"I said I'll call you," she said. "You ever known me not to follow through with a threat?"

She drove him crazy and she brought out the worst in him, but the woman knew how to make him laugh. "Don't wait too long," he said. "I might forget who you are."

"Don't you wish."

Of everything in his life he might ever wish he could forget, Kaci Boudreaux was not on that list.

She hugged the edges of her Jeep while she marched to the driver's door. "I won't hold it against you if you don't take my call," she added.

Damn impossible woman.

He stalked around the Jeep, cradled her head, and covered her lips with his.

To make her quit talking, he told himself.

To prove to her that he wasn't a total asshole, he told himself.

To kiss a hot chick because he was a red-blooded male who liked sexy blondes, he told himself.

The truth, though, might be that he needed to know she was okay.

That she wasn't still mad at him for making her go up in that airplane today.

That she still liked him enough to want to kiss him back.

Because if she kissed him back, maybe they'd go farther.

Into her backseat. They could ditch their clothes. Explore each other's bodies. He could taste her skin, hold her breasts, bury himself in the deepest parts of her.

Lose himself.

Just be.

She pressed her hands firmly against his chest, pushing him away.

He stepped back, his shaft painfully trapped by the denim of his pants. "I didn't mean it," he said. "You're not a baby, Kaci. You're strong and unstoppable."

"Go have your fun with the boys. I can't do this tonight. But I'll call you." She hoisted herself into her Jeep.

He leaned in the open window. "Soon?"

She bit her lip again. "I got some work I need to do on me." She kissed her first three fingers, pressed them to his lips, and revved the engine. "Go on. Be a good boy and go get in trouble with your friends."

He didn't want to, but he stepped back and let her go.

And when her taillights disappeared around the corner, despite knowing he was heading back into the bar with his buddies, he felt oddly alone without Kaci there with him.

She might be a menace, but somehow, she'd become *his* menace.

☙

KACI COLLAPSED ONTO HER BED and pulled Miss Higgs in for a cuddle. "I think I'm in trouble, kitty," she whispered. She could still taste Lance on her lips and feel the heat of his touch on her scalp. "He shouldn't kiss me like that."

Miss Higgs kneaded her arm and heaved out a rusty purr.

"I know, I know." She kissed her cat's head. "I'll always have you."

Miss Higgs grunted.

"And I'm not going to Germany either. That bird? That bird was a sign. God doesn't want me in airplanes."

No answer from the cat.

Obviously, she agreed.

Kaci had a sneaky suspicion a certain sexy flyboy would give her hell when he found out she was canceling her trip to Germany, but she couldn't think about that.

Not tonight.

She lay there stroking the cat until her purrs faded. Miss Higgs's fragile chest rose and fell slowly, and a kitty snore occasionally slipped out.

But Kaci couldn't sleep.

She'd messed up more than just her plans for Germany.

She'd let herself believe she could keep things with Lance on a platonic level. That they could be reluctant friends with benefits.

But he was becoming so much more.

Ron had never called her out on anything. And she'd never trusted him enough to confess her deepest fears, her biggest secrets to him. She'd never given him a chance to understand her or a chance to help her.

She didn't like needing help.

But she'd never felt as alone as she felt tonight either.

Not when she lived at home with Momma, who never knew quite what to do with her.

Not when she was battling to prove herself after switching majors during her undergrad years, nor when she was battling for credit for her work through her graduate years.

Even when Ron had told her she could either have kids now or kiss him goodbye forever, she hadn't been lonely.

But tonight, she wished Lance were here.

Well, not *Lance*. Maybe someone just like him who would listen to her talk about what had happened between them today. Who wouldn't judge her for how terrified she'd been when she'd realized the propeller on the plane was sputtering. Who would laugh with her over her unbelievable good luck in actually hitting him in the back with a mud ball. Who would tell her that he forgave her for pitching a hissy fit and calling him names and being a general pain in the ass.

Okay, yes.

She wanted Lance here.

She wasn't sure he wanted much more than to just get her naked a few more times and then be done with her.

But he never made her feel as though he wanted her only for sex.

He made her feel funny. Unique. Worthy.

Human. Fallible but forgivable.

Lovable.

But he'd made one thing very clear today: First and foremost, he was a military man, committed to Uncle Sam.

"He's going to break my heart, Miss Higgs."

The cat slumbered on. Kaci untangled herself to flip the light off, then crawled under the covers and wrapped her body around her sleeping cat.

Lance was probably still out with his friends. Having a good time with a group of guys who hated her. And why shouldn't they?

Look what she'd done to their pig. And their keg. And she'd put a stain of cheating accusations on their pumpkin-chucking trophy. Even if she'd been trying to protect her girls, she'd smeared their good names.

But she'd fix it.

She'd make everything right.

And then, maybe, she'd be worthy of having a friend like Lance for real.

Or maybe, just maybe, she'd be worthy of something more.

## Chapter 16

L ANCE WAS READY TO CRAWL up the walls.
It had been a week, and he hadn't heard from Kaci.

He deployed in just over two weeks.

She'd probably written him off. And he shouldn't care. But the woman who had taken him out to show off her potato gun wasn't the same woman who had bought Pony a new keg.

And the difference was that Lance had almost crashed a plane he'd promised her was safe.

She'd asked for space. He could give her space.

But he needed to know she was okay.

Sunday morning, he hit the pavement in his neighborhood for a long run in the crisp November morning. And while he put the miles behind him, he made up his mind.

He'd given her plenty of space. If she never wanted to see him again after today, he'd accept that. Probably he should be grateful. But first, he'd go make sure she was doing okay.

So he could deploy with a clear conscience.

Not have anything back home distracting him.

He turned the last corner of his run, took in the sight of a perky, obnoxious blonde sipping out of a paper coffee cup on his stoop, and his heart skipped a beat.

She was in her college football best—jeans, a giant Ole Miss sweatshirt swallowing her chest, and Converse sneakers that had danglies on the laces that he suspected would be classic Rebel gear. When she spotted him, she held up a second coffee cup.

She'd brought him a peace offering.

"Didn't think you'd be up so early," she called when he hit the edge of his property.

"Disappointed?" he asked.

"You know it. Nothing I like more than subjecting unsuspecting males to my charming presence before the sun's up."

Felt good to smile at her sassiness. He wiped his forehead and took a seat next to her on the stoop. "How you been?"

"Just peachy. Beating off men with a stick, turning down promotions at work, making the news for my philanthropic work. The usual."

He reached his sweaty arms around her, pulled her to his damp chest, and squeezed her in a hug. "Missed me, huh?"

"Get off, you stinky mess!" She swatted at him, but there was no vinegar in it.

Actually—"Did you just sniff me?"

"That's disgusting. Why would I do that?"

"You did. You sniffed me."

"Just to make sure that was you and not something that died."

But she did it again.

She leaned into his space, and she sniffed.

Her pupils dilated, and unless he was way off the mark, she was squeezing her thighs together.

He grinned to himself and took a swig of the lukewarm coffee she'd brought.

She still liked him.

"Your roommate home?" she asked.

"Probably."

She sniffed. "Could've gotten a dog instead."

"Yeah, but dogs are easy. Getting a Juice Box is good training."

"For what?"

His grin dropped off, and a stray leaf floating over the street was suddenly interesting. "My commander's hinting he wants me to apply for a position as an instructor pilot in the training squadron."

"Here?"

He nodded and told himself that was neither panic nor hope he heard in her voice.

They didn't have the kind of relationship where she cared one way or another what he did.

"You want to?" she asked.

"I'd love to get out of the South, but the idea of being an IP isn't entirely repulsive." He couldn't pinpoint when it happened, but sometime in the past week, the thought of staying here, stable for a few years, pushing arrogant bucks like Juice Box and molding them into not just great pilots, but great officers, had become less appalling and more appealing.

He loved his Herc. If he were being honest, he loved mentoring Juice Box too. Inspiring pilots the way Kaci inspired her students—that was worthwhile.

And possibly the idea of seeing a little more of Kaci—recreationally, of course, not as anything serious—wasn't entirely revolting either.

He still wanted to see the rest of the country and the world, but he wasn't even thirty yet. He had time. "If I'd been married when my commander suggested being an IP, I would've jumped at the opportunity," he confessed.

"Old ball and chain would've wanted you here more often, huh?"

"*I* would've wanted to be here."

She nudged his shoulder. "Lance Wheeler, you're a big ol' softie."

"You know that moment when your life falls to shit and you realize all you have left is your career?"

"Every day, sugar."

He took another sip of coffee. Smart man wouldn't have touched that with a ten-foot pole. "Rough week?"

"I live with me. Pretty much a guarantee everything's harder than it should be."

He couldn't help an amused snort. "Might try going easier on yourself."

"Or not going so far out of my way to be right all the time," she grumbled.

"Or wrong," he teased.

She humored him with a half-smile. "Or wrong."

"Lot to be said for people who don't half-ass anything." The woman made him want to pull her into his arms and just hold her. Take care of her. Let him carry her troubles for her for a while.

As if she'd let him.

"You doing okay?" he said instead.

"I'm sorry."

"For bringing coffee?"

"For being a drama queen last weekend when you took such good care of both of us to help me."

She was making that little muscle in his chest do things it wasn't supposed to do for a woman.

He wrapped an arm around her and pressed a kiss to her hair. "You're forgiven."

"Just like that?"

"Just like that."

She leaned into him and rested her arm on his thigh. "And I'm sorry I called you a pumpkin-chucking cheater."

"Also forgiven. You want to go see my catapult?"

She shook her head.

"Who are you, and what have you done with Kaci?"

"I stuffed her in a duffel bag and threatened not to let her touch my potato gun ever again if she didn't quit being mean to people who are nice to her."

"You're not mean."

"Ain't nice either."

He didn't want her to be *nice*. And he had a feeling she wouldn't have been asked to speak at a conference in Germany if she'd spent the past ten or fifteen years being *nice*. "Who needs nice? You're interesting. Colorful. And those girls in your Physics Club would probably call you smart and inspiring and encouraging. And speaking of those girls—you paid them the prize money yourself, didn't you?"

She patted his knee. "Didn't come for a pep talk, but it's sweet of you anyway. You free on Saturday?"

She had.

She'd given her Physics Club kids the equivalent of the prize money from the pumpkin-chucking contest. He'd suspected it since the day the squadron stole her car, but she'd basically just confirmed it by avoiding the question.

This woman was something else.

"No plans that I know of," he said.

"Good. Meet me at my place at ten. I'm treating you to a date. And don't go arguing. We both know I'll win, but you'll waste a bunch of breath in the meantime." She paused. "Please."

He smothered another grin. "Sure."

She leaned back and eyeballed him. "You're not fixin' to argue?"

"Like you said. I'd just be wasting my breath."

Plus, a date planned by Kaci?

No telling what she'd come up with, but he knew one thing. It wouldn't be boring. Or ordinary.

⊂℞℧

KACI WAS SIPPING HER THIRD latte of the morning after getting back from Lance's house. Miss Higgs was snuggled in the corner of the couch. Tara came out of her bedroom in yellow pajama pants and a T-shirt proclaiming her one of the few, the proud, the weird.

She collapsed beside Kaci and smothered a yawn. "You made me a bagel. You didn't have to do that."

"I got a problem."

Tara picked up the plate and sniffed the bagel. "You're pregnant. Don't worry. I have a plan. We'll rent a house and raise it together and never tell anyone until he accidentally stumbles across us one day and realizes the baby has his eyes. And that's when things will get murky, but we'll cross that bridge when we come to it."

"Sugar, you've been writing again, haven't you?"

"One of my redneck fairy-tale guys just found out he has a secret baby, and everything clicked right before I got out of bed for how I need to handle it." She waved the bagel at Kaci's stomach. "You're not pregnant, are you?"

"Worse. You sure you should be taking accounting classes? Doesn't seem to fit you."

"Desperate times." Tara gripped her hand. "He didn't give you an STD, did he?"

"Not that bad."

"Oh, Kaci...you fell in love with him, didn't you?"

"It's not *love*. More like strong friendship. With more attachment on my end than his." The coffee rolled through her stomach like sour milk, and her hands wouldn't stop shaking.

From the caffeine?

Or from seeing Lance again?

"I thought staying away from him would straighten me out," Kaci said.

"You need to stay away from that man permanently."

"I promised him a date."

"Break it."

"My momma would skin my hide and then hang it out to dry like yesterday's laundry. Boudreaux women do *not* break dates."

Plus, if she broke the date, she wouldn't see Lance again.

The way his eyes danced when he was trying not to laugh at her. The way he rolled with all of her punches. The way he smelled after a run.

Good gravy in heaven, she'd never liked the smell of sweat, but on him, she'd barely held back from jumping in his lap and riding him.

Which was another thing her momma would've skinned her hide for.

"He's military. Strike one," Tara said. "He's a pilot. Strike two. And he just got out of a three-year relationship with a woman who practically dumped him at the altar. He's out. If you're developing feelings for him, seeing him more won't make them go away. He could've killed you in that plane last weekend. You haven't forgotten that, have you?"

"We didn't die, did we?" she whispered, though her heart shuddered and her fingers went temporarily tingly.

She'd been doing an admirable job of *not* thinking about getting on a plane to Germany in barely over a month. Canceling her tickets would make her look like a chicken. Coming down with a horrific case of the flu complicated by pneumonia, psoriasis, and an antibiotic-resistant strain of staph two hours before she was supposed to board her plane would be much better. Surely she could fake being medically quarantined for a week. Couldn't she?

"Do you know what I put him through while he was trying to help me?" Kaci said. "The man deserves a medal. The least I can do is take him out to dinner."

Even Miss Higgs snorted.

"Your date plan is to take him out to dinner?" Tara said.

Of course not. "That's what normal people do on dates, isn't it?"

"*Normal* people, Kaci. Not you."

"Hush on up. The *point* is, I owe him one last show of gratitude. Are you gonna help me figure out how to stay detached, or do I have to do this all on my own?"

Tara's bright eyes narrowed. "That's not fair. If I say I won't help you, I'm a bad friend. If I say I *will* help you, we're taking on a doomed mission. You can't detach. Not if you're already attached. And you are definitely attached. *Kaci*! You bought new underwear, didn't you? Tell me you didn't buy new underwear."

"I—"

"You *did*."

"Online. I didn't go to the store or anything. Click-and-buy doesn't count as shopping. It might not even look good."

Tara gasped. "You bought *lots* of new underwear! Oh, honey. You're going to do this, aren't you?"

Kaci's phone dinged. She checked the display and didn't even care that she knew a dopey smile was spreading over her face.

*So we're clear—what exactly should I plan on wearing next weekend?* Lance's text said.

*Nothing you wouldn't mind getting dirty*, she replied.

His answer came back almost immediately. *So if I don't mind getting my nothing dirty, I can wear that?*

Tara, who was snooping, growled. "This is *not* good, Kaci."

"You're right." Kaci typed an answer quickly. *You sure you want to risk that?*

*Knowing you? Probably not. Rather not get my nuts taken off with a potato gun.*

"Not fair that he knows me so well," Kaci said.

Tara took Kaci's latte and helped herself to a big gulp. "You need to walk away."

"Will you watch Miss Higgs for me on Saturday?"

Her friend's dark curls bounced when she nodded. "You know I will. And I'll stock more chocolate. And if you change your mind, I'll still be there. And I'll still have chocolate."

"Might need some tequila too."

"Try to grab one of his socks. Or maybe something out of his wallet. So you have something to blow up when it's over."

"Good thinking."

But Kaci had a feeling blowing up anything of Lance's wouldn't bring her any satisfaction.

Because she didn't want to let him go.

FRIDAY NIGHT LANCE STROLLED INTO his house with a smile in his heart, whistling a tune. He sidestepped Juice Box's pile of crap in the laundry room, and even the scent of burnt meat didn't kill his buzz.

He'd had a two-day mission out to Seattle this week, and tomorrow he would finally get to find out what kind of date a woman like Kaci Boudreaux would plan.

Juice Box was waving a hot pad over a smoking Crock-Pot. "Dude, how old's this thing? My mom never burns beef like this."

Lance glanced in the pot. "You put water in it?"

"Natural juices, Thumper. It's supposed to have natural juices."

He sucked in a grin. "Thought we talked about you saying *natural juices*."

"Shove it, old man. Nikki's coming over tonight."

"Same girl three weeks in a row? Reputation's gonna take a hit if word gets out."

"Different Nikki. Easier to remember their names if they're all the same."

Lance grabbed a can of peanuts from the cabinet and ignored the plush buzzard sitting on top of the mail on the counter.

Juicy had been bringing buzzards of various sizes and softness into the house the past two weeks. Kept saying someone at the squadron asked him to drop it off, but Lance knew better.

Just like he knew Devon was lying about this being a different Nikki.

The kid was trying to fit in.

"It's not the same as homemade, but Publix makes a damn good fried chicken," he said.

Juice Box grunted.

"Chicks dig it when you make brownies. Could get a box mix at the store. Already have eggs and oil here." And Lance would be spending the night at Pony's house so he wouldn't have to know what Juicy did with his girl tonight.

"We're just grabbing a bite before we head out to party. No big deal. You taking brownies to Dr. Blondie?" Juicy asked.

"She'd rather have a spring-loaded slingshot and a bag of vegetables to fling."

Juice Box dropped the whole Crock-Pot in the sink and turned to face him. "You sure you know what you're doing with this girl? She's...not all there. You know?"

Lance tossed back a handful of peanuts and let his silence speak for itself.

Juice Box didn't flinch. "I'm all about having fun with a girl for fun's sake, but you seem to be getting attached. You just got dumped, man. Seeing this chick? Not a good idea."

"Appreciate the concern." The kid was trying to be a good wingman. Lance got it. But his relationship with Kaci wasn't anyone else's business. This was for fun. A distraction. Not serious. "But you'll do better worrying over what you're going to feed your date tonight."

He left the peanut can on the counter, snagged the mail and the buzzard, and headed to the master bedroom.

Juicy was wrong. Lance had this under control. Tomorrow was about fun. Curiosity.

Hanging out with a woman who was more than she seemed, but who knew this wasn't serious.

That was his story, and he was sticking to it.

## Chapter 17

WHEN LANCE PULLED INTO KACI'S parking lot Saturday morning to the sight of her Jeep parked sideways across two spaces with a canoe on the top, he might've felt another of those unwelcome happy pangs in his heart.

For all the trials she brought with her, she knew how to show a guy a good time.

She stepped out of the redbrick apartment building, tight hips swinging in painted-on jeans, shitkicker boots on her tiny feet, and a gauzy white blouse hanging open over a pink tank top that expertly put her breasts on display. Her hair was tucked up under a ball cap and her eyes were hidden behind big sunglasses. She swung a hard-sided lunch cooler while she marched to her Jeep.

He'd been too tied up with managing his ex-bride-to-be and wedding plans this past summer to go floating. A day on the river sounded damn perfect.

He hopped out of his truck. "You pack beer?" he called.

"Does a fish have scales? Of course I packed beer. Hope you like peanut butter and jalapeño sandwiches."

"Sure. Love fluffernutters best though."

She gave him a mock stern glare. "You been snooping in my cabinets?"

"Yep."

He reached her side and looped his arms around her back. She smelled like sunscreen and marshmallows, and the combination went not just to his head, but it also made his groin twitch and his heart beat faster.

"Hope you know how to paddle," she said. "Gonna be cold if we fall in."

"Just gives me an excuse to warm you up."

She shivered, but her grin told him it was a good shiver. "Don't go making promises you can't follow through on. Glad to see you wore something trashy." She thumped the big Bama *A* on his chest, then slid out of his arms. "Let me go say bye to Miss Higgs, and we can get going. You got a hat?"

While she disappeared inside, he retrieved his own ball cap from his truck, along with the small tackle box and collapsible fishing pole he kept tucked behind his seat.

Twenty minutes later, they were flying down the road, old-school country rock blaring from the speakers. She'd let him drive—"Whatever the gentleman wishes," she'd said with an overly dramatic sigh—and given him full control of the radio.

Other than the way she kept checking her phone—worried about her cat, she said—Kaci's sass was back in full force today. They bashed each other's college football teams. She insulted his pumpkin-chucking skills. He teased her about her aim. And when he pulled the Jeep to a stop at the river an hour later, he realized he'd been smiling almost the entire ride.

Wasn't something he could've said about his time with Allison. Or even with his buddies.

"You put this thing up here yourself?" he asked her while he untied the canoe.

"Could've if I'd wanted to," she replied.

"You want to get it down?"

"Nope."

"You sure? I could do the woman's work and get out lunch while you do the big manly things."

She tilted her sunglasses to hit him with the full effect of her sharp blue eyes. "Sugar, big manly things are why we have wars. And if you don't want to walk home, I suggest you get that canoe down and hope you can beat me to the back of it. Because I know you'd take a bunch of ribbing if those friends of yours found out you let a woman push off the bank for you."

"Only because they'd be jealous."

She laughed, and that spot behind his breastbone went warm. Her phone beeped, and she dove for it.

"All okay?" Lance asked.

A soft smile came over her lips. "Yep." She flashed the screen so he could see a picture of her furball stretched across a laptop keyboard.

"Your cat's running a computer?"

"I've kept her technological skills a secret from the government for years. Don't betray us and make me hurt you."

She was chaos incarnate, and Lance couldn't remember the last time he'd enjoyed unpredictability so much.

Also, she turned out to be a moderately terrible canoer. Every time she tried to paddle, they ended up sideways. The first few times, she blamed him.

And he let her.

But eventually, she swung her body around on her bench. The canoe rocked. Lance grabbed one side and tried to center himself. He didn't mind getting tipped, but they were pretty far downstream and it was November. Even southern Georgia would be nippy if they were sopping wet.

"I give up," she announced. "I got the principles down. I can tell you all about the laws of fluids and motion and momentum and inertia, but I can't for the life of me make my body work right."

"Everyone has to have a flaw," he said gravely. "Wouldn't want you to be perfect."

She cracked up, and he grinned.

"You hush," she said. "Just because I got enough flaws for the both of us—"

"Or for all of the state," he said helpfully.

She reached into the river and flicked cold water at him. "I was fixin' to treat you to a little something extra at lunch, but I'm reconsidering."

"No, you're not."

Her pearly whites flashed in a big smile. "Got me there."

She was crazy and she was loud and she was bullheaded, but

she was more too. He had a funny feeling he'd only begun to see the Kaci under the surface. He slid his paddle back into the water and pointed them back downriver. "What's your research about?"

He hadn't asked if she was still planning on going to Germany, and he didn't want to be disappointed if she was bailing.

Based on the way her eyes slid to the side when she propped her elbows on her knees and settled her chin in her hands, he had a feeling she didn't want him to know either. "Just some stuff I've been working on," she said.

"About…"

"Efficient combustion."

"For what applications?"

"Gas engines."

He waited. Moved his paddle to the other side of the canoe. Dipped it in the water, pulled back. They slid through the river, picking back up with the natural current while the sun glinted off the ripples.

"You're going to Germany to stand up in front of an audience and say, 'Hi, I'm Dr. Boudreaux, and I study efficient combustion in gas engines'?" he prompted.

Her cheeks went pink. "We're on a river. Don't need to open the floodgates."

"Is it proprietary?"

"No."

"Is it boring?"

"If you're trying to bait me, you'll do better with the fish."

"Why don't you want to talk about it?"

She shifted, and he thought she was going to spin back around and face front. Even with her cap and sunglasses shielding half her face, he could tell by the set of her lips that she didn't want to tell him anything.

About Germany *or* her research.

"When I was in college, I dated a guy who tried to pass off one of my research papers as his own," she finally said. "I dated another one who almost got me kicked out of school when he cheated off one of my tests. And I used to talk to my ex about my research. He's a chemist, but we work with similar concepts and principles sometimes. He put out a paper about his theories on my research, and it got picked up by a couple magazines, and he's been trying to convince the higher-ups that I should come work on his team in the chemistry department so our joint brains can improve on what I've already done."

Lance's grip tightened on his oar. He made himself unclench his jaw. "That's a dickhead move."

"My dean isn't having it, and Ron's got his knickers in a twist over being called a sexist pig and me not wanting to go to therapy with him. So half my lab time is getting eaten up in playing university politics and dodging my ex-husband."

He squeezed his eyes shut. Now would be a nice time for a fish to jump in their canoe. A pumpkin to fly out of the sky and cannonball into the river. Hell, he would take coming face-to-face with a bear or a tiger for a distraction. Because he couldn't stop himself from pondering a dangerous question.

"I don't want to know," he muttered to himself.

"Why I married a big ol' geezer?" Kaci said. "He was probably just a dirty old man, but he treated me like he cared about my mind. He talked to me like I understood him instead of like I needed it told to me slow. I looked up to him. And then things just…happened. He got orders and offered me a ring so I'd go with him, and I was too young to realize I was just running away from one more place I didn't fit in. I fit better with him, but I didn't fit all the way. Not the way a wife should've."

She wasn't the type of woman who'd appreciate it, but he had an overwhelming desire to beat the shit out of her ex.

"He wanted kids," she added quietly. "I don't know if I want kids or not, but I didn't want 'em with him."

"You tell him that?"

"I took a blowtorch to his car and figured that was a good enough message."

This woman was nuts. But he wasn't entirely certain it was her fault. "This trip today isn't a trap, is it?"

She smiled, but even he could tell it wasn't a happy smile.

"You're one of the good guys. When we're done, it's gonna be my
fault, and even I won't be able to find a way to twist it otherwise."

His heart flipped. "Kaci—"

"You got planes to fly and bad guys to take down. I got kids to
teach and engine efficiency to improve. We're fun, but we both
know we're not forever."

She was right, but he still wanted to tell her she was wrong.

He wasn't in this forever. Hell, he was deploying soon. Getting
out of Georgia, away from Gellings, just *away*.

But he wasn't as desperate to go. His life wasn't suffocating him
anymore, and he knew he'd still get out and see the world.

Sure, time was part of it. Time and distance from his broken
engagement helped.

But the other part was Kaci. She wasn't just a distraction. He
couldn't put into words exactly what she was—nor did he want
to—but he knew it was something more.

She reached for the cooler between them. "Was that your stomach or mine? All this fresh air gives me an appetite. Jerky? Trail
mix? Beer?"

He steered the canoe toward the riverbank. "You really pack
fluffernutter sandwiches?"

"You know it."

They pulled the canoe to shore under a canopy of pine and
oak trees. Straggly bushes dotted the bank. Just a few feet farther
in, they were in a semi-private alcove, listening to the river go
by. Kaci unpacked a massive quilt for a picnic blanket, a stack of
peanut butter and marshmallow fluff sandwiches, chips, beef jerky,
grapes and apples, and set out a second cooler with an assortment
of microbrew beers in bottles.

Lance kicked off his shoes and stretched out on the quilt. Blue
sky peeked through the trees. Leaves rustled in the breeze. A lock
of Kaci's hair had fallen out of her cap and across her cheek while
she set their lunch out. "You come out here often?" he asked.

"Just once, this past spring. My Physics Club kids all got together
for a day trip. They were disappointed I didn't bring my potato
gun."

"Still waiting for you to pull out some firecrackers or a collapsible catapult."

She shoved a beer at him. "Hush, you."

He set aside the beer and snagged her hand. When he tugged, she didn't resist but instead curled up beside him, her hand resting over his heart. He flipped her hat off, and all those silky blond strands cascaded down onto his shoulder. "Pretty day," he murmured.

"Peaceful," she replied on a sigh.

"You like peaceful?"

"More than I like to admit."

He traced a slow circle on her hand. "Nobody watching. You could go to sleep."

She inched her leg along his. "*You* could go to sleep."

Even through their clothes, her touch set his skin on fire. His pulse ricocheted through his veins, and all his blood surged south of his belt. "Didn't say *I* wanted peaceful," he said.

"Sugar, you're with me. Not wanting peaceful is a given."

"Not always." He rolled them so she was on her back beneath him.

Her fingers settled on his cheeks.

He pulled her sunglasses off and tossed them aside. Her eyes were big blue questions, a peek at the vulnerabilities and insecurities she kept hidden from the world. She was full of big talk, but he'd seen her with her students. He'd seen her *fight* for her students.

Kaci Boudreaux had a soft side he suspected few people were privileged enough to know about. "Kaci—"

"No talking," she whispered.

He should argue, but she tilted her lips up and brushed them against his.

He'd missed her kisses. Her touch. Her laugh. Her smart mouth. Her bravado.

That soft side.

He was deploying soon. She'd damn well better go to Germany, and who knew if she'd still be here when he got back? She could be recruited to go work for a university overseas.

When he left, he didn't want to leave with regrets.

He wanted to leave with good memories.

So he lowered his mouth, suckled her bottom lip, and lost himself in the world that was Kaci.

◦◦◦

K ACI WOKE UP WITH A start when her Jeep stopped moving. A steady pitter-patter of raindrops plinked off the canoe up top.

They were home.

She needed to go check on Miss Higgs.

"You know you drool in your sleep?" Lance was aiming those soft, kind eyes at her again. Not the smoky, *let's get naked again* eyes he'd used for two more stops along the river, or the amused *you're being obnoxious, but it's strangely enjoyable* eyes he'd used when she'd been, well, *her* all afternoon.

But the gentle, understanding *we can still be friends after we quit sleeping together* eyes he'd used the few times she'd reminded him that they were temporary.

As if he knew exactly how bad she'd fallen for him, but he didn't want to embarrass her by pointing it out.

Because he was *that* kind of nice.

"Kace? You awake?"

She forced herself upright and rubbed at a kink in her neck. "Shoot, if you'd driven any slower, we would've been going backwards. How many old grandpas passed us on the way?"

"Twenty or thirty," he said with a smirk.

It should've taken another ten minutes to get to her place, and she suspected he knew it as well as she did.

"Any of 'em moon us?"

"Just the one. You need to put the canoe away somewhere?"

"Rented it from the school." She stifled a yawn. "I'll return it Monday."

His fingers tangled in her hair. "Best date I've had in a long time," he said softly.

Her heart swelled. She stifled her smartass *imagine if it'd been with a nice girl* comment and instead leaned closer to him. "Doesn't have to be over. I mean, I guess we're even for the flight stuff, but if you wanted to come up…"

She let her words taper off, because his easy smile tilted down. Sympathy overtook his dark eyes.

He was done with her. Finished. Tired of her.

Their deal was over.

She lunged for her door. "Never mind. You got things to do. Don't let me keep you."

"I'm flying tomorrow," he said. "Crew rest starts in thirty minutes."

Nice excuse. But dang if her heart didn't feel as if it were being squeezed like an underinflated balloon at the thought of him up in the air. "Sure. Fly good tomorrow."

"You like camping?" he said.

"Old-fashioned or pampered?"

"Either." But that snicker-grin said he'd laugh at her if she asked for a camper or a cabin.

"You know I can't resist a good campfire."

"Good. I'll pick you up Friday night."

Her pulse fluttered, and she couldn't even muster a sassy *but what if I have plans?* "I'll take care of the firewood."

He hooked a hand behind her neck and pulled her in for a lingering kiss.

She didn't want to stop at a kiss. She wanted to toss him in the backseat and have her way with him. They had twenty-nine minutes still.

And spending the day with him hadn't been enough.

She splayed her hands across his chest. His heart thumped beneath the solid wall of muscle.

He pulled out of the kiss and rested his head on her shoulder. His breath came in ragged gasps that pulled at something deeper and higher than the longing between her legs. "I cannot understand how you can be this sexy," he said.

Captain Swaggery Pilot God was one to talk. "It's a gift."

He chuckled, his breath hot through her thin blouse. "Suppose it is." He pressed his lips to her collarbone one last time before reaching for his own door handle. "I'd offer to carry something inside, but I'm afraid of the lecture I'd get."

"Wimp," she teased.

If he carried something inside, maybe he'd stay.

He winked at her. "Don't miss me too much this week."

"You're not even going to offer me your shirt as an umbrella?" She was bordering on pathetic, but she didn't want him to leave.

Who knew if he'd come to his senses before Friday and change his mind about camping?

He treated her to a wicked grin. "I'm gonna sit in my truck and watch your shirt get wet."

"Your momma would be appalled."

"Yep," he agreed.

One more flash of that boyish grin, and he was climbing out of her Jeep. Raindrops pelted his Bama shirt. He lifted his hand in a wave before he dashed the four parking spaces over to his truck.

Kaci touched three fingers to her lips and told herself the comforting lie that another date—an *overnight* date, complete with a bonfire and probably her potato gun—wasn't any big deal.

They were friends.

With benefits.

And she could totally handle it.

⁘

"YOU'RE HOPELESS," TARA DECLARED TEN minutes later.

Kaci dropped her coolers in the kitchen. "Yep," she agreed. "But I'm a pretty satisfied hopeless."

She joined Tara on the couch, where Miss Higgs was squeezed between Tara's belly and her laptop. "Write anything good today?" she asked.

"No. My dang hillbilly Sleeping Beauty story fell apart when I couldn't convince my brilliant astrophysicist princess to kiss the weirdo passed out in the room over the bar." She slid a meaningful look at Kaci. "You could learn a thing or two from her."

"You haven't even asked how it went."

"Don't have to. You're still wearing that sappy grin."

"I know it's not serious with Lance," Kaci told the dark TV screen. "But it's dang fun hanging out with a guy who seems to like me for me."

Miss Higgs shuddered out a snore.

"Has she been eating okay the last few days?" Tara asked.

Shivers prickled Kaci's skin. "She's been a little picky, but she's always been persnickety like that."

Tara didn't call her out on the way she was stretching that truth so thin even a blind man could've seen through it.

Miss Higgs had been *ridiculously* picky about her food this week. And Kaci had been telling herself it was simply because the cat was crotchety.

She reached over and scratched the kitty's head too.

"She's a sweet cat," Tara whispered.

"She found me after a horrific beauty pageant," Kaci murmured. "I was fixin' to toss a homemade cherry bomb into a dumpster behind the auditorium, and this little white ball of fluff charged me. She'd speared a wine cork with one of her teeth, so it looked like she was smoking a short, fat cigar. She kinda wobbled like she'd been drinking the wine too. But she stopped me from tossing that cherry bomb and probably stopped me from ending up in juvie."

"Only you, Kaci."

"My momma said she probably had fleas and we couldn't keep her, but I threatened to rip the shoulder pads out of my pageant dress and then cut up all the ruffles, so we compromised. Miss Higgs got to come home and have a flea bath, and I agreed to enter the Miss Grits pageant." She stroked her fingers softly over her cat's fluffy head. "She hated Ron."

"She's a good judge of character."

"She's getting old." Kaci's throat went tight.

"Here." Tara lifted the cat and gingerly put her in Kaci's lap. "I think you two need each other tonight."

Kaci buried her face in Miss Higgs's fur. The cat's rusty purr vibrated against her chest.

She'd moved to Georgia determined to find stability.

But even though she had no intention of moving, life kept changing on her anyway.

❧

THE WEATHER HAD TAKEN A chilly turn, but despite the overcast skies, Kaci's Physics Club was happy at their booth on the campus mall on Wednesday for Club Day during Spirit Week. She approached the group from behind, bringing pizzas for her kids who were manning lunch hour. Running out for food had been a good excuse to get off campus and run home.

Miss Higgs hadn't touched her food today.

Or yesterday.

Not even when Kaci offered her fresh tuna.

Wanda Hamm was watching Miss Higgs again today while Tara was at class and her study group. Thank goodness, because if Kaci had walked into her empty apartment an hour ago and seen her cat sleeping as peacefully as she was on the Hamms' couch, she would've lost it. She'd picked up the cat and snuggled her, relieved to still feel that rusty purr going, but the sympathy had shone bright in Wanda's eyes.

She shook away the melancholy and dread and concentrated instead on the Physics Club booth.

Unlike her lectures, where she suspected a good number of the kids would rather be sleeping no matter how hard she tried to make physics interesting, these girls *wanted* to be here. She had sixteen kids in the Physics Club, and she'd do everything she could to inspire their love of how things worked. Especially the twelve girls.

The boys too—she'd take any kid interested in science—but when her daddy died, she'd lost the one parent who understood how to nurture her curiosity. Momma thought her time would've been better spent learning how to catch a husband than in figuring out how to build a better catapult.

Kaci might have to fight harder and longer to keep her job simply because she was a woman. But she reached the students. She worked hard to make it worth their while to come to class, to make physics fun and applicable to life.

She knew how to lay a foundation that would prepare them to be astrophysicists, rocket scientists, and chemical engineers. But more importantly, she knew how to lay that foundation in a way that made her students fall in love with the beauty of it.

And she'd dang well fight with everything she had to stay here, teaching these kids until her position was secure, no matter what any of her fellow professors—Ron included—said or did.

"Hey, you want to help us make lightning?" Zada called to a high school girl on a campus tour with her parents. Jess was demonstrating how to separate salt and pepper for several members of the football team. Two other students were laughing with the Eta Zeta Beta girls at the next booth, and it only took Kaci a moment to realize they were telling the story of how far their pumpkin had gone when they'd launched it off Ichabod at the Gellings Fall Fest.

She knew Jess was having boyfriend troubles, and Zada had recently taken an extra four hours a week at her job in the registrar's office because her finances were tight, but they were *here*.

Her kids were going places. They'd do great things one day.

There was plenty to be happy about today, even if part of her heart was breaking.

"Dr. Boudreaux, back me up here," Jess said. "These guys don't believe physics has anything to do with football."

Her voice dripped with pity for the boys, and Kaci found herself stifling an unlikely smile. "There's physics at work in *every* bit of football. Ever take a hit? That's force. Toss a ball? Gravity and friction play into how far it goes."

"You'd win more if you took Dr. Boudreaux's Physics 101," Jess said.

A groan went up among the boys, and several of the physics kids giggled.

"More to life than winning," Kaci said. "Who wants pizza?"

Half her students—and the football players—attacked the boxes. She had an hour before her Wednesday afternoon lecture, and Jess and Zada seemed to have a handle on entertaining the passersby, so Kaci let herself drift into the back to watch and to be on hand for any other questions.

"Kaci," an unfortunately familiar male voice said to her right, "nice booth."

She refused to let the man see her twitch, and she dug deep not to be offended at his dry delivery with the barest hint of a suggestion that the Physics Club shouldn't have a banner with flowers and hearts on it. "Ron, likewise."

There wasn't a chemistry club, but the chemistry honor society was down at the other end of the mall.

And she could wish all she wanted to that Ron had stayed on his half of the campus, but since he hadn't, she truly did need to deal with her ex-husband. She could help Lance get rid of his wedding rings, she could call people cheaters till she was blue in the face, but since the airplane incident, she'd come to realize dealing with her problems was far better than launching them out of cannons.

"What can I do for you today?" she said.

He perched against a massive oak that had been around longer than the James Robert campus and scuffed his loafers against an exposed root. "I've been doing everything I can think of to show you I want you back, that I want to take care of you and be the kind of husband you deserve, but I can't do that if we can't talk."

"You're not my husband anymore." Keeping her voice even was easier than it should've been. She wasn't mad. She was just done. And she didn't care enough to fight. "We're better the way we are than the way we were."

"*I'm* not."

"You are, sugar."

"I get it, Kaci. I know you don't want to put your research on hold to have kids right now. I know your job's important. To you. To the world. We can fix this."

There was nothing to fix, but instead of being angry with him, she simply felt sad. She kept her voice down and watched her kids to make sure none of them were listening in. "You need to let go, Ron."

"If you'd come to therapy with me—"

"You ask your therapist if it's better to be with a woman who loves you or with a woman who doesn't. I'm not trying to be cruel, but wouldn't it be worse for me to lie to you?"

"Is this about that kid you're messing around with?"

Her heart slammed into her ribs.

Lance wasn't hers. He was fun, he was smart, he was brave, and he wasn't hers.

She suddenly had more sympathy for Ron. "It's about me not being a good fit for you."

He shoved away from the tree. "I knew you could hold a grudge, but this is extreme, even for you."

That did it. A red haze spiked in her vision. "Because you know better than me what I want? What I *need*? Because you're the man, and my female parts interfere with my ability to think and act rationally?"

"Now you're being ridiculous."

"I'm not the one who won't take *no* for an answer."

"Um, Dr. Boudreaux?" Zada squinted her dark eyes, flicking glances between Kaci and Ron. "We need another aluminum plate."

Kaci turned her best disappointed-professor glare on Ron. She kept her voice low, but she suspected everyone was listening. "You bring up personal issues here again, I'm filing a harassment complaint with the chancellor. My job is no place to bring your emotional baggage."

She left him standing there and forced a smile while she turned to dig through the supplies under the pizza table. Her face was hot, but she kept her voice steady and concentrated on the solid, comforting physics principles Zada demonstrated for the prospective student.

She didn't want to be the woman who had married Ron Kelly. She didn't want to keep fighting for professional respect. She didn't want to have to resort to empty threats of harassment charges—which she would *never* file for fear of being labeled a whiner—to make her point.

She simply wanted to teach these kids, do her research, and go home to her undefined and most likely short-lived relationship with one of the best men she'd had the privilege of knowing. She wanted not to have to think about Germany next month. She wanted Miss Higgs to live forever.

Maybe Ron was right.

Maybe therapy was a good idea.

# Chapter 18

L ANCE PULLED UP TO KACI'S apartment late Friday afternoon with a light heart and a truck full of camping supplies.
Some he hadn't used in years. Others were new.

Despite being there to pick up the craziest woman he'd ever
known, his soul was at peace. His pulse surged in anticipation.
Campfires and starry skies and temperatures just low enough to
require sharing body heat to keep warm.

Yeah, this would be one hell of a good weekend. Best way to
spend his last weekend in Georgia before he deployed.

He took the steps two at a time to her floor and rapped on her
door. But it wasn't Kaci who answered.

Instead, it was her curly-haired friend. "This isn't a good time."
Her lips were set in a grim line, and her eyes dared him to contradict her. She started to shut the door on him, but Lance was
quick with sticking a foot in.

"We have plans," he said.

"Not tonight."

What the hell? "Did her ex-husband do something?"

"We could solve *that*," she murmured.

He wasn't too fond of her bloodthirsty undertones, but he'd be
happy to take care of Kaci's ex himself if the jackass was making
more trouble.

A sniffle came from inside the room. His heart knocked on his
ribs with a pang. He pushed at the door. "Is that Kaci? Why's she
crying? What happened?"

"Tell him to go away," Kaci called. Her voice was sassless with a watery weight to it.

Lance folded his arms and glared at her friend.

"Oh, yeah, that's gonna make us both change our minds," she said. But despite the way she cocked her hip out—just like Kaci would've—she also backed away and let the door open wider.

He didn't wait to ask if that was an invitation.

But when he stepped around her and caught sight of Kaci curled up in the blue-checkered chair beside her couch, her eyes puffy and her chin wobbly while she rocked her ancient cat, part of him wished he'd stayed outside.

"We're gonna have to reschedule," Kaci said without looking at him.

A piece of his heart sliced off and flopped to the carpet. "Aw, Kace, I'm sorry."

"Hush your tongue. She's not gone yet."

Her friend sized him up, silently asking if he was man enough to stay or smart enough to leave.

No-brainer. Obviously.

He crossed the room to squat by Kaci's side.

She squeezed her eyes shut. A tear slipped down her cheek.

That little drop of moisture seared his soul.

She couldn't sass her way through this. Couldn't use her bull-headed stubbornness to stop it. Couldn't even devise a physics theory that would make it make sense.

He brushed a hand over her ponytail and pressed a kiss to her temple.

Her whole body shuddered.

The cat didn't seem to notice. It lay there in her arms, wrapped in a towel, eyes closed, head lolling like a rag doll with every rock of Kaci's body.

And Lance didn't know what to do. He didn't know how to fix this.

He *wanted* to.

Because he didn't like feeling powerless?

Or because he wanted to fix it for Kaci?

"Please leave," she whispered.

His chest ached and his throat was thick. "Having a heart doesn't make you weak, Kace," he whispered.

Her lips trembled. "I need to be alone."

Tara tilted her head toward the door. Her eyes were wet too, but the rest of her seemed to dare him to comment on it. "Been here longer than you have, Captain Studmuffin," she said. "We'll call if we need you."

They wouldn't call.

Kaci didn't need him.

But it would've been damn nice if she *wanted* him.

And wanting her to want him was the last thing he needed. This was supposed to be casual. A distraction. He was wheels-up on his way to the Middle East in five days.

Kaci was right.

They should've just said their goodbyes last week and been done with it.

He squeezed her arm. "She was lucky to have you," he said.

And he showed himself out the door.

S HE WAS GONE.
    Miss Higgs was gone.

Despite what she'd told Lance, Miss Higgs had been gone for near on ten minutes, but Kaci still couldn't let go.

The door clicked shut behind Lance, and the floodgates opened. It started as a trickle of tears, and soon she was full-out sobbing.

Miss Higgs had given her last purr to the world.

One day Tara would get a real job and move out and probably find a new man who adored her. Her students would graduate and be replaced with more students with the same problems. Her momma was bound to give up in complete frustration one of these days.

And Kaci would be completely alone.

Tara squeezed into the chair with her and wrapped both Kaci and Miss Higgs's body into a warm squishy hug. "I'll go get him back," Tara said, her voice thick with tears too.

"Don't leave me," Kaci choked out.

Tara hugged her harder.

"*Ever*," Kaci added.

"Aw, Kaci…" Tara touched gentle fingers to Miss Higgs's head. "Honey, I don't think—"

"I know." Her kitty was gone. Her constant companion through the ups and downs of the past eighteen years. "I just need another minute."

Or another eighteen years.

Who else would curl up with her every night for eighteen years? Who else would be waiting by the door when she got home every night? Who else would ever keep as many secrets?

Her gaze drifted to the door.

Lance wouldn't.

No matter how much she wanted him to.

Tara put her head to Kaci's shoulder and sighed. "Wish I could blame just the grief for you wishing he was still here."

Kaci wiped her tears on her sleeve. "Hush or I'll send you away too."

"No, you won't."

She was right. Kaci would've tied her to a chair before she let her leave. "Why is it the one I don't want can't leave me alone, and the one I want is willing to give me space?"

"Because men are idiots."

Men weren't the only ones. "No comment on the one I want?"

"He seems like a great guy," Tara conceded. "And I'll save my *buts* for tomorrow."

Kaci pulled Miss Higgs to her chest one last time.

"You know," Tara said softly, "she'd want you to go to Germany."

She swallowed another lump in her throat. "I know," she whispered.

THE THING ABOUT NOT OFFICIALLY dating a stubborn, take-care-of-herself woman was that it felt wrong to leave, but also too close to a real relationship to stay.

Getting serious with a woman wasn't something Lance needed. Though Kaci was into a lot of the same things he hadn't even realized he'd missed while he'd been with Allison, he wanted the freedom of *not* being tied up with pleasing someone else.

Not long-term.

But her cat was dying. And he had a heart. He would've felt bad for anyone saying goodbye to a beloved pet.

Especially Kaci.

Had to be killing her to hurt bad enough that she let it show. And it had to be killing her that anyone saw her suffering.

The lady didn't like to look weak.

When he got home, he dragged his tent and a sleeping bag into the backyard.

He could see the stars just as well from here, he reasoned. Didn't have to add an hour or two on the road to enjoy it.

The fact that he'd be close by if Kaci happened to need— *want*—him had nothing to do with it.

She was a big girl. She could take care of herself.

Juice Box stepped out onto the patio near the pool. "Thought you were camping."

"Thought you had a date."

Juicy dangled a beer can and flashed a cocky grin. "Night's young. She'll be here."

"Nikki again?"

"Yeah, but I'm running out of Nikkis to date. Might have to learn another name soon."

"Don't have to try so hard," Lance said. "Nothing wrong with settling when you've found the right one."

Juice Box tossed himself into a plastic lawn chair while Lance set up his tent. "Who's looking for the right one? I'm just having fun."

Couldn't fault the kid. Lance had said the same thing when he'd been fresh out of pilot training too. "Are you?"

"Am I what?"

"Having fun."

"Fuck yeah."

"Glad to hear it."

Maybe Juicy *was* having the time of his life.

But when Lance had been all over the party scene, it had always felt…flat.

He'd never quite fit in. Not as well as Cheri had. They'd been together for joint undergrad pilot training in Oklahoma, but then Cheri had left for fighter training in Texas while Lance had been sent here to Gellings. So when he'd gotten to his first real squadron and met Allison, who preferred Friday night movies at home, baked cookies for fun, and could make conversation with everyone from a guy like Juice Box to a wall, he'd seen the answer to all of his needs.

A woman who didn't like to party but could fix up a meal to feed an army and engage everyone from freshly enlisted eighteen-year-olds to four-star generals. In short, the perfect officer's wife.

The antithesis of Kaci, that was for sure.

Except Kaci had something Allison never had.

She had Lance's full, undivided attention. Even when he'd been on the flight deck this past week, she'd been in the back of his mind.

He'd always been able to shut Allison out and just do his job.

But tonight, he couldn't get the image of Kaci's grief out of his mind.

Once the tent was up, he hauled his old charcoal grill from the garage, pulled the legs off, and tossed in his spare firewood.

"Got marshmallows?" Juice Box asked.

"In the truck."

They roasted hot dogs and marshmallows. Juicy's date—the same Nikki, obviously—showed up after a while, and the two of them took off. "Be safe," Lance called after them.

"Yes, Dad," Juicy shot back with an amused grin.

Kaci didn't text.

Or call.

Or email.

Lance had been at field training the summer between his sophomore and junior years of college when his family dog died.
Sunflower had only been nine years old. They'd thought she'd
live another four, five, six years, but she'd been hit by a car. He'd
told himself men didn't cry over dogs. Plus, Cheri hadn't cried.
Hell if he would.

But he'd missed that dog. And he'd spent more hours than he
could count wondering if she'd been scared. If she'd felt any pain.
If he could've saved her if he'd been there.

He poked at a log in the fire.

Kaci's cat was ancient. She'd had a good life, and she'd obviously
been loved.

But goodbyes sucked.

And Lance had a feeling he had a goodbye of his own coming
soon.

As fun as Kaci had been, he was deploying soon. He had to put
his job first.

Period.

Maybe not tonight—he wasn't cruel—but soon, he had to leave.

K ACI PULLED HER JEEP TO a stop in front of Lance's house
shortly after nine. She tightened her sloppy ponytail, wiped
her face with a spare makeup removal cloth she found in her
purse, and refused to look at the towel in the passenger seat.

Wood smoke drifted through the crisp night. She wrapped her
knit cardigan tighter around herself. When no one answered her
knock at the door, she followed the campfire smell into the backyard.

She hadn't been back here yet, but she wasn't surprised to find
a big lawn and an inground pool. The yard fit both the neighborhood and what she would've expected Lance to want to give his
former fiancée.

He was stretched out on a sleeping bag next to a dwindling fire pit. When the privacy fence gate clinked shut behind her, he sat up.

She couldn't read his expression in the dark. He lifted his arm, an open invitation for a hug. The empty hole in her chest pulsed.

"The vet has her body." She curled up next to him and swiped at her eyes. "Said I can pick up her ashes on Thursday."

He wrapped her tight, warm and solid and dependable, and pressed a lingering kiss to her hair. His capable hands stroked her back, and she had to fight against another wave of tears.

She wouldn't even let her momma know she'd cried for Miss Higgs, but she trusted Lance.

She'd trust Lance with her life.

She had, in fact. "Can I ask a huge favor?" she whispered.

"Of course."

"I mean really huge. Like I-don't-have-the-right-to-ask, bigger-than-anything-I've-ever-asked-another-human-soul-before, even-bigger-than-the-bows-my-momma-put-on-my-pageant-dresses huge."

"If I say yes, do I get to see pictures of those pageant dresses?"

If she wasn't so terrified he'd say no, she might appreciate the teasing. As it was, the very act of gathering enough courage to ask, of opening up to him even more tonight, was suffocating her. "Will you go to Germany with me?"

His surprised jerk away didn't surprise her.

But it didn't give her any confidence he'd say yes either.

"I'll pay for your ticket, and I'll buy your meals and everything," she rushed on. "I know it's asking a lot, for you to take a week of leave to go to Germany, but I can't—I don't—I can't get on that plane. I can't. Except I think I can if you're with me. I trust you. I know you can get me there. And I need to go. I *have* to go."

"Kaci—"

No. No, that was the *I'm going to say no* voice. "I'm not asking for forever." Her voice caught, and she hated herself for it. Because forever with Lance—no, she couldn't go there tonight too. "I'm just asking for this one little thing. Which I know is a big thing. Because I—I need you. I don't need anybody, but I need you. I need you to come with me."

He raked a hand over his hair and blew out a breath. "You don't need me to go."

She did.

Hypnosis wouldn't get her on that plane. Antianxiety meds wouldn't get her on that plane. But Lance—the idea of him sitting beside her, holding her hand, promising she'd be okay—he was what she needed to fly. "I do. I need you. I can't get on that plane if you're not there with me. You—you fix things. You fix *me*. Nobody else. Just you."

He scrubbed a hand over his face. "Kaci, I'm deploying in five days."

Her whole world crystallized into a fragile sphere dangling at the edge of a cliff. "You're leaving."

"You can do this, Kace. You can get on that plane, and you're going to be fine."

Rocks broke off the cliff and tumbled into the abyss, and her world teetered with them. Her chest squeezed so hard she couldn't breathe. Her stomach was screwed tight. Her eyes burned. "You're leaving," she said again.

"It's my job—"

"You knew." She pulled back and hugged herself. "You knew you were leaving this whole time."

Even in the dark, she could see him shifting into *careful with the wounded animal* mode.

That was what she was.

A wounded, broken animal. Fighting for survival.

"Never know exact dates until a week or two out, but the rotation's pretty regular," he said quietly.

He'd known.

And he hadn't told her.

Was he *ever* going to tell her? Or had he simply been planning on leaving?

Because they weren't supposed to be here. They weren't serious. They weren't committed. They weren't even *dating*.

But she loved him anyway.

He was everything she didn't want—a military man, a pilot, emotionally unavailable after being jilted—but he was also everything she needed.

He believed in her.

He challenged her.

He accepted her.

But his job still came first. As it always would. She'd been something to do between his breakup and his deployment.

He didn't love her.

And why should he?

She should be all cried out, but she stifled a sob as she scrambled to her feet.

"Kaci—"

"Be safe over there," she choked out.

He was right on her heels. "Let me drive you home."

"I'm fine."

"You're not."

She jerked her arm out of his grasp. "I. Am. Fine. Go on. Go back to your campfire. Go on your deployment. Go have fun with your buddies. Thank you for everything, Captain Wheeler, but it's apparently time for both of us to move on. We both got what we wanted, and that's that."

He let her go.

And that might have been what hurt most of all.

⌒⌒

IF KACI'S MOMMA COULD SEE her, there would be cucumber slices and Preparation H for her eyes, an emergency hot oil treatment for her hair, and a lecture about not letting anyone see you cry.

But her momma wasn't here, and Tara had baked brownies, and Kaci was just *done*.

She slammed a box of tissues on the counter beside the fresh brownies and dug into the whole pan with a fork.

"You know what we need?" she said around a mouthful of

chocolate therapy. "We need a club. You and me. An Officers' Ex-Wives Club."

Tara handed over a glass of milk. "Can we make flyers and T-shirts?"

"Knock yourself out, sugar."

But Kaci wasn't recruiting. She didn't want new friends.

Because they'd leave one day too.

And she didn't know how she'd survive.

"Can we make a divorce survival kit too?" Tara said.

"That the same as a heartbreak survival kit?" Kaci used a tissue, then attacked the brownies again.

It wasn't helping.

"Aw, honey." Tara pulled her in for a hug. "Want me to go toilet paper his house?"

She shook her head against Tara's shoulder.

"I can turn him into an impotent evil stepfather in my redneck fairy tales, but honestly, I kinda don't think they'll sell well enough to really get any satisfaction out of smearing his name. I really need to get a better day job."

"He can't go to Germany with me," Kaci whispered.

"Would it help if I come?"

"Can you land an airplane if the pilots die and the engines fall off?"

"No, but I'm good with chocolate, Xanax, and buying overpriced airport water bottles. I'll even let you read one of the fairy tales I'm working on. You might *want* the plane to go down to save you before it's over."

"Hush your tongue." Kaci shivered.

Tara squeezed harder. "You have important things to do you in your lifetime, Kaci. The world needs you. This conference in Germany is just the start. When you're ninety-eight years old, the world will be a better place because of what you've done and because of what you've taught your students to do. God won't let you die on that plane or any other plane. Understand?"

She didn't, but she nodded into Tara's shoulder again anyway.

She had to get on that plane.

With or without Lance.

Tara was right. She *had* to go to Germany.

For herself. For her profession. For the world.

But professional accolades, job satisfaction, and her pride all felt hollow tonight.

Because for the first time since she'd switched majors at eighteen years old, there was something she cared about more than she cared about physics.

And he didn't care back.

## Chapter 19

AFTER HER LECTURE MONDAY AFTERNOON, Kaci made a trip to the chemistry building. She'd posted flyers in the student center, in the humanities and mathematics and business studies buildings, and now, she was entering enemy territory.

Not that she was here to pick a fight, even if a fight might've soothed that unsettled, off-kilter part of her soul that had been aching since Friday night.

Fighting with Ron wouldn't solve anything. So she stapled her flyer to the bulletin board inside the double glass doors, then turned to go.

And ran smack into the first man who'd set her on the path to realizing just how much she needed more girlfriends who understood.

Ron slid a glance at the bulletin board, and the tendon in his neck tightened. "Seriously, Kaci?"

She'd known she'd be baiting the beast by posting flyers for the Officers' Ex-Wives Club in his building, but she hadn't expected him to see her do it. But the truth was, James Robert College had a good number of nontraditional students. She didn't see many in the Physics Department, but they were there. With the base so close by, many of those nontraditional students were former military wives, like Tara, going back to school after years of unsteady work experience due to frequent moves and the unwillingness of employers to take a chance on someone who might not be around more than a few years.

"Chancellor-approved," she said to Ron with a nod toward her flyer. "Have a nice day."

She started to step around him, but he blocked her way. "I'm not an officer anymore Kaci. You can stay here. I can stay here. We can stay here together."

"We're not *together*, Ron. We never were. You never loved me enough to ask me what I wanted out of life, and frankly, I never did you the same courtesy."

"Okay. What do you want? What can I do?"

"You can *listen*. And you can accept what I'm saying. And what I'm saying is that I've moved on, and you need to do the same."

He pointed to the flyer. "Like this? This is how you're moving on?"

"That ain't about you. It's about me." And Lance. Her heart flopped over in her chest. This was *definitely* about getting over Lance.

"Bullshit," Ron said.

"See? Right there. You can't *listen*. You don't hear me. I'm not saying what you want me to say, so you disregard it."

"I don't—" He stopped himself, and his dark eyes narrowed. "You've never been the most rational person. Can't fault me for trying to make you see clearer logic and push past your stubborn side."

"Nope. But I can tell you that my logic isn't yours to clear anymore, and my stubborn side isn't yours to deal with anymore." And the man who brought out the best in her, who made her look at logic clearer and who had the patience to accept her stubborn side, didn't want her.

Ron's lips parted. "You're serious."

"Been serious this whole time."

She could see the light dawning. The understanding that she wasn't rejecting him to hold a grudge or to make him pay or out of spite. That she honestly, truly didn't want a second chance to be his wife. His jaw sagged, and he leaned against the wall beside the bulletin board. "I moved across the country for you."

"Ask next time. And *listen*."

This time, when she stepped around him, he didn't stop her.

"And stay the hell out of Germany," she added as she pushed through the doors and into the frosty late autumn day.

Because she might be able to make peace with Ron Kelly, ex-husband, but she needed to make sure he knew she was done with Dr. Kelly, research intruder, too.

Besides, Kaci only had so much maturity in her for one day.

L ANCE COULDN'T GET HIS HEAD on straight. Monday, he forgot his ID card and the squadron patch on his flight suit. Tuesday, he locked himself out of the house and almost missed a squadron meeting.

He just forgot.

He was deploying *tomorrow*, and his brain was simply gone.

Because he couldn't stop wondering how Kaci was doing. If she was dealing with her grief okay. If she was mad at him for not telling her he was deploying. If she'd gone back to the bar and hooked up with someone else. If he needed to worry about a pumpkin landing in his pool or his truck disappearing.

If she'd talk to him if he called.

If he should just wise up and quit thinking about her.

But he couldn't. It was as though when she'd left his house last Friday, she'd taken her chaos with her. But he'd adapted. He needed chaos. So he was making his own.

And that wasn't a good omen for this deployment.

Or that ache he'd been ignoring in his chest.

So Tuesday, when he should've been heading to sleep early before the long flight overseas tomorrow, Lance surrendered.

He needed to see her. He needed her to tell him to leap off the ramp of his C-130 without a parachute.

He needed to know she was planning to go to Germany.

Her Jeep was in its parking place, so he let himself into the building and took the steps to her apartment.

This time last week, he'd been happy in his willful ignorance about Kaci's impact on his life. Today, his feet were in concrete boots. His heart bounced erratically.

And for the first time since he'd set foot in his first ROTC class as a freshman in college, his career, his calling, was a thorn in his side.

A white sign with pink curlicues announcing this as the site of the first Officers' Ex-Wives Club meeting gave him pause.

But he knocked anyway.

He needed to see Kaci.

He needed her to sass him. To tell him his ego was overinflated at the idea that he'd hurt her.

To assure him he *hadn't* hurt her.

But the sign on the door wasn't reassuring.

Her smile melted off her face when her gaze landed on him. "Evening, Captain."

He opened his mouth, but, "Hey," was all that came out.

She lifted her brows. *You got something to say, or you come here to take in the scenery?* She didn't say it, but he heard it anyway. If his heart hadn't sped up and his gut twisted, he might've smiled.

"Just wanted to check on you," he said. "You doing okay?"

Blue sparks flashed in her eyes, but the fluttering of her pulse in that soft spot of her neck told him she was just as uneven as he was. "With my cat dying, or with finding out a *friend* didn't think it was worth telling me he was leaving the country soon?"

"Yes."

"Let me ask you, sugar. How would you be doing?"

Damn shitty, if he were being honest. "I asked around my squadron. Got a buddy who's almost as good a pilot as I am who's happy to go to Germany with you if you want. I'd trust him with my life. And I'll pay for his hotel room."

"Sweet of you, but there's no need. I'm perfectly capable of getting on an airplane by myself."

Her pupils had dilated and her breathing was shallow, but she blinked twice, then lifted her nose and stared him down as if she were daring him to call her on showing an ounce of fear.

"I'd go with you myself if I could," he said. Hell, he *wanted* to go her. He wanted to hold her. Kiss her. Spend a whole *week* in a hotel with her. Yeah, he'd have to give her up during her conference hours, but he'd go to whatever parts of the conference he could. Watching her give a keynote speech about her research sounded oddly erotic.

"Like I said. No need. Anything else I can help you with tonight?"

This wasn't sass. This was bullheaded push-through-it-until-he-goes-away. "Kaci, look, I'm sorry I didn't tell you about my deployment. I didn't think we'd get as…close as we did."

She pursed her lips together. Her chest rose and fell quickly beneath her James Robert College sweatshirt, and her fingers curled into a ball.

"I've missed you," he said.

"You need to leave."

The strain in her voice twisted a screw in his heart. "If I'd known it was important to you, I would've told you I was leaving. I didn't realize—I *ignored* that it was important. And I'm sorry. If I could change it—"

"You can't, Lance. You can't change it. And you can't change me, and you can't change you. So I'm gonna tell you the same thing I told my ex-husband this week. You need to go. I need to move on. You need to move on. And you standing here won't change that."

His knees wobbled, and lightning shot through his veins. She was dumping him. Truly, finally, without question.

They weren't even together, but she was dumping him. "Kaci, you are the smartest, funniest, craziest woman I've ever met."

"Don't do this," she whispered.

He swallowed. This wasn't happening. Two women, polar opposites, both wanting nothing to do with him in the span of less than three months. "I love spending time with you. I thought you liked hanging out with me too. Can we—all I'm asking is for some time. Some of *your* time. I want to call you. I want to send you email. I want to—I want to see you when I get back. You're…" What? Special? How cliché could he get? "You're *you*. And I'm not ready to let you go."

"To what end?"

To having her in his life. In his home. In his bed. Every night. "I-I don't know."

"You know what I know?" Her lower lip trembled. "I know I told you I need you. I know you know I don't need *anyone*. But when I need you, you're gonna be halfway around the world, serving your country. And the next time I need you, you might be there, or you might not. Depends on what the military needs from you. And that's real honorable of you. But I'm not honorable. I'm selfish. I want to come first. When I finally hit that brick wall, when I have to get on another plane, when I'm sick, when someone I love dies, when my life falls apart, I *need* to come first. So long as you're married to Uncle Sam, you can't promise me that. So I'm gonna keep on taking care of me. And I'm gonna wish you the best, but this? Us? It can't be anymore."

Panic scrambled his brain cells. "Kaci, you are the strongest woman I know—"

"I play a good game. That's it. You of all people should know that. And if you don't, then I guess I probably don't know you all that well either."

"That's it?" Something new surged through his veins. Panic still, but a red-hot anger on top of it. "You're telling me we're done because of my job? You're chickening out because of my job."

"Chickening out of *what*? What are we, Lance? Because last I checked, I was just something for you to do while you got over being dumped."

He tensed. "You can stand there and say that with a straight face after everything we've been through together?"

"You gonna stand there and pretend you love me?" Her voice was soft, but strong as only Kaci could be. "Because if you can't stand there and tell me you love me, if you can't promise me you'll put *us* first, if I can't be your world and your galaxy and your universe, then there's nowhere else for us to go. I can't be your friend, Lance. I love you too much to settle for less than everything."

He felt as though someone had taken a jackhammer to his heart.

"I'm not saying I don't—" He swallowed hard. His gut churned. Was that fear? Dread? Guilt? "We've barely known each other two months," he tried.

She blinked rapidly against shiny eyes. "What was that you said a minute ago? *After all we've been through?* And that's the best you've got? Go to hell, Lance Wheeler. I'm sure I'll see you there someday."

The door slammed with the staccato bang of a gunshot, and Lance found himself nose-first in her sign for her damn club.

He balled his hands into fists and barely held back from banging on the door. Punching the wall. Punching himself.

She was right.

He wasn't in love with her.

And if she was crazy enough to think friendship had to equal love, then he was better off without her.

No matter what that bitter taste in his mouth, the sour roiling in his stomach, and the raw wounds on his heart suggested.

## Chapter 20

L ANCE HAD BEEN ON ENOUGH deployments the past five years to know the routines.

Despite his issues since Friday, his pre-deployment checklists were done, checkrides all signed off, bags packed, and the normal anticipation was licking at his heels. He knew his mission, and he knew he needed to be ready to get out there and get troops and supplies where they needed to be.

But Wednesday morning, while family and friends gathered on the flight line for one last goodbye before the squadron went wheels-up, something was missing.

Allison had been there for Lance's past two deployments, but he didn't miss her today. She'd always been pragmatic—*Not like you and Goose are battling the MiGs,* she'd joked both times. *You'll be home soon.*

He'd shrugged off the comparison both times too, though he hadn't forgotten it. His passion for being in the air wasn't about being *Top Gun* great. Didn't have any need to prove he was the best. He just wanted to be one with the sky, serving his country.

Today, his parents weren't coming either. He had a better shot of running into Cheri overseas than he did of seeing her here stateside. Neither of which bothered him—yeah, he was missing the holidays this year, but so was Cheri. They'd go home together and celebrate in the spring.

He skimmed a glance about the crowd, ears tuned for a sassy twang, even though he knew *she* wasn't coming either.

She'd said as much last night.

And now, there was a hollow spot under his breastbone, and he felt as though he were leaving things unsettled here.

He'd miss her.

"You want me to send pictures of the pool parties?" Juice Box asked with a smirk.

God help him, he was leaving his house in Juice Box's care. "You'll freeze your nuts off."

"Depends on who I bring with me."

"So much to learn, Juicy. So much to learn."

Juice Box angled closer and dropped his voice. "You nervous?"

He had been on his first deployment, and he had no doubt that was what the kid was thinking about. He'd taken Lance's spot in the next rotation so Flincher wouldn't have to deploy again before he got orders to a new base. "Old hat by now. I'll show you around when you get there. But I'll fly back over there and kick your ass if I get home and find my house broken."

Juicy's brows relaxed. So did his shoulders. "Cranky old man."

"Captain Wheeler?" A brunette with a pixie haircut, round cheeks, and a ruby smile squinted at him. "I'm Madeline Scott. Evan's wife." She put a hand to her round belly. "I just wanted to say thank you."

Flincher stepped to his wife's side, holding a squirming little girl with two tiny pigtails that made her look like she had horns. "Still owe you, man."

"Nah," Lance said. "Doing me the favor. Good to get in the extra flight hours."

But he wasn't as excited to get out of Georgia as he'd been two months ago.

And that little blondie Flincher was holding was making Lance think about his favorite blonde.

Again.

Would she go to Germany? Would she take any more crap from her fellow professors?

Would she get back together with her ex-husband?

Lance nearly growled.

"You need anything, you let us know," Madeline said. "Is your family here today?"

"Just me."

The insta-pity in her eyes made his joints twitch. She patted his arm. "We'll make sure to send you extra care packages. Hope you like drawings. Izzy here's crazy with a crayon these days."

"You don't have to—"

"Yes, we do," Flincher said.

*We.*

Flincher had a family. The sweet wife, the adorable tot, one more on the way. Even Pony had a few buddies out to see him off.

But not Lance.

Because he'd fucked up with the only person in the world who would've wanted to be here for him.

⸙

TWO WEEKS INTO DECEMBER, KACI and Tara hadn't found any new members for their club, but they were doing just fine on their own.

Kaci had gone to her doctor for antianxiety medicine. She'd made appointments to meet with fellow physicists from Austria, Japan, and six other countries while she was in Germany, and she had a hypothesis niggling at her that she wanted to investigate as soon as she got back. Her speech was ready and approved by the dean, and even her cranky, girl-hating, fellow physics professors hadn't been able to find fault with it.

Ron had canceled his plans to attend the conference too.

The Physics Club kids were tweaking Ichabod in anticipation of a watermelon-flinging contest coming in June that was within driving distance and, with Kaci's endorsement, three of them had been selected for scholarships from the James Robert Physics Association alumni group.

Life was good.

Except she kept checking the base's webpage for Lance's squadron.

It had been a slow news week when Lance and his buddies

shipped out a few weeks ago, so they'd been covered on the local news.

Tara had been working that night, and even though Kaci knew she should've put on a movie or streamed a TV show, she'd recorded the news and then watched, craning for any glimpse of Lance, reaching for Miss Higgs, who wasn't there, stifling tears when Lance himself came on for an interview, steady and authoritative and heart-stopping in his aviator sunglasses and green flight suit.

And she might've rewound it to watch it again.

And another one or two—dozen—times.

He was doing what he was born to do. Kicking ass and taking names. Keeping the world safe.

So she needed to do what she was born to do. Make the world better through physics.

She was trying not to throw up the night before her flight when Tara got home from her shift at Jimmy Beans. "You okay?" Tara asked.

Kaci mumbled a *mmph* and nodded. Then tried to telepathically sent Tara a message asking how her final went, since she was pretty sure if she opened her mouth, she'd puke.

Tara missed the message.

"Here. I picked up some ginger mints for you. They'll help settle your stomach." Tara climbed onto Kaci's bed and peered in the pink suitcase. "Wow. Is that an Hermès scarf? What else are you hiding in your closet?"

"You pass your finals?" Kaci croaked out.

"Hope so." Tara twirled a curl around her finger. "You're going to do great, Kaci. You know that, right?"

That was what everyone kept telling her. "I still wish he was coming with me." Admitting the truth was painful, but admitting the truth to Tara was also a relief.

"Aw, honey," Tara whispered.

"I just want him to hug me again. I want to hear his voice again. When Ron and I broke up, I didn't miss him. Because I never wanted to hug him. His voice wasn't special. I didn't want to have his babies. But Lance—I would've had Lance's babies, Tara. I don't even know if I want kids, and I would've had his babies."

Tara squeezed her in a hug. "You're going to be okay, Kaci. You have bigger things to do."

"I just *miss* him."

"His roommate came into Jimmy Beans last night."

Kaci's nose wrinkled.

Tara plopped down on the bed. "Sounds like it's been an easy deployment so far for the guys over there. Devon said you can stop by anytime. His girlfriend slugged him. Nikki's a grad student in the English department, and she kinda offered to help me with my redneck fairy tales. She's doing research into the ways storytelling is shifting because of the digital marketplace, so I'm sorta going to be the subject of her master's thesis. But I'll meet with her at her place. Or alone here. I told Devon he's not allowed to know where we live."

Kaci rubbed the sore spot to the left of her breastbone. "Do what you need to do, sugar. Life goes on."

So long as her plane was airworthy tomorrow. And the other one, too, that would bring her back from Germany.

Where she'd actually be closer to Lance than she was today.

"I can still drop everything and go with you tomorrow," Tara said. She'd never once come out and said she knew Kaci was terrified to fly, but Kaci knew she knew.

She'd probably known since the night Kaci came home complaining that some hot guy in a bar had kissed her and run away. Because that was the kind of friend Tara was.

"I got this," Kaci said.

Her fingers were numb, but she'd be fine. She'd get on that plane. She'd have the time of her professional life in Germany. She'd come home.

And life would go on.

Really, it was good that she and Lance had called it quits. If they were still dating, she'd be doing that helpless female thing, begging him to save her, and she'd be making excuses not to get on the plane.

She squeezed her eyes shut.

If she'd never met Lance, she wouldn't be getting on that plane tomorrow.

She was going because he'd believed in her.

She was going because he called her strong.

She was going because he'd gone out of his way to show her planes were safe and then delivered her safely to the ground even *with* engine problems.

She owed it to him to do this. To not toss her cookies. To not cry. To not cause a scene.

And to *enjoy* it.

"And did I tell you we have a new club member?" Tara added with a sly grin.

"No!"

"Mrs. Sheridan."

"The *base commander's wife*?"

"Yep. Turns out, the commander's her second husband. She was married to another military guy before that, and she thinks the ex-wives club is awesome. She's offered to be either a full member or an advisor, whatever we want or need. She's *not* planning on divorcing General Sheridan, but she does believe in supporting both current *and* former military spouses."

"Shut the front door."

"So, anyway, you have to go kick ass in Germany. Because we need you to get back home and put more flyers all over campus and town. Okay?"

Kaci nodded. "I'll do my best."

✐

DEPLOYMENTS DIDN'T LEAVE MUCH DOWNTIME, but Lance found a few hours a week to catch up on email. He could also call Cheri toll-free through the base phone system, so he'd been bothering his twin as often as humanly possible.

It helped center him.

Unlike his previous deployments, his head still wasn't all here.

He gritted his way through it, digging deep for his focus, especially when he was flying, but he kept forgetting little things. Getting agitated by a boot string breaking or for leaving his sunglasses in the wrong place or forgetting his password.

He'd thought Kaci was the chaos in his life.

But he was beginning to suspect she'd been his balance.

After all the time he'd put into anticipating getting the hell out of Georgia, Georgia was exactly where he wanted to be.

Just before Christmas, he did something he knew he'd regret. He Googled Kaci's name.

Because he had to know.

The top story was written in English, but it might as well have been gibberish. Lance was hardly an imbecile, but all the physics lingo being tossed around made his head hurt. The point, though, was that she'd done it.

She'd made it to Germany.

And from the nontechnical bits he could pick out of the articles he found in his three hours before he was due on the flight line, he learned that she'd aced her presentation.

*Groundbreaking.*

*Game-changing.*

*Brilliant.*

He found an article from back home, written two days after she'd gotten back, summing everything up in layman's terms. *Biofuels are only half the battle, local physicist says.* Kaci's research was paving the way toward improving engine efficiency, with an eye toward zero net energy loss. She'd been asked to go to Sweden in May and to an energy conference in California in the fall.

Before he could think better of it, he copied the link to the news story and switched to his mail program.

❧

KACI'S FIRST CHRISTMAS WITHOUT MISS Higgs was weird. Momma hovered more than she usually did, as though the loss of the cat had thrown her off too. Kaci wasn't sleeping well in her old bedroom, and those things she'd always taken for granted—Momma's rigid posture, the desperate need to get back to her own life, cat hair on the Jell-O mold—were all missing.

She slipped into her old bedroom—still decorated in the muted yellows and blues that Momma insisted were good for her constitution—under the guise of needing a post-Christmas-dinner nap, and pulled out her laptop.

The mashed potatoes had inspired an idea about a key point she was missing with her new hypothesis, and she wanted to write it down before she forgot it. While she was on her computer, she switched over to check email.

And lost her breath.

*Wheeler, Lance (Capt, USAF)* had sent her a message.

She hovered the mouse over the checkbox beside the message, debating if she should simply delete it.

They hadn't parted on *bad* terms. They'd parted on *we have different lives* terms.

Mildly embarrassing *different lives* terms, what with her slipping out that she loved him, but still. Not *bad* terms.

She couldn't be a military wife and still meet her professional goals, and when he was finally far enough from his breakup that he could see clearly, he'd realize he was just having fun, and they weren't destined soul mates like Tara's couples in her books.

But Kaci could *read* the email from Lance. Reading it didn't mean she had to respond.

Or care.

Her heart swelled.

Too late. She already cared.

And she probably always would.

With a defeated sigh, she clicked on the message.

*Proud of you*, was all it said, with a link below to the article from the Gellings paper.

*I'm freaking proud of me too, you dolt,* she wanted to reply.

Or maybe *Shove it, flyboy.*

But she'd discovered her pride wasn't the best at speaking for her.

She hesitated longer than she wanted to admit, looking for hidden messages between the three words. Ten letters. Ten letters could say so much. But these ten letters said so little.

True, they said he'd been thinking of her enough to read an article about her and forward it to her. Or that one of his squadron buddies had hacked his email and sent her a message to screw with them both. Or possibly she was asleep, and he hadn't actually sent the email, but she wished he had.

She growled at herself.

She was thirty-freaking-four years old. If she couldn't reply to a simple email from a *friend*, she had more issues than she thought.

*Thank you*, she typed. And then she hit *Send* before she could overthink it.

*Thank you* was appropriate. He'd gotten her there. He'd taken her up on her first airplane ride. He'd believed in her. He'd challenged her. He'd held her. He'd pushed her.

And he'd taken five minutes out of his deployment to let her know he was thinking about her.

She hadn't seen the man in over a month, and he still tied her up in needy, emotional knots.

Of all the men she'd known in her life, none had treated her like Lance did. Some men wanted her for her body. Others for her brains. She'd known a few who had dug her potato gun.

But Lance had honestly seemed to like *her*. All of her. The redneck parts. The physicist parts. The female parts. The obnoxious parts.

Regardless of anything she'd said to him, what she'd done to him, he kept coming back.

He could've been perfect for her.

But she would never ask a man to sacrifice something she wasn't willing to sacrifice herself to be with him. She wasn't willing to give up her tenure-track position, which meant she wasn't willing to move away from Gellings.

So how could she ask Lance to leave the military for her?

And why would he want to?

She found Momma working at her desk in the pristine den,

vacuum marks still visible in the plush carpet. Momma's reading glasses were perched on the end of her nose while she stared at the monitor.

"Enough beauty rest for one day?" Momma said.

Kaci curled up in the plush round chair beneath a hanging sweet potato plant. "If you'd known what was gonna happen to Daddy, would you have still married him?"

One of Momma's perfectly plucked eyebrows went up. *"Age is no excuse to lower your beauty standards,"* she'd said on more occasions than Kaci cared to count. "Are you reconsidering your separation from Colonel Kelly?"

Kaci hugged a mauve throw pillow. "No."

Momma pulled off her glasses and swiveled soundlessly to face Kaci in the corner. "Had we known what your father's fate would be, it's far more likely he would've left *me* to save me from the grief."

"Would you have let him?"

"Of course not."

Kaci found a smile.

"I take it you've been dating again."

"If that's what kids these days are calling it."

Momma's cheek twitched.

"We're over," Kaci added softly. "I was just wishing one of us could've been a little different."

"You wouldn't like him if he were different, and if the man has any sense at all, he wouldn't like you if you were different either."

Some days, every once in a while, Momma was Kaci's favorite person.

But then there were moments like this when her brilliance was as irritating as a mosquito bite in a place she couldn't reach.

Because she was right.

Lance probably wouldn't like her if she were different. If she changed her mind about what she wanted out of her career, he wouldn't respect her as much.

And then where would she be?

"I think I'm better off single," Kaci said.

"All the best of us are."

⁓⊙⌒

L ANCE WAS BACK IN HIS bunk, staring at his two-word reply
 from Kaci, when Pony came in with a stack of boxes. "Mail
call. We got presents."

Mail. One of the highlights of deploying.

"Shit, Thumper. Ain't that your ex-fiancée?"

He took the shoebox-size package Pony thrust at him and
glanced at the return label. "Huh."

He hadn't heard from her since September. But that was her
name and address in the return sender field.

And sending a deployment care package was exactly the sort of
thing Allison would do. Because it was the patriotic thing to do.

Doing it for him was a little weird, but the weirder part was that
he didn't feel anything seeing her name on the box.

No anger. No regret. No excitement.

Now, if Kaci had sent a care package—

He tossed aside the box from Allison and examined the other
three boxes Pony had piled at his feet. One from his parents, one
from Cheri—the dork, she was deployed too—and one from
Flincher and his family.

None from Kaci.

Not that she had reason to send him anything.

He had a feeling he was lucky to get two words in an email
from her.

"My wife left me after my first deployment," Pony said.

Lance shot a look at his buddy. "You were married?"

"Not long. I reconnected with a high school girlfriend and
eloped to Vegas. Knew it wouldn't last when her care packages
pissed me off. She sent crossword puzzle books and a photo
album of her dog."

Lance grunted. No wonder Pony didn't talk about his ex-wife.

"Got one from a family friend once though." Pony sliced open
the first of his seven boxes. "Oreos, Lucky Charms, and a stack of

*Star Wars* books. Looked her up when I got home. Was ready to propose, but she was dating someone, so I just said thanks. Funny thing. She wouldn't stand out in a crowd, but when she smiled..." He shook his head. "Sometimes the chicks *get* us. And there's a connection. But we're too late."

Lance glanced at his tablet again. "Or we picked the wrong career."

"Fuck that excuse. I got thirteen years in. Seven more, I can retire. She loves me? We'll make it work."

"I've got six in, and I'm sticking around until they put stars on my shoulders."

"You take a three-year tour in the training squadron and a four-year follow-on at Gellings, you'll be in as long as I am now. Difference, though, is you got a girl you miss who'd be happy at Gellings for another seven years. All I have is a job." Pony lifted a pair of socks decorated with mustaches and grimaced. "And a bunch of family with weird senses of humor."

"You think this is just a job?"

"It's more than a job. But it's not enough to be my entire life."

Lance picked up the box from Cheri and balanced it on his knee.

Did he want a job in the training squadron?

It *would* mean staying in Georgia. Teaching and training and mentoring more kids like Juice Box.

Whom Lance actually missed, in a little-brother kind of way.

But staying in Georgia, even for a job that sounded appealing, meant he'd be close to Kaci.

There were plenty of women in the world who made good wives to military members. Plenty of women who wouldn't write him off because he deployed, because he moved every few years, because he might not come home one day.

But none of those women who would've loved him despite his job were Kaci Boudreaux.

And even here, halfway around the world, weeks after he'd last seen her, he couldn't get her out of his mind.

*Chapter 21*

ON A BLUSTERY SATURDAY AFTERNOON in late March, Kaci took her Physics Club kids back out to the fairgrounds to test their improvements to Ichabod. After her last disaster with launching pumpkins, she'd called in advance to make sure the field was open and that they could use it for test-firing.

She'd also asked Tara to pass along to Lance's roommate that she was firing pumpkins, just in case she aimed the wrong way and put their squadron bar in danger again.

Tara had found it hilarious. Apparently Nikki and Devon-slash-Juice Box had too. And so the message had been passed along, and Kaci had asked Zada to take the lead in making sure they were aiming away from the houses when they arrived at the field this morning.

A small cluster of Civil War reenactors were also set up on the firing line. And instead of a catapult, they had a cannon.

Her redneck heart gave an indignant squeak. She'd always wanted to fire a cannon.

"Aren't they a little far south?" Zada whispered. "I didn't think there were any Civil War battles in this part of the state."

"Love of the Confederacy isn't always tied to a battleground," Kaci murmured back.

Her six students went to work setting up Ichabod.

Kaci willfully ignored the cannon dudes.

She'd had a lot of practice at willfully ignoring things in the past few months.

Willfully ignoring that she'd committed to getting on two more airplanes to speak at two more conferences. Willfully ignoring that she still had two more years of teaching before she could go before the tenure board, and that she still hadn't made friends with the old cronies who would decide her fate. She kept half hoping at least one or two would retire before then.

Willfully ignoring that Lance's squadron was supposed to be home sometime today since Devon-slash-Juice Box had left earlier this week.

Not straining for sounds of cargo planes or casting glances at the sky every few minutes.

She pinched her lips together and resisted stomping.

He'd kept emailing—short notes every few days to every few weeks, which she responded to in equally short terms—but that didn't change anything.

He was still a military pilot first and foremost, and she was still a physics professor who needed job stability.

Zada jogged past. "I'll grab the vegetables," she called behind her.

Pumpkins were scarce, and the imported watermelons Kaci had found were expensive, so her students were using cloth bags stuffed with potatoes for a few test runs on Ichabod. She wrenched her eyes away from the sky and stepped over to watch the girls load the catapult.

"That potato's face looks like Zada's ex-boyfriend."

"Let's crush him."

"Smashed potato face, coming up. Hey, anybody want to go to the movies tonight?"

"Excuse me. Is one of you Dr. Boudreaux?" A rotund gentleman whose Confederacy uniform was bursting at the buttons stopped at the edge of their group.

"That's me, sugar. What can we do for you?"

"We got word you might could help us fire our cannon."

She swiveled her attention between the man and his cannon, but her gaze snagged on something else at the edge of the cluster of Civil War reenactors.

A tall, lanky, dark-haired captain in a flight suit and aviator sunglasses.

Her heart skipped a beat.

No, it skipped about six beats, and then it tripped over itself catching back up.

"I've always wanted to fire a cannon," she whispered.

The Civil War soldier grinned. "That's what that young feller over there said when he asked us to come out and practice today."

No.

Oh, no no no.

He was *not* using her redneck nature to get to her heart.

She'd kill him. She'd stuff *him* in that cannon and see how far he could fly.

Why couldn't he just let her go?

"Man just got back from war," the soldier said. "Can't leave him hanging, miss."

Whispers went up among her students. "Is that your boyfriend, Dr. Boudreaux?"

"Are you dating one of the cheaters?"

"Oh, wow, military guys are seriously hot."

Kaci shushed them. "What's it matter to him if I fire your cannon?" she asked the Confederate soldier.

"Man seems to have his heart tied up in it, miss."

Lance stood at parade rest, legs spread, hands tucked behind his back, straight-faced. A well-trained specimen waiting.

Waiting for what?

For her to kick a boot up his rear end?

Or for her to launch herself at him and never let go?

Because if her heart could've laid out her future and written her destiny, she'd be in his arms, breathing him in, touching him, tasting him, never letting him go again.

But he was still in that danged flight suit, still in his military uniform, still acting every bit the military man.

She was stuck in a tug-of-war between her heart and her self-preservation. And by the way that swollen organ was knocking around her chest, she was pretty sure her heart was winning.

"I'll fire it for you, Dr. Boudreaux," Zada whispered.

Kaci's legs moved on their own. She wasn't marching—no, this time, she was wobbling.

He wasn't here just to torture her.

Was he?

The closer she got, the more clearly she could see that Lance *wasn't* in his military best. His blue hat was crooked. Out-of-regs stubble dotted his cheeks and chin. And his uniform wasn't entirely right—was it his rank? Or was he missing a patch somewhere?

He pressed his lips together.

She couldn't see his eyes, but she felt his gaze.

*Oh*, she felt his gaze. Seeking her. Demanding she come closer. Pulling her in.

When she stopped in front of him, she could barely breathe. Her chest was tight, her heart defying some laws of physics, her eyes hot and wet.

He'd left.

Miss Higgs had died, he'd left, and she'd had to get on that airplane by herself.

And she'd survived all of it.

But she wasn't sure she could survive finding out why he was here.

He licked his lips. Ducked his head. Looked at her again. "Don't think the cannon can put them into orbit, but I was hoping you'd help me chuck some MREs anyway."

Her pulse tripped. If he wanted to chuck military rations out of a cannon, did he mean he wanted to get out of the military? Or just that he was tired of eating bad food while he was gone?

"Don't play with me," she whispered.

"Volunteered to be an IP. Here. Got three years without deployments while I teach new officers to fly 130s, and I can ask to stay another four back in the 946th after that."

Seven years.

He could stay here, at Gellings, right down the road from James Robert College, for the next seven years.

She curled her arms around herself. "And then?"

"Then you name it, Kace. Anything." He started to reach for her. She veered back. He yanked his sunglasses off and dropped his hands. "You want me to get out, I'll get out. You want me to pull strings and get us to Germany so you can go teach and research over there, I'll pull every damn string I can. I'll take a year remote in Korea so I can come back here to Gellings again. Anything. I just—I miss you. I want you. God, Kaci, I *need* you."

He *needed* her? "Nobody needs me," she whispered.

Suddenly she was wrapped up in him, a capable hand cradling her head against his shoulder, his viselike grip a steel beam holding her against his hot, hard body while his voice resonated in her ears. "Kaci, so many people need you. Your friends need you. Your students need you. *I* need you. You're everything missing in my life. You're my light. You're my laughter. You're my love. You're my home. I didn't want to be in the sandbox. I didn't want to be at my house. I didn't want to be back here at the squadron. I wanted to be with you. The last four months, all I've wanted is to be with you. Wherever you are. I want to be with you."

*This.* This was everything she'd ever wanted. Everything she'd ever needed. She couldn't have let him go if her life depended on it. "Did you fall and hit your head over there?"

His chuckle rumbled against her body, and her long-dormant feminine parts stirred to life.

"God, I've missed you," he whispered into her hair.

"Maybe I'm still mad at you."

His fingers trailed down her neck. "I hope so. I have a lot of groveling and apologizing and making amends to do. I should've told you I was leaving. I should've told you how much I cared. I'll make it all up to you though. Please, Kaci. Please let me love you."

As if she could tell him no for anything. He could've asked her to go with him to the moon.

He was here.

He'd missed her.

He knew her, and he still wanted her.

He *loved* her.

"Is this good quiet or bad quiet?" he whispered.

"I missed you too." She lifted her face to his. The worry and vulnerability and just plain exhaustion etched in his expression tugged at her soul. "Oh, Lance." She cupped his cheeks, went up on tiptoe, and pressed her lips to his.

She couldn't *not* kiss him.

A low groan rumbled out of his chest. He sucked her lower lip into his mouth, and she forgot where she was, forgot what day it was, forgot her own name.

Her name didn't matter.

All that mattered was that she was his. And time and distance and airplanes couldn't change that.

Cheers went up all around them.

She reluctantly pulled out of his kiss. "My students," she whispered.

He grinned, then pressed another kiss to her cheek. "And the cannon."

She laughed and wiped her eyes.

He knew her too well.

She might not have wanted another military man in her life, but she was keeping this one.

And she wouldn't want him any other way.

❧

SIX MONTHS AGO, THE LAST place Lance would've expected to find true contentment was on his couch with a fully clothed woman talking his ear off. But tonight, despite his body being tired from the long flight home, he couldn't stop smiling, and that sassy twang was utter music to his ears.

"And when we landed in Germany, that pilot had the nerve to ask everyone to come back and fly their airline again. Like the dang man thought we all should've liked it as much as you crazy people do."

He slid his fingers through her silky hair and lost himself in her unique Kaci scent. "Can I go with you in May?"

She arched a brow at him. "Oh, I see what's going on. You're thinking you found yourself an easy way to go on fancy vacations."

"I see right through you, Dr. Boudreaux."

Her blue eyes sparkled, and she leaned up to nuzzle his cheek. "Don't go telling anybody else," she whispered.

"I'll keep your secret," he whispered back, "but it might cost you."

She wasn't an easy woman by any stretch of the imagination, but she was *his* woman. She'd keep him on his toes. She'd pull crazy shit. She'd probably frustrate the hell out of him some days.

But this woman had more love hidden in that big ol' heart of hers than the world would ever know.

And when she shifted on the couch to straddle him, that beautiful smile glowing, her eyes full of mischief, her fingers igniting a trail of anticipation across his skin, he knew he was the luckiest man in the world to have all of her love.

# *Epilogue*

*Three months later…*

IF KACI HAD TO BE running late to meet the high school student group she was mentoring for summer semester, at least she had a good excuse. "My shoe!" she called to Lance. "I can't find my danged shoe."

He hopped around the bed, tugging his jeans back up. "Did it go in the bathroom?"

"Looked there."

"The closet?"

"Sugar, think *harder*."

He barked out a laugh. "This shoe?"

Sure enough, there was her sandal sitting right on top of that danged stuffed Alabama elephant he kept on his dresser just to torment her.

Or maybe in retribution for her putting Rebel, the Ole Miss black bear, on her dresser.

Her Lance was a mighty fine sport, all things considered. "Hand it over. I gotta get going."

"Nope. You know the rules. If Big Al has it, he gets to keep it. Unless…"

"I think I just paid that debt, thank you very much." They'd had a houseguest the past few days—one of Lance's old college buddies was moving to town, and he'd crashed with them while he was house-hunting—and between the boys sitting out back catching up late into the night and Kaci's schedule at James Robert with the summer semester starting this week, she and Lance hadn't had much opportunity to talk.

Or kiss.

Or make love.

Until about an hour or so ago.

And now Kaci was late to meet her group. "Can I pay you back later?"

Lance plucked the shoe off his elephant's trunk. "Promise?"

"You know I can't tell you no for anything." She'd even let him put a diamond ring on her finger a few weeks back. Dang man had used her fears against her and proposed on the airplane ride to Sweden.

Not that she could've told him no for anything, even if they'd been safely on the ground.

Plus, he'd let her touch his catapult.

This man was her everything.

Tara was afraid they were moving too fast, but Kaci's heart knew what it wanted, and Lance knew what he was getting himself into.

She'd never known anyone who loved her so much just for being her.

And she loved him more than she'd ever known she could love another person. So much so, in fact, that she'd promised him she'd be open-minded about his career and where *he* needed to go when his seven years at Gellings were up.

For all that he'd been willing to sacrifice for her, how could she not?

He handed over her shoe—and stole a kiss in the process—but the doorbell rang before they got too distracted.

Lance tossed a T-shirt over his head. "Go easy on those kids tonight." He gave her an affectionate tap on the butt, then strolled out the bedroom door.

She slipped into her shoes and grabbed her bag. She had twenty high school kids to entertain tonight as part of a summer program for teenagers interested in STEM careers, and she was looking forward to it. As she breezed out of the bedroom, Lance's snort of laughter stopped her.

His buddy Jackson, their recent houseguest, was back. Dark-haired and slow-drawled, he was the very epitome of the perfect military gentleman. "Thought you were headed over to Alabama by now," Kaci said.

He flashed her a dimpled grin. "Won't be in your hair long, Miss Kaci. Just forgot to leave y'all a thank-you gift for letting me crash here."

"He means he forgot to leave *you* a thank-you gift," Lance said.

Kaci glanced at the clock.

She was seriously late.

But that plastic bag Lance held out for her was clunky and bulky, and that box sticking out the top—"Did you bring me firecrackers from over the border?"

Firecrackers were illegal in Georgia, but plentiful in Alabama.

Both men were grinning now. "Heard tell you might could use some," Jackson said.

"Jackson Davis, it's a good thing I'm an engaged woman, or Lance might have to fight you for me."

"All his idea," Jackson said. "I would've messed up and brought you flowers."

"Owe me really big now, Kace," Lance said.

She certainly did. "Y'all come back anytime," she said to Jackson. "Bring your pup with you next time. Can't wait to meet her." She gave Lance one last quick kiss, then darted out the door.

And two hours later, she was sitting in Jimmy Beans, wishing Tara still worked the night shift instead of at her new accounting day job. Because after Kaci sent her high school program students off on a physics-themed scavenger hunt, guided by Zada and a few of the other girls here for the summer, she saw a sight she recognized all too well.

A young woman with light honey-brown hair and professional clothes, a backpack at her feet, and an untouched drink at her table, darting glances around the shop as though she were looking for someone. Bleak loneliness was etched in her pretty eyes.

Kaci snagged her phone.

*Hope you know I meant it when I told you I was fixin' to keep up my*

*Officers' Ex-Wives Club,* she typed to Lance. *Because I think I just found a girl who needs a friend.*

She sipped her latte and watched her potential new friend.

The woman had nontraditional student written all over her. She was older than most of the students on campus, and she kept grabbing her ring finger, then glancing at it as though she'd forgotten a ring wasn't there.

Kaci's phone buzzed in her hand. *Go use that big heart of yours. But don't go getting any ideas about leaving me. I need you too much.*

She smiled as she stood and made her way to the other woman's table.

That man didn't need her.

But being loved by Lance Wheeler was better than fireworks, potato guns, and catapults combined.

And even her redneck heart agreed.

# The Complete Jamie Farrell Book List

## THE MISFIT BRIDES SERIES:

*Blissed (CJ and Natalie)*
*Matched (Will and Lindsey)*
*Smittened (Mikey and Dahlia)*
*Sugared (Josh and Kimmie)*
*Married (Max and Merry)*

### The Officers' Ex-Wives Club Series:

*Her Rebel Heart (Lance and Kaci)*
*Southern Fried Blues (Jackson and Anna Grace)*
*Moonshine & Magnolias (Zack & Shelby)*

### Standalone Books

*Mr. Good Enough (Trent and Maddie)*
*Sweet Serendipity, a Hope Falls Kindle World Novella (Wyatt and Skye)*

# Acknowledgments

THIS BOOK WOULDN'T HAVE HAPPENED without the nudging from Rachel, Kait, and everyone else who loved Kaci in *Southern Fried Blues*. Thank you for your notes, your encouragement, and your volunteering as tribute in exchange for Kaci's book being written. I hope *Her Rebel Heart* has lived up to expectations!

To my amazing Feisty Belles!! Y'all make this job fun on the hard days, and I couldn't have named half the characters in this book without you. Special thanks to Rhonda Brant and Holly Ruzycki for suggesting Kaci's ex-husband's name and to K'Tee Bee for inspiring the name of Lance's ex. And more special thanks to Zada Koury, Brittany Shivers, Julianna Santiago, Jess Peterson, and Wanda and Gerald Hamm for letting me use your names and parts of your names in this book.

A huge shout-out to my amazing editorial team, Deb Nemeth, Pauline Colette, and Jessica Snyder. You all are simply amazing! And a round of applause to Kim Killion at The Killion Group for the new covers for the entire Officers' Ex-Wives Club series.

To my family, you are my heart. Thank you for your love and support and undying belief in me. I love you!

# About the Author

JAMIE FARRELL IS A BESTSELLING author of feel-good contemporary romances. She believes love, laughter, and bacon are the most powerful forces in the universe. Her debut novel, *Southern Fried Blues*, was a finalist in the National Readers' Choice Awards and the National Excellence in Romance Fiction Awards. *Blissed*, the first book in her Misfit Brides series, received a starred review in Publishers Weekly Magazine.

A native Midwesterner, Jamie has lived in the South the majority of her adult life. When she's not writing, she and her military hero husband are busy raising three hilariously unpredictable children.

Jamie can be reached at www.JamieFarrellBooks.com.

CPSIA information can be obtained
at www.ICGtesting.com
Printed in the USA
LVOW12s1301230917
549812LV00001B/137/P